Darkness & Dawn 2:

Beyond the Great Oblivion

Other books by George Allen England available from Leonaur

Darkness & Dawn 1
The Vacant World

Darkness & Dawn 3:
The After Glow

Darkness & Dawn 2:

Beyond the Great Oblivion

George Allen England

LEONAUR

Darkness & Dawn 2: Beyond the Great Oblivion
by George Allen England

Published by Leonaur Ltd

Contents original to this edition and its presentation in this form
copyright © 2005 Leonaur Ltd

ISBN (10 digit): 1-84677-036-X (hardcover)
ISBN (13 digit): 978-1-84677-036-4 (hardcover)

ISBN (10 digit): 1-84677-028-9 (softcover)
ISBN (13 digit): 978-1-84677-028-9 (softcover)

http://www.leonaur.com

Publisher's Notes

The views expressed by the author do not necessarily reflect
those of the publishers.

In the interests of authenticity, the spellings, grammar and place
names used in this book have been retained from the original
edition.

To Robert H. Davis
Unique inspirer of plots
Do I dedicate this, my trilogy
G.A.E.

1. Beginnings

A thousand years of darkness and decay! A thousand years of blight, brutality, and atavism; of Nature overwhelming all man's work, of crumbling cities and of forgotten civilization, of stupefaction, of death! A thousand years of night!

Two human beings, all alone in that vast wilderness -- a woman and a man.

The past, irrevocable; the present, fraught with problems, perils. and alarms; the future -- what?

A thousand years!

Yet, though this thousand years had seemingly smeared away all semblance of the world of men from the cosmic canvas, Allan Stern and Beatrice Kendrick thrilled with as vital a passion as though that vast, oblivious age lay not between them and the time that was.

And their long kiss, there in sight of their new home -- to be alone there in that desolated world -- was as natural as the summer breeze, the liquid melody of the red-breast on the blossomy apple-bough above their heads, the white and purple spikes of odorous lilacs along the vine-grown stone wall, the gold and purple dawn now. breaking over the distant reaches of the river.

Thus were these two betrothed, this sole surviving pair of human beings.

Thus, as the new day burned to living flame up the inverted bowl of sky, this woman and this man pledged each other their love and loyalty and trust.

Thus they stood together, his left arm about her warm, lithe body, clad as she was only in her tigerskin. Their eyes met and held true, there in the golden glory of the dawn. Unafraid, she read the message in the depths of his eyes, the invitation, the command; and they both foreknew the future.

Beatrice spoke first, flushing a little as she drew toward him.

"Allan," she said with infinite tenderness, even as a mother might speak to a well-loved son, "Allan, come now and let me dress your wound. That's the first thing to do. Come, let me see your arm."

He smiled a little, and with his broad, brown hand stroked back the spun silk of her hair, its mass transfixed by the raw gold pins he had found for her among the ruins of New York.

"No, no!" he objected. "It's nothing -- it's not worth bothering about. I'll be all right in a day or two. My flesh heals almost at once, without any care. You don't realize how healthy I am."

"I know, dear, but it must hurt you terribly!"

"Hurt? How could I feel any pain with your kiss on my mouth?"

"Come!" she again repeated with insistence, and pointed toward the beach where their banca lay on the sand.

"Come, I'll dress your wound first. And after I find out just how badly you're injured --"

He tried to stop her mouth with kisses, but she evaded him.

"No, no!" she cried. "Not now -- not now!"

Allan had to cede. And now presently there he knelt on the fine white sand, his bearskin robe opened and flung back, his well-knit shoulder and sinewed arm bare and brown.

"Well, is it fatal?" he jested. "How long do you give me to survive it?" as with her hand and the cold limpid water of the Hudson she started to lave the caked blood away from his gashed triceps.

At sight of the wound she looked grave, but made no comment. She had no bandages; but with the woodland skill she had developed in the past weeks of life in close touch with nature, she bound the cleansed wound with cooling leaves and fastened them securely in place with lashings of leather thongs from the banca.

Presently the task was done. Stern slipped his bearskin back in place. Beatrice, still solicitous, tried to clasp the silver buckle that held it; but he, unable to restrain himself, caught her hand in both of his and crushed it to his lips.

Then he took her perfect face between his palms, and for a long moment studied it. He looked at her waving hair, luxuriant and glinting rich brown gleams in the sunlight; her thick, arched brows and hazel eyes, liquid and full of mystery as woodland pools; her skin, sun-browned and satiny, with abundant tides of life-blood coursing vigorously in its warm flush; her ripe lips. He studied her, and loved and yearned toward her; and in him the passion leaped up like living flames.

His mouth met hers again.

"My beloved!" breathed he.

Her rounded arm, bare to the shoulder, circled his neck; she hid her face in his breast.

"Not yet -- not yet!" she whispered.

On the white and pink flowered bough above, the robin, unafraid, gushed into a very madness of golden song. And now the sun, higher risen, had struck the river into a broad sheet of spun metal, over which the swallows -- even as in the olden days -- darted and spiraled, with now and then a flick and dash of spray.

Far off, wool-white winding-sheets of mist were lifting, lagging along the purple hills, clothed with inviolate forest.

Again the man tried to raise her head, to burn his kisses on her mouth. But she, instilled with the eternal spirit of woman, denied him.

"No, not now -- not yet!" she said; and in her eyes he read her meaning. "You must let me go now, Allan. There's so much to do; we've got to be practical, you know."

"Practical! When I -- I love --"

"Yes, I know, dear. But there's so much to be done first." Her womanly homemaking instinct would not be gainsaid. "There's so much work! We've got the place to explore, and the house to put in order, and -- oh, thousands of things! And we must be very sensible and very wise, you and I, boy. We're not children, you know. Now that we've lost our home in the Metropolitan Tower, everything's got to be done over again."

"Except to learn to love you!" answered Stern, letting her go with reluctance.

She laughed back at him over her fur-clad shoulder as her sandaled feet followed the dim remnants of what must once have been a broad driveway from the river road along the beach, leading up to the bungalow.

Through the encroaching forest and the tangle of the degenerate apple-trees they could see the concrete walls, with here or there a bit of white still gleaming through the enlacements of ancient vines that had enveloped the whole structure -- woodbine, ivy, wisterias, and the maddest jungle of climbing roses, red and yellow, that ever made a nest for love.

"Wait, I'll go first and clear the way for you," he said cheerily. His big bulk crashed down the undergrowth. His hands held back the thorns and briers. Together they slowly made way toward the house.

The orchard had lost all semblance of regularity, for in the thousand years since the hand of man had pruned or cared for it Mother Nature had planted and replanted it times beyond counting. Small and gnarled and crooked the trees were, as the spine-tree souls in Dante's *dolorosa selva*.

Here or there a pine had rooted and grown tall, killing the lesser tribe of green things underneath.

Warm lay the sun there. A pleasant carpet of last year's leaves and pine-spills covered the earth.

"It's all ready and waiting for us, all embowered and carpeted for love," said Allan musingly. "I wonder what old Van Amburg would think of his estate if he could see it now? And what would he say to our having it? You know, Van was pretty ugly to me at one time about my political opinion -- but that's all past and forgotten now. Only this is certainly an odd turn of fate."

He helped the girl over a fallen log, rotted with moss and lichens. "It's one awful mess, sure as you're born. But as quick as my arm gets back into shape, we'll have order out of chaos before you know it. Some fine day you and I will drive our sixty horse-power car up an asphalt road here, and --"

"A car? Why, what do you mean? There's not such a thing left in the whole world as a car!"

The engineer tapped his forehead with his finger.

"Oh, yes, there is. I've got several models right here. You just wait till you see the workshop I'm going to install on the bank of the river with current-power, and with an electric light plant for the whole place, and with --"

Beatrice laughed.

"You dear, big, dreaming boy!" she interrupted. Then with a kiss she took his hand.

"Come," said she. "We're home now. And there's work to do."

2. Settling Down

Together, in the comradeship of love and trust and mutual understanding, they reached the somewhat open space before the bungalow, where once the road had ended in a stone-paved drive. Allan's wounded arm, had he but sensed it, was beginning to pain more than a little. But he was oblivious. His love, the fire of spring that burned in his blood, the lure of this great adventuring, banished all consciousness of ill.

Parting a thicket, they reached the steps. And for a while they stood there, hand in hand, silent and thrilled with vast, strange thoughts, dreaming of what must be. In their eyes lay mirrored the future of the human race. The light that glowed in them evoked the glories of the dawn of life again, after ten centuries of black oblivion.

"Our home now!" he told her, very gently, and again he kissed her, but this time on the forehead. "Ours when we shall have reclaimed it and made it ours. See the yellow roses, dear? They symbolize our golden future. The red, red roses? Our passion and our pain!"

The girl made no answer, but tears gathered in her eyes -- tears from the deepest wells of the soul. She brought his hand to her lips.

"Ours!" she whispered tremblingly.

They stood there together for a little space, silent and glad. From an oak that shaded the porch a squirrel chippered at them. A sparrow -- larger now than the sparrows they remembered in the time that was -- peered out at them, wondering but unafraid, from its nest under the eaves; at them, the first humans it had ever seen.

"We've got a tenant already, haven't we?" smiled Allan. "Well, I guess we sha'n't have to disturb her, unless perhaps for a while, when I cut away this poison ivy here." He pointed at the glossy triple leaf. "No poisonous thing, whether plant, snake, spider, or insect, is going to stay in this Eden!" he concluded, with a laugh.

Together, with a strange sense of violating the spirit of the past, they went up the concrete steps, untrodden now by human feet for ten centuries.

The massive blocks were still intact for the most part, for old Van Amburg had builded with endless care and with no remotest regard for cost. Here a vine, there a sapling had managed to insinuate a tap-root in some crack made by the frost, but the damage was trifling. Except for the falling of a part of a cornice, the building was complete. But it was hidden in vines and mold. Moss, lichens and weeds grew on the steps, flourishing in the detritus that had accumulated.

Allan dug the toe of his sandal into the loose drift of dead leaves and pine-spills that littered the broad piazza.

"It'll need more than a vacuum cleaner to put this in shape!" said he. "Well, the sooner we get at it, the better. We'd do well to take a look at the inside."

The front door, one-time built of oaken planks studded with hand-worked nails and banded with huge wrought-iron hinges, now hung there a mere shell of itself, worm-eaten, crumbling, disintegrated.

With no tools but his naked hands Stern tore and battered it away. A thick, pungent haze of dust arose, yellow in the morning sunlight that presently, for the first time in a thousand years, fell warm and bright across the cob-webbed front hallway, through the aperture.

Room by room Allan and Beatrice explored. The bungalow was practically stripped bare by time.

"Only dust and rust," sighed the girl. "The same story everywhere we go. But -- well, never mind. We'll soon have it looking homelike. Make me a broom, dear, and I'll sweep out the worst of it at once."

Talking now in terms of practical detail, with romance for the hour displaced by harsh reality, they examined the entire house.

Of the once magnificent furnishings, only dust-piles, splinters and punky rubbish remained. Through the rotted plank shutters, that hung drunkenly awry from rust-eaten hinges, long spears of sunlight wanly illuminated the wreck of all that had once been the lavish home of a billionaire.

Rugs, paintings, furniture, bibelots, treasures of all kinds now lay commingled in mournful decay. In what had evidently been the music room, overlooking the grounds to southward, the grand piano now was only a mass of rusted frame, twisted and broken fragments of wire and a considerable heap of wood-detritus, with a couple of corroded pedals buried in the pile.

"And this was the famous hundred-thousand-dollar harp of Sara, his daughter, that the papers used to talk so much about, you remember?" asked the girl, stirring with her foot a few mournful bits of rubbish that lay near the piano.

"*Sic transit gloria mundi!*" growled Stern, shaking his head. "You and she were the same age, almost. And now --"

Silent and full of strange thoughts they went on into what had been the kitchen. The stove, though heavily bedded in rust, retained its form, for the solid steel had resisted even the fearful lapse of vanished time.

"After I scour that with sand and water," said Stern, "and polish up these aluminum utensils and reset that broken pane with a piece of glass from upstairs where it isn't needed, you won't know this place. Yes, and I'll have running water in here, too -- and electricity from the power-plant, and --"

"Oh, Allan," interrupted the girl, delightedly, "this must have been the dining room." She beckoned from a doorway. "No end of dishes left for us! Isn't it jolly? This is luxury compared to the way we had to start in the tower!"

In the dining-room a good number of the more solid cut-glass and china pieces had resisted the shock of having fallen, centuries ago, to the floor, when the shelves and cupboards of teak and mahogany had rotted and gone to pieces. Corroded silverware lay scattered all about; and there was gold plate, too, intact save for the patina of extreme age -- platters, dishes, beakers. But of the table and the chairs, nothing remained save dust.

Like curious children they poked and pried.

"Dishes enough!" exclaimed she. "Gold, till you can't rest. But how about something to put on the dishes? We haven't had a bite since yesterday noon, and I'm about starved. Now that the fighting's all over, I begin to remember my healthy appetite!"

Stern smiled.

"You'll have some breakfast, girlie," promised he. "There'll be the wherewithal, never fear. Just let's have a look upstairs, and then I'll go after something for the larder."

They left the downstairs rooms, silent save for a fly buzzing in a spider's web, and together ascended the dusty stairs. The railing was entirely gone; but the concrete steps remained.

Stern helped the girl, in spite of the twinge of pain it caused his wounded arm. His heart beat faster -- so, too, did hers -- as they gained the upper story. The touch of her was, to him, like a lighted match flung into a powder magazine; but he bit his lip, and though his face paled, then flushed, he held his voice steady as he said:

"So then, bats up here? Well, how the deuce do they get in and out? Ah! That broken window, where the elm-branch has knocked out the glass -- I see! That's got to be fixed at once!"

He brushed webs and dust from the remaining panes, and together they peered out over the orchard, out across the river, now a broad sheet of molten gold. His arm went about her; he drew her head against his heart, fast-beating; and silence fell.

"Come, Allan," said the girl at length, calmer than he. "Let's see what we've got here to do with. Oh, I tell you to begin with," and she smiled up frankly at him, "I'm a tremendously practical sort of woman. You may be an engineer, and know how to build wireless telegraphs and bridges and -- and things; but when it comes to home-building --"

"I admit it. Well, lead on," he answered; and together they explored the upper rooms. The sense of intimacy now lay strong upon them, of unity and of indissoluble love and comradeship. This was quite another venture than the exploration of the tower, for now they were choosing a home, their home, and in them the mating instinct had begun to thrill, to burn.

Each room, despite its ruin and decay, took on a special charm, a dignity, the foreshadowing of what must be. Yet intrinsically the place was mournful, even after Stern had let the sunshine in.

For all was dark desolation. The rosewood and mahogany furniture, pictures, rugs, brass beds, all alike lay reduced to dust and ashes. A gold clock, the porcelain fittings of the bath-room, and some fine clay and meerschaum pipes in what had evidently been Van Amburg's den -- these constituted all that had escaped the tooth of time.

In a front room that probably had been Sara's, a mud-swallow had built its nest in the far corner. It flew out, frightened, when Stern thrust his hand into the aperture to see if the nest were tenanted, fluttered about with scared cries, then vanished up the broad fireplace.

"Eggs -- warm!" announced Stern. "Well, this room will have to be shut up and left. We've got more than enough, anyhow. Less work for you, dear," he added, with a smile. "We might use only the lower floor, if you like. I don't want you killing yourself with housework, you understand."

She laughed cheerily.

"You make me a broom and get all the dishes and things together," she answered, "and then leave the rest to me. In a week from now you won't know this place. Once we clear out a little foothold here we can go back to the tower and fetch up a few loads of tools and supplies --"

"Come on, come on!" he interrupted, taking her by the hand and leading her away. "All such planning will do after breakfast, but I'm starving! How about a five-pound bass on the coals, eh? Come on, let's go fishing."

3. The Maskalonge

With characteristic resourcefulness Stein soon manufactured adequate tackle with a well-trimmed alder pole, a line of leather thongs and a hook of stout piano wire, properly bent to make a barb and rubbed to a fine point on a stone. He caught a dozen young frogs among the sedges in the marshy stretch at the north end of the landing-beach, and confined them in the only available receptacle, the holster of his automatic.

All this hurt his arm severely, but he paid no heed.

"Now," he announced, "we're quite ready for business. Come along!"

Together they pushed the boat off; it glided smoothly out onto the breast of the great current.

"I'll paddle," she volunteered. "You mustn't, with your arm in the condition it is. Which way?"

"Up -- over there into that cove beyond the point," he answered, baiting up his hook with a frog that kicked as naturally as though a full thousand years hadn't passed since any of its progenitors had been handled thus. "This certainly is far from being the kind of tackle that Bob Davis or any of that gang used to swear by, but it's the best we can do for now. When I get to making lines and hooks and things in earnest, there'll be some sport in this vicinity. Imagine water untouched by the angler for ten hundred years or more!"

He swung his clumsy line as he spoke, and cast. Far across the shining water the circles spread, silver in the morning light; then the trailing line cut a long series of V's as the girl paddled slowly toward the cove. Behind the banca a rippling wake flashed metallic; the cold, clear water caressed the primitive hull, murmuring with soft cadences, in the old, familiar music of the time when there were men on earth. The witchery of it stirred Beatrice; she smiled, looked up with joy and wonder at the beauty of that perfect morning, and in her clear voice began to sing, very low, very softly, to herself, a song whereof -- save in her brain -- no memory now remained in the whole world.

"Stark vole der Fels, Tief wie das Meer,
Muss deine Liebe, muss deine Liebe sein --"

"Ah!" cried the man, interrupting her.

The alder pole was jerking, quivering in his hands; the leather line was taut.

"A strike, so help me! A big one!"

He sprang to his feet, and, unmindful of the swaying of the banca, began to play the fish.

Beatrice, her eyes a-sparkle, turned to watch; the paddle lay forgotten in her hands.

"Here he comes! Oh, damn!" shouted Stern. "If I only had a reel now --"

"Pull him right in, can't you?" the girl suggested.

He groaned, between clenched teeth-for the strain on his arm was torture.

"Yes, and have him break the line!" he cried. "There he goes, under the boat, now! Paddle! Go ahead -- paddle!"

She seized the oar, and while Stern fought the monster she set the banca in motion again. Now the fish was leaping wildly from side to side, zig-zagging, shaking at the hook as a bull-dog shakes an old boot. The leather cord hummed through the water, ripping and vibrating, taut as a fiddle-string. A long, silvery line of bubbles followed the vibrant cord.

Flash!

High in air, lithe and graceful and very swift, a spurt of green and white -- a long, slim curve of glistening power -- a splash; and again the cord drew hard.

"Maskalonge!" Stern cried. "Oh, we've got to land him -- got to! Fifteen pounds if he's an ounce!"

Beatrice, flushed and eager, watched the fight with fascination.

"If I can bring him close, you strike -- hit hard!" the man directed. "Give it to him! He's our breakfast!"

Even in the excitement of the battle Stern realized how very beautiful this woman was. Her color was adorable -- rose-leaves and cream. Her eyes were shot full of light and life and the joy of living; her loosened hair, wavy and rich and brown, half hid the graceful curve of her neck as she leaned to watch, to help him.

And strong determination seized him to master this great fish, to land it, to fling it at the woman's feet as his tribute and his trophy.

He had, in the days of long ago, fished in the Adirondack wildernesses. He had fished for tarpon in the Gulf; he had cast the fly along the brooks of Maine and lured the small-mouthed bass with floating bait on many a lake and stream. He had even fished in a Rocky Mountain torrent, and out on the far Columbia, when failure to succeed meant hunger.

But this experience was unique. Never had he fished all alone in the world with a loved woman who depended on his skill for her food, her life, her everything.

Forgotten now the wounded arm, the crude and absurd implements; forgotten everything but just that sole, indomitable thought: "I've got to win!"

Came now a lull in the struggles of the monster. Stern hauled in. Another rush, met by a paying-out, a gradual tautening of the line, a strong and steady pull.

"He's tiring," exulted Stern. "Be ready when I bring him close!"

Again the fish broke cover; again it dived; but now its strength was lessening fast.

Allan hauled in.

Now, far down in the clear depths, they could both see the darting, flickering shaft of white and green.

"Up he comes now! Give it to him, hard!"

As Stern brought him to the surface, Beatrice struck with the paddle -- once, twice, with magnificent strength and judgment.

Over the gunwale of the banca, in a sparkle of flying spray, silvery in the morning sun, the maskalonge gleamed.

Excited and happy as a child, Beatrice clapped her hands. Stern seized the paddle as she let it fall. A moment later the huge fish, stunned and dying, lay in the bottom of the boat, its gills rising, falling in convulsive gasps, its body quivering, scales shining in the sunlight -- a thing of wondrous beauty, a promise of the feast for two strong, healthy humans.

Stern dried his brow on the back of his hand and drew a deep breath, for the morning was already warm and the labor had been hard.

"Now," said he, and smiled, "now a nice little pile of dead wood on the beach, a curl of birch-bark and a handful of pine punk and grass -- a touch of the flint and steel! Then this," and he pointed at the maskalonge, "broiled on a pointed stick, with a handful of checkerberries for dessert, and I think you and I will be about ready to begin work in earnest!"

He knelt and kissed her -- a kiss that she returned -- and then, slowly, happily, and filled with the joy of comradeship, they drove their banca once more to the white and gleaming beach.

4. The Golden Age

Stern's plans of hard work for the immediate present had to be deferred a little, for in spite of his perfect health, the spear-thrust in his arm -- lacking the proper treatment, and irritated by his labor in catching the big fish -- developed swelling and soreness. A little fever even set in the second day. And though he was eager to go out fishing again, Beatrice appointed herself his nurse and guardian, and withheld permission.

They lived for some days on the excellent flesh of the maskalonge, on clams from the beach -- enormous clams of delicious flavor -- on a new fruit with a pinkish meat, which grew abundantly in the thickets and somewhat resembled breadfruit; on wild asparagus-sprouts, and on the few squirrels that Stern was able to "pot" with his revolver from the shelter of the leafy little camping-place they had arranged near the river.

Though Beatrice worked many hours all alone in the bungalow, sweeping it with a broom made of twigs lashed to a pole, and trying to bring the place into order, it was still no fit habitation.

She would not even let the man try to help her, but insisted on his keeping quiet in their camp. This lay under the shelter of a thick-foliaged oak at the southern end of the beach. The perfect weather and the presence of a three-quarters moon at night invited them to sleep out under the sky.

"There'll be plenty of time for the bungalow," she said, "when it rains. As long as we have fair June weather like this no roof shall cover me!"

Singularly enough, there were no mosquitoes. In the thousand years that had elapsed, they might either have shifted their habitat from eastern America, or else some obscure evolutionary process might have wiped them out entirely. At any rate, none existed, for which the two adventurers gave thanks.

Wild beasts they feared not. Though now and then they heard the yell of a wildcat far back in the woods, or the tramping of an occasional bulk through the forest, and though once a cinnamon bear poked his muzzle out into the clearing, sniffed and departed with a grunt of disapproval, they could not bring themselves to any realization of animals as a real peril. Their camp-fire burned high all night, heaped with driftwood and windfalls; and beyond this protection, Stern had his automatic and a belt nearly full of cartridges. They discussed the question of a possible attack by some remnants of the Horde; but common sense assured them that these creatures would -- such as survived -- give them a wide berth.

"And in any event," Stern summed it up, "if anything happens, we have the bungalow to retreat into. Though in its present state, without any doors or shutters, I think we're safer out among the trees, where, on a pinch, we could go aloft."

Thus his convalescence progressed in the open air, under the clouds and sun and stars and lustrous moon of that deserted world.

Beatrice showed both skill and ingenuity in her treatment. With a clam-shell she scraped and saved the rich fat from under the skins of the squirrels, and this she "tried out" in a golden dish, over the fire. The oil thus got she used to anoint his healing wound. She used a dressing of clay and leaves; and when the fever flushed him she made him comfortable on his bed of spruce-tips, bathed his forehead and cheeks, and gave him cold water from a spring that trickled down over the moss some fifty feet to westward of the camp.

Many a long talk they had, too -- he prone on the spruce, she sitting beside him, tending the fire, holding his hand or letting his head lie in her lap, the while she stroked his hair. Ferns, flowers in profusion -- lilacs and clover and climbing roses and some new, strange scarlet blossoms -- bowered their nest. And through the pain and fever, the delay and disappointment, they both were glad and cheerful. No word of impatience or haste or repining escaped them. For they had life; they had each other; they had love. And those days, as later they looked back upon them, were among the happiest, the most purely beautiful, the sweetest of their whole wondrous, strange experience.

He and she, perfect friends, comrades and lovers, were inseparable. Each was always conscious of the other's presence. The continuity of love, care and sympathy was never broken. Even when, at daybreak, she went away around the wooded point for her bath in the river, he could hear her splashing and singing and laughing happily in the cold water.

It was the Golden Age come back to earth again -- the age of natural and pure simplicity, truth, trust, honor, faith and joy, unspoiled by malice or deceit, by lies, conventions, sordid ambitions, or the lust of wealth or power. Arcady, at last -- in truth!

Their conversation was of many things. They talked of their awakening in the tower and their adventures there; of the possible cause of the world-catastrophe that had wiped out the human race, save for their own survival; the Horde and the great battle; their escape, their present condition, and their probable future; the possibility of their ever finding any other isolated human beings, and of reconstituting the fragments of the world or of renewing the human race.

And as they spoke of this, sometimes the girl would grow strangely silent, and a look almost of inspiration -- the universal mother -- look of the race -- would fill her wondrous eye's. Her hand would tremble in his; but he would hold it tight, for he, too, understood.

"Afraid, little girl?" he asked her once.

"No, not afraid," she answered; and their eyes met. "Only -- so much depends on us -- on you, on me! What strength we two must have, what courage, what endurance! The future of the human race lies in our hands!"

He made no answer; he, too, grew silent. And for a long while they sat and watched the embers of the fire; and the day waned. Slowly the sun set in its glory over the virgin hills; the far eastern spaces of the sky grew bathed in tender lavenders and purples. Haze drew its veils across the world, and the air grew brown with evenfall.

Presently the girl arose, to throw more wood on the fire. Clad only in her loose tiger-skin, clasped with gold, she moved like a primeval goddess. Stern marked the supple play of her muscles, the unspoiled grace and strength of that young body, the swelling warmth of her bosom. And as he looked he loved; he pressed a hand to his eyes; for a while he thought -- it was as though he prayed.

Evening came on -- the warm, dark, mysterious night. Off there in the shallows gradually arose the million-voiced chorus of frogs, shrill and monotonous, plaintive, appealing -- the cry of new life to the overarching, implacable mystery of the universe. The first faint silvery powder of the stars came spangling out along the horizon. Unsteady bats began to reel across the sky. The solemn beauty of the scene awed the woman and the man to silence. But Stern, leaning his back against the bole of the great oak, encircled Beatrice with his arm.

Her beautiful dear head rested in the hollow of his throat; her warm, fragrant hair caressed his cheek; he felt the wholesome strength and sweetness of this woman whom he loved; and in his eyes -- unseen by her -- tears welled and gleamed in the firelight.

Beatrice watched, like a contented child, the dancing showers of sparks that rose, wavering and whirling in complex sarabands -- sparks red as passion, golden as the unknown future of their dreams. From the river they heard the gentle lap-lap-lapping of the waves along the shore. All was rest and peace and beauty; this was Eden once again -- and there was no serpent to enter in.

Presently Stern spoke.

"Dear," said he, "do you know, I'm a bit puzzled in some ways, about -- well, about night and day, and temperature, and gravitation, and a number of little things like that. Puzzled. We're facing problems here that we don't realize fully as yet."

"Problems? What problems, except to make our home, and -- and live?"

"No, there's more to be considered than just that. In the first place, although I have no timepiece, I'm moderately certain the day and night are shorter now than they used to be before the smash-up. There must be a difference of at least half an hour. Just as soon as I can get around to it, I'll build a clock, and see. Though if the force of gravity has changed, too, that, of course, will change the time of vibration of any pendulum, and so of course will invalidate my results. It's a hard problem, right enough."

"You think gravitation has changed?"

"Don't you notice, yourself, that things seem a trifle lighter -- things that used to be heavy to lift are now comparatively easy?"

"M-m-m-m-m -- I don't know. I thought maybe it was because I was feeling so much stronger, with this new kind of outdoor life."

"Of course, that's worth considering," answered Stern, "but there's more in it than that. The world is certainly smaller than it was, though how, or why, I can't say. Things are lighter, and the time of rotation is shorter. Another thing, the pole-star is certainly five degrees out of place. The axis of the earth has been given an astonishing twist, some way or other.

"And don't you notice a distinct change in the climate? In the old days there were none of these huge, palm-like ferns growing in this part of the world. We had no such gorgeous butterflies. And look at the new varieties of flowers -- and the breadfruit, or whatever it is, growing on the banks of the Hudson in the early part of June!

"Something, I tell you, has happened to the earth, in all these centuries; something big! Maybe the cause of it all was the original catastrophe; who knows? It's up to us to find out. We've got more to do than make our home, and live, and hunt for other people -- if any are still alive. We've got to solve these world problems; we've got work to do, little girl. Work -- big work!"

"Well, you've got to rest now, anyhow," she dictated. "Now, stop thinking and planning, and just rest! Till your wound is healed, you're going to keep good and quiet."

Silence fell again between them. Then, as the east brightened with the approach of the moon, she sang the song he loved best -- *Ave Maria, Gratia Plena* -- in her soft, sweet voice, untrained, unspoiled by false conventions. And Stern, listening, forgot his problems and his plans; peace came to his soul, and rest and joy.

The song ended. And now the moon, with a silent majesty that shamed human speech, slid her bright silver plate up behind the fret of trees on the far hills. Across the river a shimmering path of light grew, broadening; and the world beamed in holy beauty, as on the primal night.

And their souls drank that beauty. They were glad, as never yet. At last Stern spoke.

"It's more like a dream than a reality, isn't it?" said he. "Too wonderful to be true. Makes me think of Alfred de Musset's 'Lucie.' You remember the poem?

" *'Un soir, nous etions seuls,*
J'etais assis pres d'elle . . .'"

Beatrice nodded. "Yes, I know!" she whispered. "How could I forget it? And to think that for a thousand years the moon's been shining just the same, and nobody --"

"Yes, but is it the same?" interrupted Stern suddenly, his practical turn of mind always reasserting itself. "Don't you see a difference? You remember the old-time face in the moon, of course. Where is it now? The moon always presented only one side, the same side, to us in the old days. How about it now? If I'm not mistaken, things have shifted up there. We're looking now at some other face of it. And if that's so it means a far bigger disarrangement of the solar system and the earth's orbit and more things than you or I suspect!

"Wait till we get back to New York for half a day, and visit the tower and gather up our things. Wait till I get hold of my binoculars again! Perhaps some of these questions may be resolved. We can't go on this way, surrounded by perpetual puzzles, problems, mysteries! We must --"

"Do nothing but rest now!" she dictated with mock severity.

Stern laughed.

"Well, you're the boss," he answered, and leaned back against the oak. "Only, may I propound one more question?"

"Well, what is it?"

"Do you see that dark patch in the sky? Sort of a roughly circular hole in the blue, as it were -- right there?" He pointed. "Where there aren't any stars?"

"Why -- yes. What about it?"

"It's moving, that's all. Every night that black patch moves among the stars, and cuts their light off; and one night it grazed the moon -- passed before the eastern limb of it, you understand. Made a partial eclipse. You were asleep; I didn't bother you about it. But if there's a new body in the sky, it's up to us to know why, and what about it, and all. So the quicker --"

"The quicker you get well, the better all around!"

She drew his head down and kissed him tenderly on the forehead with that strange, innate maternal instinct which makes women love to "mother" men even ten years older than themselves.

"Don't you worry your brains about all these problems and vexations tonight, Allan. Your getting well is the main thing. The whole world's future hangs on just that! Do you realize what it means? Do you?"

"Yes, as far as the human brain can realize so big a concept. Languages, arts, science, all must be handed down to the race by us. The world can't begin again on any higher plane than just the level of our collective intelligence. All that the world knows today is stored in your brain-cells and mine! And our speech, our methods, our ideals, will shape the whole destiny of the earth. Our ideals! We must keep them very pure!"

"Pure and unspotted," she answered simply. Then with an adorable and feminine anticlimax:

"Dear, does your shoulder pain you now? I'm awfully heavy to be leaning on you like this!"

"You're not hurting me a bit. On the contrary, your touch, your presence, are life to me!"

"Quite sure you're comfy, boy?"

"Positive."

"And happy?"

"To the limit."

"I'm so glad. Because I am, too. I'm awfully sleepy, Allan Do you mind if I take just a little, tiny nap?"

For all answer he patted her, and smoothed her hair, her cheek, her full, warm throat.

Presently by her slow, gentle breathing he knew she was asleep.

For a long time he half-lay there against the oak, softly swathed in his bear-skin, on the odorous bed of fir, holding her in his arms, looking into the dancing firelight.

And night wore on, calm, perfumed, gentle; and the thoughts of the man were long, long thoughts -- thoughts "that do often lie too deep for tears."

5. Deadly Peril

Pages on pages would not tell the full details of the following week -- the talks they had, the snaring and shooting of small game, the fishing, the cleaning out of the bungalow, and the beginnings of some order in the estate, the rapid healing of Stern's arm, and all the multifarious little events of their new beginnings of life there by the river-bank.

But there are other matters of more import than such homely things; so now we come to the time when Stern felt the pressing imperative of a return to the tower. For he lacked tools in every way; he needed them to build furniture, doors, shutters; to clear away the brush and make the place orderly, rational and beautiful; to start work on his projected laboratory and power-plant; for a thousand purposes.

He wanted his binoculars, his shotgun and rifles, and much ammunition, as well as a boat-load of canned supplies and other goods. Instruments, above all, he had to have.

So, though Beatrice still, with womanly conservatism, preferred to let well enough alone for the present, and stay away from the scene of such ghastly deeds as had taken place on the last day of the invasion by the Horde, Stern eventually convinced and over-argued her; and on what he calculated to be the 16th day of June, 2912 -- the tenth day since the fight-they set sail for Manhattan. A favoring northerly breeze, joined with a clear sky and sunshine of unusual brilliancy, made the excursion a gala time for both. As they put their supplies of fish, squirrel-meat and breadfruit aboard the banca and shoved the rude craft off the sand, both she and he felt like children on an outing.

Allan's arm was now so well that he permitted himself the luxury of a morning plunge. The invigoration of this was still upon him as, with a song, he raised the clumsy skin sail upon the rough-hewn mast. Beatrice curled down in her tiger-skin at the stern, took one of the paddles, and made ready to steer. He settled himself beside her, the thongs of his sail in his hand. Thus happy in comradeship, they sailed away to southward, down the blue wonder of the river, flanked by headlands, wooded heights, crags, cliffs and Palisades, now all alike deserted.

Noon found them opposite the fluted columns of gray granite that once had borne aloft the suburbs of Englewood. Stern recognized the conformation of the place; but though he looked hard, could find no trace of the Interstate Park road that once had led from top to bottom of the Palisades, nor any remnant of the millionaires' palaces along the heights there.

"Stone and brick have long since vanished as structures," he commented. "Only steel and concrete have stood the gaff of uncounted years! Where all that fashion, wealth and beauty once would have scorned to notice us, girl, now what's left? Hear the cry of that gull? The barking of that fox? See that green flicker over the pinnacle? Some new, bright bird, never dreamed of in this country! And even with the naked eye I can make out the palms and the lianas tangled over the verge of what must once have been magnificent gardens!"

He pointed at the heights.

"Once," said he, "I was consulted by a sausage-king named Breitkopf, who wanted to sink an elevator-shaft from the top to the bottom of this very cliff, so he could reach his hundred-thousand-dollar launch in ease. Breitkopf didn't like my price; he insulted me in several rather unpleasant ways. The cliff is still here, I see. So am I. But Breitkopf is -- elsewhere."

He laughed, and swept the river with a glance.

"Steer over to the eastward, will you?" he asked. "We'll go in through Spuyteu Duyvil and the Harlem. That'll bring us much nearer the tower than by landing on the west shore of Manhattan."

Two hours later they had run past the broken arches of Fordham, Washington, and High Bridges, and following the river -- on both banks of which a few scattered ruins showed through the massed foliage -- were drawing toward Randall's and Ward's islands and Hell Gate.

Wind and tide still favored them. In safety they passed the ugly shoals and ledges. Here Stern took the paddle, while Beatrice went to the bow and left all to his directing hand.

By three o'clock in the afternoon they were drawing past Blackwell's Island. The Queensboro Bridge still stood, as did the railway bridges behind them; but much wreckage had fallen into the river, and in one place formed an ugly whirlpool, which Stern had to avoid by some hard work with the paddle.

The whole structure was sagging badly to southward, as though the foundations had given way. Long, rusted masses of steel hung from the spans, which drooped as though to break at any moment. Though all the flooring had vanished centuries before, Stern judged an active man could still make his way across the bridge.

"That's their engineering," gibed he, as the little boat sailed under and they looked up like dwarfs at the legs of a Colossus. "The old Roman bridges are good for practically eternity, but these jerry steel things, run up for profits, go to pieces in a mere thousand years! Well, the steel magnates are gone now, and their profits with them. But this junk remains as a lesson and a warning, Beta; the race to come must build better than this, and sounder, every way!"

On, on they sailed, marveling at the terrific destruction on either hand -- the dense forests now grown over Brooklyn and New York alike.

"We'll be there before long now," said Allan. "And if we have any luck at all, and nothing happens, we ought to be started for home by nightfall. You don't mind a moonlight sail up the Hudson, do you?"

It was past four by the time the banca nosed her way slowly in among the rotten docks and ruined hulks of steamships, and with a gentle rustling came to rest among the reeds and rushes now growing rank at the foot of what had once been Twenty-Third Street.

A huge sea-tortoise, disturbed, slid off the sand-bank where he had been sunning himself and paddled sulkily away. A blue heron flapped up from the thicket, and with a frog in its bill awkwardly took flight, its long neck crooked, legs dangling absurdly.

"Some mighty big changes, all right," commented Stern. "Yes, there's got to be a deal of work done here before things are right again. But there's time enough, time enough -- there's all the time we need, we and the people who shall come after us!"

They made the banca fast, noting that the tide was high and that the leather cord was securely tied to a gnarled willow that grew at the water's edge. Half an hour later they had made their way across town to Madison Avenue.

It was with strange feelings they once more approached the scene of their battle against such frightful odds with the Horde. Stern was especially curious to note the effect of his Pulverite, not only on the building itself but on the square.

This effect exceeded his expectations. Less than two hundred feet of the tower now stood and the whole western facade was but a mass of cracked and gaping ruin.

Out on the Square the huge elms and pines had been uprooted and flung in titanic confusion, like a game of giants' jack-straws. And vast conical excavations showed, here and there, where vials of the explosive had struck the earth. Gravel and rocks had even been thrown over the Metropolitan Building itself into the woodland glades of Madison Avenue. And, worse, bits of bone -- a leg-bone, a shoulder-blade, a broken skull with flesh still adhering -- here or there met the eye.

"Mighty good thing the vultures have been busy here," commented Stern. "If they hadn't, the place wouldn't be even approachable. Gad! I thank my stars what we've got to do won't take more than an hour. If we had to stay here after dark I'd surely have the creeps, in spite of all my scientific materialism! Well, no use being retrospective. We're living in the present and future now; not the past. Got the plaited cords Beatrice? We'll need them before long to make up our bundle with."

Thus talking, Stern kept the girl from seeing too much or brooding over what she saw. He engaged her actively on the work in hand. Until he had assured himself there was no danger from falling fragments in the shattered halls and stairways that led up to the gaping ruin at the truncated top of the tower he would not let her enter the building, but set her to fashioning a kind of puckered bag with a huge skin taken from the furrier's shop in the Arcade, while he explored.

He returned after a while, and together they climbed over the debris and ruins to the upper rooms which had been their home during the first few days after the awakening.

The silence of death that lay over the place was appalling -- that and the relics of the frightful battle. But they had their work to do; they had to face the facts.

"We're not children, Beta," said the man. "Here we are for a purpose. The quicker we get our work done the better. Come on, let's get busy!"

Stifling the homesick feeling that tried to win upon them they set to work. All the valuables they could recover they collected -- canned supplies, tools, instruments, weapons, ammunition and a hundred and one miscellaneous articles they had formerly used.

This flotsam of a former civilization they carried down and piled in the skin bag at the broken doorway. And darkness began to fall ere the task was done.

Still trickled the waters of the fountain in Madison Forest through the dim evening aisles of the shattered forest. A solemn hush fell over the dead world; night was at hand.

"Come, let's be going," spoke the man, his voice lowered in spite of himself, the awe of the Infinite Unknown upon him. "We can eat in the banca on the way. With the tide behind us, as it will be, we ought to get home by morning. And I'll be mighty glad never to see this place again!"

He slung a sack of cartridges over his shoulder and picked up one of the cord loops of the bag wherein lay their treasure-trove. Beatrice took the other.

"I'm ready," said she. Thus they started.

All at once she stopped short.

"Hark! What's that?" she exclaimed under her breath.

Far off to northward, plaintive, long-drawn and inexpressibly mournful, a wailing cry re-echoed in the wilderness -- fell, rose, died away, and left the stillness even more ghastly than before.

Stern stood rooted. In spite of all his aplomb and matter-of-fact practicality, he felt a strange thrill curdle through his blood, while on the back of his neck the hair drew taut and stiff.

"What is it?" asked Beatrice again.

"That? Oh, some bird or other, I guess. It's nothing. Come on!"

Again he started forward, trying to make light of the cry; but in his heart he knew it well.

A thousand years before, far in the wilds near Ungava Bay, in Labrador, he had heard the same plaintive, starving call -- and he remembered still the deadly peril, the long fight, the horror that had followed.

He knew the cry; and his soul quivered with the fear of it; fear not for himself, but for the life of this girl whose keeping lay within the hollow of his hand.

For the long wail that had trembled across the vague spaces of the forest, affronting the majesty and dignity of night and the coming stars with its blood-lusting plaint of famine, had been none other than the summons to the hunt, the news of quarry, the signal of a gathering wolf-pack on their trail.

6. Trapped!

"That's not the truth you're telling me, Allan," said Beatrice very gravely. "And if we don't tell each other the whole truth always, how can we love each other perfectly and do the work we have to do? I don't want you to spare me anything, even the most terrible things. That's not the cry of a bird -- it's wolves!"

"Yes, that's what it is," the man admitted. "I was in the wrong. But, you see -- it startled me at first. Don't be alarmed, little girl! We're well armed you see, and --"

"Are we going to stay here in the tower if they attack?"

"No. They might hold us prisoners for a week. There's no telling how many there may be. Hundreds, perhaps thousands. Once they get the scent of game, they'll gather for miles and miles around; from all over the island. So you see --"

"Our best plan, then, will be to make for the banca?"

"Assuredly! It's only a matter of comparatively few minutes to reach it, and once we're aboard, we're safe. We can laugh at them and be on our homeward way at the same time. The quicker we start the better. Come on!"

"Come!" she repeated. And they made their second start after Stern had assured himself his automatic hung easily in reach and that the guns were loaded.

Together they took their way along the shadowy depths of the forest where once Twenty-Third Street had lain. Bravely and strongly the girl bore her half of the load as they broke through the undergrowth, clambered over fallen and rotten logs, or sank ankle-deep in mossy swales.

Even though they felt the danger, perhaps at that very moment slinking, sneaking, crawling nearer off there in the vague, darkling depths of the forest, they still sensed the splendid comradeship of the adventure. No longer as a toy, a chattel, an instrument of pleasure or amusement did the idea of woman now exist in the world. It had altered, grown higher, nobler, purer -- it had become that of mate and equal, comrade, friend, the indissoluble other half of man.

Beatrice spoke.

"You mustn't take more of the weight than I do, Allan," she insisted, as they struggled onward with their burden. "Your wounded arm isn't strong enough yet to --"

"S-h-h-h!" he cautioned. "We've got to keep as quiet as possible. Come on -- the quicker we get these things aboard and push off the better! Everything depends on speed!"

But speed was hard to make. The way seemed terribly long, now that evening had closed in and they could no longer be exactly sure of their path. The cumbersome burden impeded them at every step. In the gloom they stumbled, tripped over vines and creepers, and became involved among the close-crowding boles.

Suddenly, once again the wolf-cry burst out, this time reechoed from another and another savage throat, wailing and plaintive and full of frightful portent.

So much nearer now it seemed that Beatrice and Allan both stopped short. Panting with their labors, they stood still, fear-smitten.

"They can't be much farther off now than Thirty-Fifth Street," the man exclaimed under his breath. "And we're hardly past Second Avenue yet -- and look at the infernal thickets and brush we've got to beat through to reach the river! Here, I'd better get my revolver ready and hold it in my free hand. Will you change over? I can take the bag in my left. I've got to have the right to shoot with!"

"Why not drop everything and run for the banca?"

"And desert the job? Leave all we came for? And maybe not be able to get any of the things for Heaven knows how long? I guess not!"

"But, Allan --"

"No, no! What? Abandon all our plans because of a few wolves? Let 'em come! We'll show 'em a thing or two!"

"Give me the revolver, then -- you can have the rifle!"

"That's right -- here!"

Each now with a firearm in the free hand, they started forward again. On and on they lunged, they wallowed through the forest, half carrying, half dragging the sack which now seemed to have grown ten times heavier and which at every moment caught on bushes, on limbs and among the dense undergrowth.

"Oh, look -- look there!" cried Beatrice. She stopped short again, pointing the revolver, her finger on the trigger.

Allan saw a lean, gray form, furtive and sneaking, slide across a dim open space off toward the left, a space where once First Avenue had cut through the city from south to north.

"There's another!" he whispered, a strange, choked feeling all around his heart. "And look -- three more! They're working in ahead of us. Here, I'll have a shot at 'em, for luck!"

A howl followed the second spurt of flame in the dusk. One of the gray, gaunt portents of death licked, yapping, at his flank.

"Got you, all right!" gibed Stern. "The kind o' game you're after isn't as easy as you think, you devils!"

But now from the other side, and from behind them, the slinking creatures gathered. Their eyes glowed, gleamed, burned softly yellow through the dusk of the great wilderness that once had been the city's heart. The two last humans in the world could even catch the flick of ivory fangs, the lolling wet redness of tongues -- could hear the soughing breath through those infernal jaws.

Stern raised the rifle again, then lowered it.

"No use," said he quite calmly. "God knows how many there are. I might use up all our ammunition and still leave enough of 'em to pick our bones. They'll be all around us in a minute; they'll be worrying at us, dragging us down! Come on -- come on, the boat!"

"Light a torch, Allan. They're afraid of fire."

"Grand idea, little girl!"

Even as he answered he was scrabbling up dry kindling. Came the rasp of his flint.

"Give 'em a few with the automatic, while I get this going!" he commanded.

The gun spat twice, thrice. Then rose a snapping, snarling wrangle. Off there in the gloom a hideous turmoil grew.

It ended in screams of pain and rage, suddenly throttled, choked, and torn to nothing. A worrying, rending, gnashing told the story of the wounded wolf's last moment.

Stern sprang up, a dry flaming branch of resinous fir in his hand. The rifle he thrust back into the bag.

"Ate him, still warm, eh?" he cried. "Fine! And five shots left in the gun. You won't miss, Beta! You can't!"

Forward they struggled once more.

"Gad, we'll hang to this bag now, whatever happens!" panted Stern, jerking it savagely off a jagged stub. "Five minutes more and we'll -- arrh! would you?"

The flaring torch he dashed full at a grisly muzzle that snapped and slavered at his legs. To their nostrils the singe of burned hair wafted. Yelping, the beast swerved back.

But others ran in and in at them; and now the torch was failing. Both of them shouted and struck; and the revolver stabbed the night with fire.

Pandemonium rose in the forest. Cries, howls, long wails and snuffing barks blent with the clicking of ivories, the pad-pad-pad of feet, the crackling of the underbrush.

All around, wolves. On either side, behind, in front, the sliding, bristling, sneaking, suddenly bold horrors of the wild.

And the ring was tightening; the attack was coming, now, more and more concertedly. The swinging torch could not now drive them back so fast, so far.

Strange gleams shot against the tree-trunks, wavered through the dusk, lighted the harsh, rage-contracted face of the man, fell on the laboring, skin-clad figure of the woman as they still fought on and on with their precious burden, hoping for a glimpse of water, for the river, and salvation.

"Take -- a tree?" gasped Beatrice.

"And maybe stay there a week? And use up -- all our ammunition? Not yet -- no -- no! The boat!"

On, ever on, they struggled.

A strange, unnatural exhilaration filled the girl, banishing thoughts of peril, sending the blood aglow through every vein and fiber of her wonderful young body.

Stern realized the peril more keenly. At any moment now he understood that one of the devils in gray might hurl itself at the full throat of Beatrice or at his own.

And once the taste of blood lay on those crimson tongues -- goodby!

"The boat -- the boat!" he shouted, striking right and left like mad with the smoky, half- extinguished flare.

"There -- the river!" suddenly cried Beatrice.

Through the columns of the forest she had seen at last the welcome gleam of water, starlit, beautiful and calm. Stern saw it, too. A demon now, he charged the snarling ring. Back he drove them; he turned, seized the bag, and again plunged desperately ahead.

Together he and Beatrice crashed out among the willows and the alders on the sedgy shore, with the vague, shifting, bristling horror of the wolf-pack at their heels.

"Here, beat 'em off while I cut the cord -- while I get the bag in -- and shove off!" panted Stern.

She seized the torch from his hand. Up he snatched the rifle again, and with a pointblank volley flung three of the grays writhing and yelling all in the mud and weeds and trampled cattails on the river verge.

Down he threw the gun. He turned and swept the dark shore, there between the ruins of the wharves, with a keen reconnoitering glance.

What? What was this?

There stood the aged willow to which the banca had been tied. But the boat -- where was it?

With a cry Stern leaped to the tree. His clutching hands fumbled at the trunk.

"My God! Here's -- here's the cord!" he stammered. "But it's -- been cut! The boat -- the boat's gone!"

7. A Night of Toil

An hour later, from the gnarled branches of the willow -- up into which Stern had fairly flung her, and where he had himself clambered with the beasts ravening at his legs -- the two sole survivors of the human race watched the glowering eyes that dotted the velvet gloom.

"I estimate a couple of hundred, all told," judged Allan. "Odd we never ran across any of them before tonight. Must be some kind of a migration under way -- maybe some big shift of game, of deer, or buffalo, or what-not. But then, in that case, they wouldn't be so starved, so dead-set on white meat as they seem to be."

Beta shifted her place on a horizontal limb.

"It's awfully hard for a soft wood," she remarked. "Do you think we'll have to stay here long, dear?"

"That depends. I don't see that the fifteen we've killed since roosting here have served as any terrible examples to the others. And we're about twenty cartridges to the bad. They're not worth it, these devils. We've got to save our ammunition for something edible till I can get my shop to running and begin making my own powder. No; must be there's some other and better way."

"But what?" asked the girl. "We're safe enough here, but we're not getting any nearer home -- and I'm so hungry!"

"Same here," Stern coincided. "And the lunch was all in the boat; worse luck! Who the deuce could have cut her loose? I thought we'd pretty effectually cleared out those Hinkmatinks, or whatever the Horde consisted of.

But evidently something, or somebody, is still left alive with a terrific grudge against us, or an awful longing for navigation."

"Was the cord broken or cut?"

"I'll see."

Stern clambered to a lower branch. With the trigger-guard of his rifle he was able to catch the cord. All about the trunk, mean-while, the wolves leaped snarling. The fetid animal smell of them was strong upon the air -- that, and the scent of blood and raw meat, where they had feasted on the slain.

With the severed cord, Allan climbed back to where Beatrice sat.

"Hold the rifle, will you?" asked he. A moment, and by the quick showers of sparks that issued from his flint and steel, he was examining the leather thong.

"Cut!"

"Cut? But then, then --"

"No tide or wind to blame. Some intelligence, even though rudi-mentary, has been at work here -- is at work -- opposed to us."

"But what?"

"No telling. There may be more things in this world yet than either of us dream. Perhaps we committed a very grave error to leave the apparently peaceful little nook we've got, up there on the Hudson, and tackle this place again. But who could ever have thought of anything like this after that terrible slaughter?"

They kept silence a few minutes. The wolves now had sunk to a plane of comparative insignificance. At the very worst Stern could annihilate them, one by one, with a lavish expenditure of his ammunition. Unnoticed now, they yelped, and scratched and howled about the tree, sat on their haunches, waiting in the gloom, or sneaked -- vague shadows -- among the deeper dusks of the forest.

And once again the east began to glow, even as when he and she had watched the moon rise over the hills beyond the Hudson; and their hearts beat with joy for even that relief from the dark mystery of solitude and night.

After a while the man spoke.

'It's this way," said he. "Whoever cut that cord and either let the banca float away or else stole it, evidently doesn't want to come to close quarters for the present, so long as these wolves are making themselves friendly.

"Perhaps, in a way, the wolves are a factor in our favor; perhaps, without them, we might have had a poisoned arrow sticking into us, or a spear or two, before now. My guess is that we'll get a wide berth so long as the wolves stay in the neighborhood. I think the anthropoids, or whoever they were, must have been calculating on ambushing us as we came back, and expected to 'get' us while we were hunting for the boat.

"They didn't reckon on this little diversion. When they heard it they probably departed for other regions. They won't be coming around just yet, that's a safe wager. Mighty lucky, eh? Think what hard targets we'd make, up here in this willow, by moonlight!"

"You're right, Allan. But when it comes daylight we'll make better ones. And I don't know that I enjoy sitting up here and starving to death, with a bodyguard of wolves to keep away the Horde, very much more than I would taking a chance with the arrows. It's two sixes, either way, and not a bit nice, is it?"

"Hang the whole business! There must be some other way-some way out of this infernal pickle! Hold on -- wait -- I -- I almost see it now!"

"What's your plan, dear?"

"Wait! Let me think, a minute!"

She kept silence. Together they sat among the spreading branches in the growing moonlight. A bat reeled overhead, chippering weakly. Far away a whippoorwill began its fluty, insistent strain. A distant cry of some hunting beast echoed, unspeakably weird, among the dead, deserted streets buried in oblivion. The brush crackled and snapped with the movements of the wolf-pack; the continued snarling, whining, yapping, stilled the chorus of the frogs along the sedgy banks.

"If I could only snare a good, lively one!" suddenly broke out Stern.

"What for?"

"Why, don't you see?" And with sudden inspiration he expounded. Together, eager as children, they planned. Beatrice clapped her hands with sheer delight.

"But," she added pensively, "it'll be a little hard on the wolf, won't it?"

Stern had to laugh.

"Yes," he assented; "but think how much he'll learn about the new kind of game he tried to hunt!"

Half an hour later a grim old warrior of the pack, deftly and securely caught by one hind leg with the slip-noosed leather cord, dangled inverted from a limb, high out of reach of the others.

Slowly he swung, jerking, writhing, frothing as he fought in vain to snap his jaws upon the cord he could not touch. And night grew horrible with the stridor of his yells.

"Now then," remarked Stern calmly, "to work. The moonlight's good enough to shoot by. No reason I should miss a single target."

Followed a time of frightful tumult as the living ate the dying and the dead, worrying the flesh from bones that had as yet scarcely ceased to move. Beatrice, pale and silent, yet very calm, watched the slaughter. Stern, as quietly methodical as though working out a reaction, sighted, fired, sighted, fired. And the work went on apace. The bag of cartridges grew steadily lighter. The work was done long before all the wolves had died. For the survivors, gorged to repletion, some wounded, others whole, slunk gradually away and disappeared in the dim glades, there to sleep off their cannibal debauch.

At last Stern judged the time was come to descend.

"Bark away, old boy!" he exclaimed. "The louder the better. You're our danger-signal now. As long as those poor, dull anthropoid brains keep sensing you I guess we're safe!"

To Beatrice he added:

"Come now, dear. I'll help you down. The quicker we tackle that raft and away, the sooner we'll be home!"

"Home!" she repeated. "Oh, how glad I'll be to see our bungalow again! How I hate the ruins of the city now! Look out, Allan -- you'll have to let me take a minute or two to straighten out in. You don't know how awfully cramped I am!"

"Just slide into my arms -- there, that's right!" he answered, and swung her down as easily as though she had been a child. Her arms went round his neck; their lips met and thrilled in a long kiss.

But not even the night-breeze and the moon could now beguile them to another. For there was hard, desperate work to do, and time was short.

A moment they stood there together, under the old tree wherein the wolf was dangling in loud-mouthed rage.

"Well, here's where I go at it!" exclaimed the man.

He opened the big sack. Fumbling among the tools, he quickly found the ax.

"You, Beta," he directed, "get together all the plaited rope you can take off the bag, and cut me some strips of hide. Cut a lot of them. I'll need all you can make. We've got to work fast -- got to clear out of here before sunrise or there may be the devil to pay!"

It was a labor of extraordinary difficulty, there in those dense and dim-lit thickets, felling a tall spruce, limbing it out and cutting it into three sections. But Stern attacked it like a demon. Now and again he stopped to listen or to jab the suspended wolf with the ax-handle.

"Go on there, you alarm-signal!" he commanded. "Let's have plenty of music, good and loud, too. Maybe if you deliver the goods and hold out -- well, you'll get away with your life. Otherwise, not!"

Robinson Crusoe's raft had been a mere nothing to build compared with this one that the engineer had to construct there at the water's edge, among the sedges and the reeds For Crusoe had planks and beams and nails to help him; while Stern had naught but his ax, the forest, and some rough cordage.

He had to labor in the gloom, as well, listening betimes for sounds of peril or stopping to stimulate the wolf. The dull and rusty ax retarded him; blisters rose upon his palms, and broke, and formed again. But still he toiled.

The three longitudinal spruce timbers he lashed together with poles and with the cords that Beatrice prepared for him. On these, again, he laid and lashed still other poles, rough-hewn.

In half an hour's hard work, while the moon began to sink to the westward, he had stepped a crude mast and hewed a couple of punt-poles.

"No use our trying to row this monstrosity," he said to Beatrice, stopping a moment to dash the sweat off his forehead with a shaking hand. "We either rig the skin sack in some way as a sail, or we drift up with the tide, tie at the ebb, and so on -- and if we make the bungalow in three days we're lucky!

"Come on now, Beatrice. Lend a hand here and we'll launch her! Good thing the tide's coming up- -she almost floats already. Now, one, two, three!"

The absurd raft yielded, moved, slid out upon the marshy water and was afloat!

"Get aboard!" commanded Allan. "Go forward to the *salon de luxe*. I'll stow the bag aft, so."

He lifted her in his arms and set her on the raft. The bag he carefully deposited at what passed for the stern. The raft sank a bit and wallowed, but bore up.

"Now then, all aboard!" cried Stern.

"The wolf, Allan, the wolf! How about him?"

"That's right, I almost plumb forgot! I guess he's earned his life, all right enough."

Quickly he slashed the cord. The wolf dropped limp, tried to crawl, but could not, and lay panting on its side, tongue lolling, eyes glazed and dim.

"He'll be a horrible example all his life of what it means to monkey with the new kind of meat," remarked Allan, clambering aboard. "If wolves or anthropoids can learn, they ought to learn from him!"

Strongly, steadily, they poled the raft out through the marshy slip, on, on, past the crumbling wreckage of the pier-head.

"Now the tide's got us," exclaimed Allan with satisfaction, as the moonlit current, all silver and rippling with calm beauty, swung them up-stream.

Beatrice, still strong, and full of vigorous, pulsing life, in spite of the long vigil in the tree and the hard night of work, curled up at the foot of the rough mast, on the mass of fir-tips Stern had piled there.

"You steer, boy," said she, "and I'll go to work on making some kind of sail out of the big skin. By morning we ought to have our little craft under full control.

"It's one beautiful boat, isn't it?" mocked Stern, poling off from a gaunt hulk that barred the way.

"It mayn't be very beautiful," she answered softly, "but it carries the greatest, purest, noblest love that ever was since the world began -- it carries the hope of the whole world, of all the ages -- and it's taking us home!"

8. The Rebirth of Civilization

A month had hardly gone, before order and peace and the promise of bountiful harvests dwelt in and all about Hope Lodge, as they had named the bungalow.

From the kitchen, where the stove and the aluminum utensils now shone bright and free from rust, to the bedrooms where fir-tips and soft skin rugs made wondrous sleeping places, the house was clean and sweet and beautiful again. Rough-hewn chairs and tables, strong, serviceable and eloquent of nature -- through which this rebirth of the race all had to come -- adorned the rooms. Fur rugs covered the floors.

In lieu of pictures, masses of flowers and great sprays of foliage stood in clay pots of Stern's own manufacture and firing. And on a rustic book-case in their living room, where the big fireplace was, and where the southern sun beat warmest in, stood their chief treasure -- a set of encyclopedias.

Stern had made leather bindings for these, with the deft help of Beatrice. The original bindings had vanished before the attacks of time and insects centuries before. But the leaves were still intact. For these were thin sheets of nickel, printed by the electrolysis process.

"Just a sheer streak of luck," Stern remarked, as he stood looking at this huge piece of fortune with the girl. "Just a kindly freak of fate, that Van Amburg should have bought one of Edison's first sets of nickel-sheet books.

"Except for the few sets of these in existence, here and there, not a book remains on the surface of this entire earth. The finest hand-made linen paper has disintegrated ages ago. And parchment has probably crinkled and molded past all recognition. Besides, up-to-date scientific books, such as we need, weren't done on parchment. We're playing into gorgeous luck with these encyclopedias, for everything I need and can't remember is in them. But it certainly was one job to sort those scattered sheets out of the rubbish-pile in the library and rearrange them."

"Yes, that was hard work, but it's done now. Come on out into the garden, Allan, and see if our crops have grown any during the night!"

The grounds about the bungalow were a delight to them. Like two children they worked, day by day, to enlarge and beautify their holdings, their lands won back from nature's greed.

Though wild fruits -- some new, others familiar -- and fish and the plentiful game all about them offered abundant food, to be had for the mere seeking, they both agreed on the necessity of re-establishing agriculture. For they disliked the thought of being driven southward, with the return of each successive winter. They wanted, if advisable, to be able to winter in the bungalow. And this meant some provision for the unproductive season.

"It won't always be summer here, you know," Stern told her. "This Eden will sometime lie wet and dreary under the winter rains that I expect now take the place of snow. And the eternal curse of Adam -- toil -- is not yet lifted even from us two sur-vivors of the fifteen hundred million that once ruled the earth. We, and those who shall come after, must have the old-time foods again. And that means work!"

They had cleared a patch of black, virgin soil, in a sunny hollow. Here Stern had transplanted all the wild descendants of the vegeta-bles and grains of other time which in his still limited explorations he had come across.

The work of clearing away the thorns and bushes, the tangled lianas and tall trees, was severe; but it strengthened him and hard-ened his whip-cord muscles till they ridged his skin like iron. He burned and pulled the stumps, spaded and harrowed and hoed all by hand, and made ready the earth for the reception of its first crop in a thousand years.

He recalled enough of his anthropology and botany from uni-versity days to recognize the reverted, twisted and stringy little de-generate wild-potato root which had once served the Aztecs and Pueblo Indians for food, and could again, with proper cultivation, be brought back to full perfection. Likewise with the maize, the squash, the wild turnip, and many other vegetable forms.

"Three years of cultivation," he declared, "and I can win them back to edibility. Five, and they'll be almost where they were before the great catastrophe. As for the fruits, the apple, cherry, and pear, all they need is care and scientific grafting.

"I predict that ten years from today, orchards and cornfields and gardens shall surround this bungalow, and the heritage of man shall be brought back to this old world!"

"Always giving due credit to the encyclopedia," added Beatrice.

"And to you!" he laughed happily. "This is all on your account, anyhow. If I were alone in the world, you bet there'd be no gardens made!"

"No, I don't believe there would," she agreed, a serious look on her face. "But, then," she concluded, smiling again, "you aren't alone, Allan. You've got me!"

He tried to catch her in his arms, but she evaded him and ran back toward the bungalow.

"No, no, you've got to work," she called to him from the porch. "And so have I. Goodby!" And with a wave of the hand, a strong, brown hand now, slim and very beautiful, she vanished.

Stern stood in thought a moment, then shook his head, and, with a singular expression, picked up his hoe, and once more fell to cultivating his precious little garden-patch, on which so infinitely much depended. But something lay upon his mind; he paused, reflecting ; then picked up a stone and weighed it in his hand, tried another, and a third.

"I'm damned," he remarked, "if these feel right to me! I've been wondering about it for a week now -- there's got to be some answer to it. A stone of this size in the old days would certainly have weighed more. And that big boulder I rooted out from the middle of the field -- in the other days I couldn't have more than stirred it.

"Am I so very much stronger? So much as all that? Or have things grown lighter? Is that why I can leap farther, walk better, run faster? What's it all about, anyhow?"

He could not work, but sat down on a rock to ponder. Numerous phenomena occurred to him, as they had while he had lain wounded under the tree by the river during their first few days at the bungalow.

"My observations certainly show a day only twenty-two hours and fifty-seven minutes long; that's certain," he mused. "So the earth is undoubtedly smaller. But what's that got to do with the mass of the earth? With weight? Hanged if I can make it out at all!

"Even though the earth has shrunk, it ought to have the same power of gravitation. If all the molecules and atoms really were pressed together, with no space between, probably the earth wouldn't be much bigger than a football, but it would weigh just that much, and a body would fall toward it from space just as fast as now. Quite a hefty football, eh? For the life of me I can't see why the earth's having shrunk has affected the weight of everything!"

Perplexed, he went back to his work again. And though he tried to banish the puzzle from his mind it still continued to haunt and to annoy him.

Each day brought new and interesting activities. Now they made an expedition to gather a certain kind of reeds which Beatrice could plat into cordage and basketry; now they peeled quantities of birch-bark, which on rainy days they occupied themselves in splitting into thin sheets for paper. Stern manufactured a very excellent ink in his improvised laboratory on the second floor, and the split and pointed quills of a wild goose served them for pens in taking notes and recording their experiences.

"Paper will come later, when we've got things a little more settled," he told her. "But for now this will have to do."

"I guess if you can get along with skin clothing for a while, I can do with birch-bark for my correspondence," she replied laughing. "Why not catch some of those wild sheep that seem so plentiful on the hills to westward? If we could domesticate them, that would mean wool and yarn and cloth -- and milk, too, wouldn't it? And if milk, why not butter?"

"Not so fast!" he interposed. "Just wait a while -- we'll have cattle, goats, and sheep, and the whole business in due time; but how much can one pair of human beings undertake? For the present we'll have to be content with what mutton-chops and steaks and hams I can get with a gun -- and we're mighty lucky to have those!"

Singularly enough, and contrary to all beliefs, they felt no need of salt. Evidently the natural salts in their meat and in the fruits they ate supplied their wants. And this was fortunate, because the quest of salt might have been difficult; they might even have had to boil sea-water to obtain it.

They felt no craving for sweets, either; but when one day they came upon a bee-tree about three-quarters of a mile back in the woods to westward of the river, and when Stern smoked out the bees and gathered five pounds of honey in the closely platted rush basket lined with leaves, which they always carried for miscellaneous treasure-trove, they found the flavor delicious. They decided to add honey to their menu, and thereafter always kept it in a big pottery jar in their kitchen.

Stern's hunting, fishing and gardening did not occupy his whole time. Every day he made it a rule to work at least an hour, two if possible, on the thirty-foot yawl that had already begun to take satisfactory shape on the timber ways which now stood on the river bank.

All through July and part of August he labored on this boat, building it stanch and true, calking it thoroughly, fitting a cabin, stepping a fir mast, and making all ready for the great migration which he felt must inevitably be forced upon them by the arrival of cool weather.

He doubted very much, in view of the semitropic character of some of the foliage, whether even in January the temperature would now go below freezing; but in any event he foresaw that there would be no fruits available, and he objected to a winter on flesh foods. In preparation for the trip he had built a little "smoke-house" near the beach, and here he smoked considerable quantities of meat -- deer-meat, beef from a wild steer which he was so fortunate as to shoot during the third week of their stay at the bungalow, and a good score of hams from the wild pigs which rooted now and then among the beech growth half a mile downstream.

Often the girl and he discussed this coming trip, of an evening, sitting together by the river to watch the stars and moon and that strange black wandering blotch that now and then obscured a portion of the night sky -- or perchance leaning back in their huge, rustic easy chairs lined with furs on the broad piazza; or again, if the night were cool or rainy, in front of their blazing fire of pine knots and driftwood, which burned with gorgeous blues and greens and crimsons in the vast throat of Hope Lodge fireplace.

Other matters, too, they talked of -- strange speculations, impossible to solve, yet filling them with vague uneasiness, with wonder and a kind of mighty awe in face of the vast, unknowable mysteries surrounding them; the forces and phenomena which might, though friendly in their outward aspect, at any time precipitate catastrophe, ruin and death upon them and extinguish in their persons all hopes of a world reborn.

The haunting thought was never very far away: "Should either one of us be killed -- what then?"

One day Stern voiced his fear.

"Beatrice," he said, "if anything should ever happen to me, and you be left alone in a world which, without me, would become instantly hostile and impossible, remember that the most scientific way out is a bullet. That's my way if anything happens to you! Understand?"

She nodded, and for a long time that day the silence of a great pact weighed upon their souls.

9. Planning The Great Migration

Stern rigged a tripod for the powerful field-glasses he had rescued from the Metropolitan Building, and by an ingenious addition of a wooden tube and another lens carefully ground out of rock crystal, succeeded in producing (on the right-hand barrel of the binoculars) a telescope of reasonably high power. With this, of an evening, he often made long observations, after which he would spend hours figuring all over many sheets of the birch bark, which he then carefully saved and bound up with leather strings for future reference.

In Van's set of encyclopedias he found a fairly large celestial map and thorough astronomic data. The results of his computations were of vital interest to him.

He said to Beatrice one evening:

"Do you know, that wandering black patch in the sky moves in a regular orbit of its own? It's a solid body, dark, irregular in outline, and certainly not over five hundred miles above the surface of the earth."

"What can it be, dear?"

"I don't know yet. It puzzles me tremendously. Now, if it would only appear in the daytime once in a while, we might be able to get some information or knowledge about it; but, coming only at night, all it records itself as is just a black, moving thing. I'm working on the size of it now, making some careful studies. In a while I shall probably know its area and mass and density. But what it is I cannot say -- not yet."

They both pondered a while, absorbed in wonder. At last the engineer spoke again.

"Beta," said he, "there's another curious fact to note. The axis of the earth itself has shifted more than six degrees, thirty minutes!"

"It has? Well -- what about it?" And she went on with her platting of reed cordage.

"You don't seem much concerned about it!"

"I'm not. Not in the least. It can shift all it wants to, for all of me. What hurt does it do? Doesn't it run just as well that way?"

Stern looked at her a moment, then laughed.

"Oh, yes; it runs all right," he answered. "Only I thought the announcement that the pole-star had thrown up its job might startle you a bit. But I see it doesn't. So far as practical results go, it accounts for the warmer climate and the decreased inclination to the plane of the ecliptic; or, rather, the decreased --"

"Please, please, don't!" she begged. "There's nothing really wrong, is there?"

"Well, that depends on how you define it. Probably an astronomer might think there was something very much wrong. I make it that the orbit of the earth has altered its relative length and width by --"

"No figures, Allan, there's a dear. You know I'm awfully bad at arithmetic. Tell me what it means, won't you?"

"Well, it means, for one thing, that we've maybe spent a far longer time on this earth since the cataclysm than we even dare suspect. It may be that what we've been calculating as about a thousand years, is twice that, or even five times that -- no telling. For another thing, I'm convinced by all these changes, and by the diminution of gravity and by the accelerated rate of revolution of the earth --"

"Allan dear, please hand me those scissors, won't you?"

Stern laughed again.

"Here!" said he. "I guess I'm not much good as a lecturer. But I tell you one thing I'm going to do, and that's a one best bet. I'm going to have a try at some really big telescope before a year's out, and know the truth of this thing!"

"A big telescope! Build one, you mean?"

"Not necessarily. All I need is a chance to make some accurate observations, and I can find out all I need to know. Even though I have been out of college for -- let's see --"

"Fifteen hundred years, at a guess," she suggested.

"Yes, all of that. Even so, I remember a good bit of astronomy. And I've got my mind set on peeking through a first-class tube. If the earth has broken in two, or anything like that, and our part is skyhooting away toward the unknown regions of outer space beyond the great ring of the Milky Way and is getting into an unchartered place in the universe -- as it seems to be -- why, we ought to have a good look at things. We ought to know what's what, eh?

"Then there's the moon I want to investigate, too. No man except myself has even seen the side that's now turned toward the earth. No telling what a good glass mightn't show.

"That's so, dear," she answered. "But where can you find the sort of telescope you need?"

"In Boston -- in Cambridge, rather. The Harvard observatory has the biggest one within striking distance. What do you say to our making our trial trip in the boat, up the Sound and around Cape Cod, to Boston? We can spend a week there, then slant away for wherever we may decide to pass the winter. How does that suit you, Beta?"

She put away her work, and for a moment sat looking in at the flames that went leaping up the huge boulder chimney. The room glowed with warmth and light that drove away the cheerlessness of a foggy, late August drizzle.

"Do you really think we're wise to -- to leave our home, with winter coming on?" she asked at length, pensively, the firelight casting its glow across her cheek and glinting in her eyes.

"Wise? Yes. We can't stay here, that's certain. And what is there to fear out in the world? With our firearms and our knowledge of fire itself, our science and our human intelligence, we're far more than a match for all enemies, whether of the beast-world or of that race of the Horde. I hate, in a way, to revisit the ruins of New York, for more ammunition and canned stuffs. The place is too ghastly, too hideous, now, after the big fight.

"Boston will be a clean ground for us, with infinite resources. And as I said before, there's the Cambridge observatory. It's only two or three miles back in the forest, from the coast; maybe not more than half a mile from some part of the Charles River. We can sail up, camp on Soldiers' Field, and visit it easily. Why not?"

He sat down on the tiger-rug before the fire, near the girl. She drew his head down into her lap; then, when he was lying comfortably, began playing with his thick hair, as he loved so well to have her do.

"If you think it's all right, Allan," said she, "we'll go. I want what you want."

"That's my good girl!" exclaimed the engineer. "We'll be ready to start in a few days now. The boat's next thing to finished. What with the breadfruit, smoked steer and buffalo meat, hams and canned goods now on our shelves, we've certainly got enough supplies to stock her a two months' trip.

"Even with less, we'd be safe in starting. You see, the world's lain untouched by mankind for so many centuries that all the blighting effect of man's folly and greed and general piracy has vanished.

"The soil's got back to its natural state, animal life abounds, and so long as I still have a good supply of cartridges, we can live almost anywhere. Anthropoids? I don't think there's much danger. Oh, yes, I remember the line of blue smoke we saw yesterday over the hills to westward; but what does that prove? Lightning may have started a fire -- there's no telling. And we can't always stay here, Beta, just because there may be dangers out yonder!"

He flung one arm toward the vast night, beyond the panes where the mist and storm were beating cheerlessly.

"No, we can't camp down here indefinitely. Now's the time to start. As I say, we've got all of sixty days' of downright civilized food on hand, for a good cruise in the *Adventure*. The chance of finding other people somewhere is too precious not to make any risk worthwhile."

Silence fell between them for a few minutes. Each saw visions in the flames. The man's thoughts dwelt, in particular, on this main factor of a possible rediscovery of other human beings somewhere.

More than the girl, he realized the prime importance of this possibility. Though he and she loved each other very dearly, though they were all in all each to the other, yet he comprehended the loneliness she felt rather than analyzed -- the infinite need of man for man, of woman for woman -- the old social, group-instinct of the race beginning to reassert itself even in their Eden.

Each of them longed, with a longing they hardly realized as yet, to hear some other human voice, to see another face, clasp another hand and again feel the comradeship of man.

During the past week or so, Stern had more than once caught himself listening for some other sound of human life and activity. Once he had found the girl standing on a wooded point among the pines, shading her eyes with her hand and watching downstream with an attitude of hope which spoke more fluently than words. He had stolen quietly away, saying nothing, careful not to break her mood. For he had understood it; it had been his very own.

The mood expressed itself, at times, in long talks together of the seeming dream-age when there had been so many millions of men and women in the world. Beatrice and Stern found themselves dwelling with a peculiar pleasure on memories and descriptions of throngs.

They would read the population statistics in Van's encyclopedia, and wonder greatly at them, for now these figures seemed the unreal chimeras of wild imaginings.

They would talk of the crowded streets, the "L" crushes and the jams at the Bridge entrance; of packed cars and trains and overflowing theaters; of great concourses they had seen; of every kind and condition of affairs where thousands of their kind had once rubbed elbows, all strangers to each other, yet all one vast kin and family ready in case of need to succor one another, to use the collective intelligence for the benefit of each.

Sometimes they indulged in fanciful comparisons, trying to make their present state seem wholly blest.

"This is a pretty fine way to live, after all," Stern said one day, "even if it is a bit lonesome at times. There's no getting up in the morning and rushing to an office. It's a perpetual vacation! There are no appointments to keeps no angry clients kicking because I can't make water run up-hill or make cast-iron do the work of tool-steel. No saloons or free-lunches, no subways to stifle the breath out of us, no bills to pay and no bill collectors to dodge; no laws except the laws of nature, and such as we make ourselves; no bores and no bad shows; no politics, no yellow journals, no styles --"

"Oh, dear, how I'd like to see a milliner's window again!" cried Beatrice, rudely shattering his thin-spun tissue of optimism. "These skin-clothes, all the time, and no hats, and no chiffons and no -- no nothing, at all! Oh, I never half appreciated things till they were all taken away!"

Stern, feeling that he had tapped the wrong vein, discreetly withdrew; and the sound of his calking-hammer from the beach, told that he was expending a certain irritation on the hull of the *Adventure*.

One day he found a relic that seemed to stab him to the heart with a sudden realization of the tremendous gap between his own life and that which he had left.

Hunting in the forest, to westward of the bungalow, he came upon what at first glance seemed a very long, straight, level Indian mound or earthwork; but in a moment his trained eye told him it was a railway embankment.

With an almost childish eagerness he hunted for some trace of the track; and when, buried under earth-mold and rubbish, he found some rotten splinters of metal, they filled him with mingled pleasure and depression.

"My God!" he exclaimed, "is it possible that here, right where I stand, countless thousands of human beings once passed at tremendous velocity, bent on business and on pleasure, now ages long vanished and meaningless and void? That mighty engines whirled along this bank, where now the forest has been crowding for centuries? That all, all has perished -- forever?

"It shall not be!" he cried hotly, and flung his hands out in passionate denial. "All shall be thus again! All shall return -- only far better! The world's death shall not, cannot be!"

Experiences such as these, leaving both of them increasingly irritated and depressed as time went on, convinced Stern of the imperative necessity for exploration. If human beings still existed anywhere in the world, he and she must find them, even at the risk of losing life itself. Years of migration, he felt, would not be too high a price to pay for the reward of coming once again in contact with his own species. The innate gregariousness of man was torturing them both.

Now that the hour of departure was drawing nigh, a strange exultation filled them both -- the spirit of conquest and of victory.

Together they planned the last details of the trip.

"Is the sail coming along all right, Beta?" asked Stern, the night when they decided to visit Cambridge. "You expect to have it done in a day or two?"

"I can finish it tomorrow. It's all woven now. Just as soon as I finish binding one edge with leather strips, it'll be ready for you."

"All right; then we can get a good, early start, on Monday morning. Now for the details of the freight."

They worked out everything to its last minutiae. Nothing was forgotten, from ammunition to the soap which Stern had made out of moose-fat and wood-ashes and had pressed into cakes; from fishing-tackle and canned goods to toothbrushes made of stiff vegetable fibers set in bone; from provisions even to a plentiful supply of birch-bark leaves for taking notes.

"Monday morning we're off," Stern concluded, "and it will be the grandest lark two people ever had since time began! Built and stocked as the *Adventure* is, she's safe enough for anything from here to Europe.

"Name the place you want to see, and it's yours. Florida? Bermuda? Mediterranean? With the compass I've made and adjusted to the new magnetic variations, and with the maps out of Van's set of books, I reckon we're good for anything, including a trip around the world.

"The survivors will be surprised to see a fully stocked yawl putting in to rescue them from savagery, eh? Imagine doing the Captain Cook stunt, with white people for subjects!"

"Yes, but I'm not counting on their treating us the way Captain

61

Cook was; are you? And what if we shouldn't find anybody, dear? What then?"

"How can we help finding people? Could a billion and a half human beings die, all at once, without leaving a single isolated group somewhere or other?"

"But you never succeeded in reaching them with the wireless from the Metropolitan, Allan."

"Never mind -- they weren't in a condition to pick up my messages; that's all. We surely must find somebody in all the big cities we can reach by water, either along the coast or by running up the Mississippi or along the St. Lawrence and through the lakes. There's Boston, of course, and Philadelphia, New Orleans, San Francisco, St. Louis, Chicago -- dozens of others-no end of places!"

"Oh, if they're only not all like New York!"

"That remains to be seen. There's all of Europe, too, and Africa and Asia -- why, the whole wide world is ours! We're so rich, girl, that it staggers the imagination -- we're the richest people that have ever lived, you and I. The 'pluses' in the old days owned their millions; but we own- -we own the whole earth!"

"Not if there's anybody else alive, dear."

"That's so. Well, I'll be glad to share it with 'em, for the sake of a handshake and a 'howdy,' and a chance to start things going again. Do you know, I rather count on finding a few scattered remnants of folk in London, or Paris, or Berlin?

"Just the same as in our day, a handful of ragged shepherds descended from the Mesopotamian peoples extinct save for them -- were tending their sheep at Kunyunjik, on those Babylonian ruins where once a mighty metropolis stood, and where five million people lived and moved, trafficked, loved, hated, fought, conquered, died -- so now, today, perhaps, we may run across a handful of white savages crouching in caves or rude huts among the debris of the Place de l'Opera, or Unter den Linden, or -- "

"And civilize them, Allan? And bring them back and start a colony and make the world again? Oh, Allan, do you think we could?" she exclaimed, her eyes sparkling with excitement.

"My plans include nothing less," he answered. "It's mighty well worth trying for, at any rate. Monday morning we start, then, little girl."

"Sunday, if you say so."

"Impatient, now?" he laughed. "No, Monday will be time enough. Lots of things yet to put in shape before we leave. And we'll have to trust our precious crops to luck, at that. Here's hoping the winter will bring nothing worse than rain. There's no help for it, whatever happens. The larger venture calls us."

They sat there discussing many many other factors of the case, for a long time. The fire burned low, fell together and dwindled to glowing embers on the hearth.

In the red gloom Allan felt her vague, warm, beautiful presence. Strong was she; vigorous, rosy as an Amazon, with the spirit and the beauty of the great outdoors; the life lived as a part of nature's own self. He realized that never had a woman lived like her.

Dimly he saw her face, so sweet, so gentle in its wistful strength, shadowed with the hope and dreams of a whole race -- the type, the symbol, of the eternal motherhood.

And from his hair he drew her hand down to his mouth and kissed it; and with a thrill of sudden tenderness blent with passion he knew all that she meant to him -- this perfect woman, his love, who sometime soon was now to be his bride.

10. Toward the Great Cataract

Pleasant and warm shone the sun that Monday morning, that September day, warm through the greenery of oak and pine and fern-tree. Golden it lay upon the brakes and mosses by the river-bank; silver upon the sands.

Save for the chippering of the busy squirrels, a hush brooded over nature. The birds were silent. A far blue haze veiled the distant reaches of the stream. Over the world a vague, premonitory something had fallen; it was summer still, but the first touch of dissolution, of decay, had laid the shadow of a pall upon it.

And the two lovers felt their hearts gladden at thought of the long migration out into the unknown, the migration that might lead them to southern shores and to perpetual plenty, perhaps to the great boon of contact once again with humankind.

From room to room they went, making all tight and fast for the long absence, taking farewell of all the treasures that during their long weeks of occupancy had accumulated there about them.

Though Stern was no sentimentalist, yet he, too, felt the tears well in his eyes, even as Beta did, when they locked the door and slowly went down the broad steps to the walk he had cleared to the river.

"Goodby," said the girl simply, and kissed her hand to the bungalow. Then he drew his arm about her and together they went on down the path. Very sweet the thickets of bright blossoms were; very warm and safe the little garden looked, cut out there from the forest that stood guard about it on all sides.

They lingered one last moment by the sun-dial he had carved on a flat boulder, set in a little grassy lawn. The shadow of the gnomon fell athwart the IX and touched the inscription he had graved about the edge:

I Mark No Hours But Bright Ones.

Beatrice pondered.

"We've never had any other kind, together -- not one," said she, looking up quickly at the man as though with a new sort of self-realization. "Do you know that, dear? In all this time, never one hour, never one single moment of unhappiness or disagreement. Never a harsh word, an unkind look or thought. 'No hours but bright ones!' Why, Allan, that's the motto of our lives!"

"Yes, of our lives," he repeated gravely. "Our lives, forever, as long as we live. But come, come -- time's slipping on. See, the shadow's moving ahead already. Come, say goodby to everything, dear, until next spring. Now let's be off and away!"

They went aboard the yawl, which, fully laden, now lay at a little stone wharf by the edge of the sweet wild wood, its mast overhung by arching branches of a Gothic elm.

Allan cast off the painter of braided leather, and with his boat-hook pushed away. He poled out into the current, then raised the sail of woven rushes like that of a Chinese junk.

The brisk north wind caught it, the sail crackled, filled and bellied hugely. He hauled it tight. A pleasant ripple began to murmur at the stern as the yawl gathered speed.

"Boston and way-stations!" cried he. But through his jest a certain sadness seemed to vibrate. As the wooded point swallowed up their bungalow and blotted out all sight of their garden in the wilderness, then as the little wharf vanished, and nothing now remained but memories, he, too, felt the solemnity of a leave-taking which might well be eternal.

Beatrice pressed a spray of golden-rod to her lips.

"From our garden," said she. "I'm going to keep it, wherever we go."

"I understand," he answered. "But this is no time, now, for retrospection. Everything's sunshine, life, hope -- we've got a world to win!"

Then as the yawl heeled to the breeze and foamed away down stream with a speed and ease that bore witness to the correctness of her lines, he struck up a song, and Beatrice joined in, and so their sadness vanished and a great, strong, confident joy thrilled both of them at prospect of what was yet to be.

By mid-afternoon they had safely navigated Harlem River and the upper reaches of East River, and were well up toward Willett's Point, with Long Island Sound opening out before them broadly.

Of the towns and villages, the estates and magnificent palaces that once had adorned the shores of the Sound, no trace remained. Nothing was visible but unbroken lines of tall, blue forest in the distance; the Sound appeared to have grown far wider, and what seemed like a strong current set eastward in a manner certainly not produced by the tide, all of which puzzled Stern as he held the little yawl to her course, sole alone in that vast blue where once uncounted thousands of keels had vexed the brine.

Nightfall found them abreast the ruins of Stamford, still holding a fair course about five or six miles off shore.

Save for the gulls and one or two quick-scurrying flights of Mother Carey's chickens (now larger and swifter than in the old days), and a single "V" of noisy geese, no life had appeared all that afternoon. Stern wondered at this. A kind of desolation seemed to lie over the region

"Ten times more living things in our vicinity back home on the Hudson," he remarked to Beatrice, who now lay 'mid-ships, under the shelter of the cabin, warmly wrapped in furs against the keen cutting of the night wind. "It seems as though something had happened around here, doesn't it? I should have thought the Sound would be alive with birds and fish. What can the matter be?"

She had no hypothesis, and though they talked it over, they reached no conclusion. By eight o'clock she fell asleep in her warm nest, and Stern steered on alone, by the stars, under promise to put into harbor where New Haven once had stood, and there himself get some much-needed sleep.

Swiftly the yawl split the waters of the Sound, for though her sail was crude, her body was as fine and speedy as his long experience with boats could make it. Something of the vast mystery of night and sea penetrated his soul as he held the boat on her way.

The night was moonless; only the great untroubled stars wondered down at this daring venture into the unknown.

Stern hummed a tune to keep his spirits up. Running easily over the monotonous dark swells with a fair following breeze, he passed an hour or two. He sat down, braced the tiller, and resigned himself to contemplation of the mysteries that had been and that still must be. And very sweet to him was the sense of protection, of guardianship, wherein he held the sleeping girl, in the shelter of the little cabin.

He must have dozed, sitting there inactive and alone. How long? He could not tell. All that he knew was, suddenly, that he had wakened to full consciousness, and that a sense of uneasiness, of fear, of peril, hung about him.

Up he started, with an exclamation which he suppressed just in time to avoid waking Beatrice. Through all, over all, a vast, dull roar was making itself heard -- a sound as though of mighty waters rushing, leaping, echoing to the sky that droned the echo back again.

Whence came it? Stern could not tell. From nowhere, from everywhere; the hum and vibrant blur of that tremendous sound seemed universal.

"My God, what's that?" Allan exclaimed, peering ahead with eyes widened by a sudden stabbing fear. "I've got Beatrice aboard, here; I can't let anything happen to her!"

The gibbous moon, red and sullen, was just beginning to thrust its strangely mottled face above the uneasy moving plain of waters. Far off to southward a dim headland showed; even as Stern looked it drifted backward and away.

Suddenly he got a terrifying sense of speed. The headland must have lain five miles to south of him; yet in a few moments, even as he watched, it had gone into the vague obliteration of a vastly greater distance.

"What's happening?" thought Stern. The wind had died; it seemed as though the waters were moving with the wind, as fast as the wind; the yawl was keeping pace with it, even as a floating balloon drifts in a storm, unfeeling it.

Deep, dull, booming, ominous, the roar continued. The sail flapped idle on the mast. Stern could distinguish a long line of foam that slid away, past the boat, as only foam slides on a swift current.

He peered, in the gloom, to port; and all at once, far on the horizon, saw a thing that stopped his heart a moment, then thrashed it into furious activity.

Off there in a direction he judged as almost due northeast, a tenuous, rising veil of vapor blotted out the lesser stars and dimmed the brighter ones.

Even in that imperfect light he could see something of the sinuous drift of that strange cloud.

Quickly he lashed the tiller, crept forward and climbed the mast, his night-glasses slung over his shoulder.

Holding by one hand, he tried to concentrate his vision through the glasses, but they failed to show him even as much as the naked eye could discern.

The sight was paralyzing in its omen of destruction. Only too well Stern realized the meaning of the swift, strong current, the roar -- now ever increasing, ever deepening in volume -- the high and shifting vapor veil that climbed toward the dim zenith.

"Merciful Heaven!" gulped he. "There's a cataract over there -- a terrible chasm -- a plunge -- to what? And we're drifting toward it at express-train speed!"

11. The Plunge!

Dazed though Stern was at his first realization of the impending horror, yet through his fear for Beatrice, still asleep among her furs, struggled a vast wonder at the meaning, the possibility of such a phenomenon.

How could a current like that rush up along the Sound? How could there be a cataract, sucking down the waters of the sea itself -- whither could it fall? Even at that crisis the man's scientific curiosity was aroused; he felt, subconsciously, the interest of the trained observer there in the midst of deadly peril.

But the moment demanded action.

Quickly Stern dropped to the deck, and, noiseless as a cat in his doe-skin sandals, ran aft.

But even before he had executed the instinctive tactic of shifting the helm, paying off, and trying to beat up into the faint breeze that now drifted over the swirling current, he realized its futility and abandoned it.

"No use," thought he. "About as effective as trying to dip up the ocean with a spoon. Any use to try the sweeps? Maybe she and I together could swing away out of the current -- make the shore -- nothing else to do -- I'll try it, anyhow."

Beside the girl he knelt.

"Beta! Beta!" he whispered in her ear. He shook her gently by the arm. "Come, wake up, girlie -- there's work to do here!"

She, submerged in healthy sleep, sighed deeply and murmured some unintelligible thing; but Stern persisted. And in a minute or so there she was, sitting up in the bottom of the yawl among the furs.

In the dim moonlight her face seemed a vague sweet flower shadowed by the dark, wind-blown masses of her hair. Stern felt the warmth, scented the perfume of her firm, full-blooded flesh.

She put a hand to her hair; her tiger-skin robe, falling back to the shoulder, revealed her white and beautiful arm.

All at once she drew that arm about the man and brought him close to her breast.

"Oh, Allan!" she breathed. "My boy! Where are we? What is it? Oh, I was sleeping so soundly! Have we reached harbor yet? What's that noise -- that roaring sound? Surf?"

For a moment he could not answer. She, sensing some trouble, peered closely at him.

"What is it, Allan?" cried she, her woman's intuition telling her of trouble. "Tell me -- is anything wrong?"

"Listen, dearest!"

"Yes, what?"

"We're in some kind of -- of --"

"What? Danger?"

"Well, it may be. I don't know yet. But there's something wrong. You see --"

"Oh, Allan!" she exclaimed, and started up. "Why didn't you waken me before? What is it? What can I do to help?"

"I think there's rough water ahead, dear," the engineer answered, trying to steady his voice, which shook a trifle in spite of him; "At any rate, it sounds like a waterfall of some kind or other; and see, there's a line, a drift of vapor rising over there. We're being carried toward it on a strong current."

Anxiously she peered, now full awake. Then she turned to Allan. "Can't we sail away?"

"Not enough wind. We might possibly row out of the current, and -- and perhaps --"

"Give me one of the sweeps quick, quick!"

He put the sweeps out. No sooner had he braced himself against a rib of the yawl and thrown his muscles against the heavy bar than she, too, was pulling hard.

"Not too strong at first, dear," he cautioned. "Don't use up all your strength in the first few minutes. We may have a long fight for it!"

"I'm in it with you -- till the end -- whichever way it ends," she answered; and in the moonlight he saw the untrammeled swing and play of her magnificent body.

The yawl came round slowly till it was crosswise to the current, headed toward the mainland shore. Now it began to make a little headway. But the breeze slightly impeded it.

Stern whipped out his knife and slashed the sheets of platted rush. The sail crumpled, crackled and slid down; and now under a bare pole the boat cradled slowly ahead transversely across the foam-streaked current that ran swiftly soughing toward the dim vapor-swirls away to the northeast.

No word was spoken now. Both Beatrice and Stern lay to the sweeps; both braced themselves and put the full force of back and arms into each long, powerful stroke. Yet Stern could see that, at the rate of progress they were making over that black and oily swirl, they could not gain ten feet while the current was carrying them a thousand.

In his heart he knew the futility of the fight, yet still he fought. Still Beatrice fought for life, too, there by his side. Human instinct, the will to live, drove them on, on, where both understood there was no hope.

For now already the current had quickened still more. The breeze had sprung up from the opposite direction; Stern knew the boiling rush of waters had already reached a speed greater than that of the wind itself. No longer the stars trembled, reflected? in the waters. All ugly, frothing, broken, the swift current foamed and leaped, in long, horrible gulfs and crests of sickening velocity.

And whirlpools now began to form. The yawl was twisted like a straw, wrenched, hurled, flung about with sickening violence.

"Row! Row!" Stern cried none the less. And his muscles bunched and hardened with the labor; his veins stood out, and sweat dropped from his brow, ran into his eyes, and all but blinded him.

The girl, too, was laboring with all her might. Stern heard her breath, gasping and quick, above the roar and swash of the mad waters. And all at once revulsion seized him -- rage, and a kind of mad exultation, a defiance of it all.

He dropped the sweep and sprang to her.

71

"Beta!" he shouted, louder than the droning tumult. "No use! No use at all! Here -- come to me!"

He drew the sweep inboard and flung it in the bottom of the yawl.

Already the vapors of the cataract ahead were drifting over them and driving in their faces. A vibrant booming shuddered through the dark air, where now even the moon's faint light was all extinguished by the whirling mists.

Heaven and sea shook with the terrible concussion of falling waters. Though Stern had shouted, yet the girl could not have heard him now.

In the gloom he peered at her; he took her in his arms. Her face was pale, but very calm. She showed no more fear than the man; each seemed inspired with some strange exultant thought of death, there with the other.

He drew her to his breast and covered her face; he knelt with her among the heaped-up furs, and then, as the yawl plunged more violently still, they sank down in the poor shelter of the cabin and waited.

His arms were about her; her face was buried on his breast. He smoothed her hair; his lips pressed her forehead.

"Goodby!" he whispered, though she could not hear.

They seemed now to hover on the very brink.

A long, racing sluicelike incline of black waters, streaked with swirls of white, appeared before them. The boat plunged and whirled, dipped, righted, and sped on.

Behind, a huge, rushing, wall-like mass of lathering, leaping surges. In front, a vast nothingness, a black, unfathomable void, up through which gushed in clouds the mighty jets of vapor.

Came a lurch, a swift plunge.

The boat hung suspended a moment.

Stern saw what seemed a long, clear, greenish slant of water. Deafened and dazed by the infernal pandemonium of noise, he bowed his head on hers, and his arms tightened.

Suddenly everything dropped away. The universe crashed and bellowed.

Stern felt a heavy dash of brine -- cold, strangling, irresistible. All grew black.

"Death!" thought he, and knew no more.

12. Trapped on the Ledge

Consciousness won back to Allan Stern -- how long afterward he could not tell -- under the guise of a vast roaring tumult, a deafening thunder that rose, fell, leaped aloft again in huge, titanic cadences of sound.

And coupled with this glimmering sense-impression, he felt the drive of water over him; he saw, vaguely as in the memory of a dream, a dim gray light that weakly filtered through the gloom.

Weak, sick, dazed, the man realized that he still lived; and to his mind the thought "Beatrice!" flashed back again.

With a tremendous effort, gasping and shaken, weak, unnerved and wounded, he managed to raise himself upon one elbow and to peer about him with wild eyes.

A strange scene that. Even in the half light, with all his senses distorted by confusion and by pain, he made shift to comprehend a little of what he saw.

He understood that, by some fluke of fate, life still remained in him; that, in some way he never could discover, he had been cast upon a ledge of rock there in the cataract -- a ledge over which spray and foam hurled, seething, yet a ledge which, parting the gigantic flood, offered a chance of temporary safety.

Above him, sweeping in a vast smooth torrent of clear green, he saw the steady downpour of the falls. Out at either side, as he lay there still unable to rise, he caught glimpses through the spume-drive, glimpses of swift white water, that broke and creamed as it whirled past; that jetted high; that, hissing, swept away, away, to unknown depths below that narrow, slippery ledge.

Realization of all this had hardly forced itself upon his dazed perceptions when a stronger recrudescence of his thought about the girl surged back upon him.

"Beatrice! Beatrice!" he gasped, and struggled up.

On hands and knees, groping, half-blinded, deafened, he began to crawl; and as he crawled, he shouted the girl's name, but the thundering of the vast tourbillions and eddies that swirled about the rock, white and ravening, drowned his voice. Vague yet terrible, in the light of the dim moon that filtered through the mists, the racing flood howled past. And in Stern's heart, as he now came to more and better understanding, a vast despair took shape, a sickening fear surged up.

Again he shouted, chokingly, creeping along the slippery ledge. Through the driving mists he peered with agonized eyes. Where was the yawl now? Where the girl? Down there in that insane welter of the mad torrent -- swept away long since to annihilation? The thought maddened him.

Clutching a projection of the rock, he hauled himself up to his feet, and for a moment stood there, swaying, a strange, tattered, dripping figure in the dim moonlight, wounded, breathless and disheveled, with bloodshot eyes that sought to pierce the hissing spray.

All at once he gulped some unintelligible thing and staggered forward.

There, wedged in a crevice, he had caught sight of something -- what it was he could not tell, but toward it now he stumbled.

He reached the thing. Sobbing with realization of his incalculable loss and of the wreckage of all their hopes and plans and all that life had meant, he fell upon his knees beside the object.

He groped about it as though blind; he felt that formless mass of debris, a few shattered planks and part of the woven sail, now jammed into the fissure in the ledge. And at touch of all that remained to him, he crouched there, ghastly pale and racked with unspeakable anguish.

But hope and the indomitable spirit of the human heart still urged him on. The further end of the ledge, overdashed with wild jets of spray and stinging drives of brine, still remained unexplored. And toward this now he crept, bit by bit, fighting his way along, now clinging as some more savage surge leaped over, now battling forward on hands and knees along the perilous strip of stone.

One false move, he knew, one slip and all was over. He, too, like the yawl itself, and perhaps like Beatrice, would whirl and fling away down, down, into the nameless nothingness of that abyss.

Better thus, he dimly realized, better, after all, than to cling to the ledge in case he could not find her. For it must be only a matter of time, and no very long time at that, when exhaustion and starvation would weaken him and when he must inevitably be swept away.

And in his mind he knew the future, which voiced itself in a half-spoken groan:

"If she's not there, or if she's there, but dead -- goodby!"

Even as he sensed the truth he found her. Sheltered behind a jutting spur of granite, Beatrice was lying, where the shock of the impact had thrown her when the yawl had struck the ledge.

Drenched and draggled in her water-soaked tiger-skin, her long hair tangled and disheveled over the rock, she lay as though asleep.

"Dead!" gasped Allan, and caught her in his arms, all limp and cold. Back from her brow he flung the brine-soaked hair; he kissed her forehead and her lips, and with trembling hands began to chafe her face, her throat, her arms.

To her breast he laid his ear, listening for some flicker of life, some promise of vitality again.

And as he sensed a slight yet rhythmic pulsing there -- as he detected a faint breath, so vast a gratitude and love engulfed him that for a moment all grew dazed and shaken and unreal.

He had to brace himself, to struggle for self-mastery.

"Beta! Beta!" he cried. "Oh, my God! You live -- you live!"

Dripping water, unconscious, lithe, she lay within his clasp, now strong again. Forgotten his weakness and his pain, his bruises, his wounds, his fears All had vanished from his consciousness with the one supreme realization --"She lives!"

Back along the ledge he bore her, not slipping now, not crouching, but erect and bold and powerful, nerved to that effort and that daring by the urge of the great love that flamed through all his veins.

Back he bore her to the comparative safety of the other end, where only an occasional breaker creamed across the rock and where, behind a narrow shelf that projected diagonally upward and outward, he laid his precious burden down.

And now again he called her name; he rubbed and chafed her. Only joy filled his soul. Nothing else mattered now. The total loss of their yawl and all its precious contents, the wreck of their expedition almost at its very start, the fact that Beatrice and he were now alone upon a narrow ledge of granite in the midst of a stupendous cataract that drained the ocean down to unknown, unthinkable depths, the knowledge that she and he now were without arms, ammunition, food, shelter, fire, anything at all, defenseless in a wilderness such as no humans ever yet had faced -- all this meant nothing to Allan Stern.

For he had her; and as at last her lids twitched, then opened, and her dazed eyes looked at him; as she tried to struggle up while he restrained her; as she chokingly called his name and stretched a tremulous hand to him, there in the thunderous half light of the falls, he knew he could not ask for greater joy, though all of civilization and of power might be his, without her.

In his own soul he knew he would choose this abandonment and all this desperate peril with Beatrice, rather than safety, comfort, luxury, and the whole world as it once had been apart from her.

Yet, as sometimes happens in the supreme crises of life, his first spoken word was commonplace enough.

"There, there, lie still!" he commanded, drawing her close to his breast. "You're all right, now -- just keep quiet, Beatrice!"

"What -- what's happened --" she gasped. "Where --"

"Just a little accident, that's all," he soothed the frightened girl. Dazed by the roaring cadence of the torrent, she shuddered and hid her face against him; and his arms protected her as he crouched there beside her in the scant shelter of the rocky shelf.

"We got carried over a waterfall, or something of that sort," he added. "We're on a ledge in the river, or whatever it is, and --"

"You're hurt, Allan?"

"No, no -- are you?"

"It's nothing, boy!" She looked up again, and even in the dim light he saw her try to smile. "Nothing matters so long as we have each other!"

Silence between them for a moment, while he drew her close and kissed her. He questioned her again, but found that save for bruises and a cruel blow on the temple, she had taken no hurt in the plunge that had stunned her. Both, they must have been flung from the yawl when it had gone to pieces. How long they had lain upon the rock they knew not. All they could know was that the light woodwork of the boat had been dashed away with their supplies and that now they again faced the world empty-handed -- provided even that escape were possible from the midst of that mad torrent.

An hour or so they huddled in the shelter of the rocky shelf till strength and some degree of calm returned and till the growing light far off to eastward through the haze and mist told them that day was dawning again.

Then Allan set to work exploring once more carefully their little islet in the swirling flood.

"You stay here, Beta," said he. "So long as you keep back of this projection you're safe. I'm going to see just what the prospect is."

"Oh, be careful, Allan!" she entreated. "Be so very, very careful, won't you?"

He promised and left her. Then, cautiously, step by step, he made his way along the ledge in the other direction from that where he had found the senseless girl.

To the very end of the ledge he penetrated, but found no hope. Nothing was to be seen through the mists save the mad foam-rush of the waters that leaped and bounded like white-maned horses in a race of death. Bold as the man was, he dared not look for long. Dizziness threatened to overwhelm him with sickening lure, its invitation to the plunge. So, realizing that nothing was to be gained by staying there, he drew back and once more sought Beatrice.

"Any way out?" she asked him, anxiously, her voice sounding clear and pure through the tumult of the rushing waters.

He shook his head, despairingly. And silence fell again, and each sat thinking long, long thoughts, and dawn came creeping grayly through the spume-drive of the giant falls.

More than an hour must have passed before Stern noted a strange phenomenon -- an hour in which they had said few words -- an hour in which both had abandoned hopes of life -- and in which, she in her own way, he in his, they had reconciled themselves to the inevitable.

But at last, "What's that?" exclaimed the man; for now a different tone resounded in the cataract, a louder, angrier note, as though the plunge of waters at the bottom had in some strange, mysterious way drawn nearer. "What's that?" he asked again.

Below there somewhere by the tenebrous light of morning he could see -- or thought that he could see -- a green, dim, vaguely tossing drive of waters that now vanished in the whirling mists, now showed again and now again grew hidden.

Out to the edge of the rocky shelf he crept once more. Yes, for a certainty, now he could make out the seething plunge of the waters as they roared into the foam-lashed flood below.

But how could this be? Stern's wonder sought to grasp analysis of the strange phenomenon.

"If it's true that the water at the bottom's rising," thought he, "then there must either be some kind of tide in that body of water or else the cavity itself must be filling up. In either case, what if the process continues?"

And instantly a new fear smote him -- a fear wherein lay buried like a fly in amber a hope for life, the only hope that had yet come to him since his awakening there in that trap sealed round by sluicing maelstroms.

He watched a few moments longer, then with a fresh resolve, desperate yet joyful in its strength, once more sought the girl.

"Beta," said he, "how brave are you?"

"How brave? Why, dear?"

He paused a moment, then replied: "Because, if what I believe is true, in a few minutes you and I have got to make a fight for life -- a harder fight than any we've made yet -- a fight that may last for hours and may, after all, end only in death. A battle royal! Are you strong for it? Are you brave?"

"Try me!" she answered, and their eyes met, and he knew the truth, that come what might of life or death, of loss or gain, defeat or victory, this woman was to be his mate and equal to the end.

"Listen, then!" he commanded. "This is our last, our only chance. And if it fails --"

12. On the Crest of the Maelstrom

Stern's observation of the rising flood proved correct. By whatever theory it might or might not be explained, the fact was positive that now the water there below them was rising fast, and that inside of an hour the torrent would engulf their ledge.

It seemed as though there must be some vast, rhythmic ebb and flux in the unsounded abysses that yawned beneath them, some incalculable regurgitation of the sea, which periodically spewed forth a part, at least, of the enormous torrent that for hours poured into that titanic gulf.

And it was upon this flux, stormy and wild and full of seething whirlpools, that Allan Stern and the girl now built their only possible hope of salvation and of life.

"Come, we must be at world!" he told her, as together they peered over the edge and now beheld the weltering flood creeping up, up along the thunderous plunge of the waterfall till it was within no more than a hundred feet of their shelter.

As the depth of the fall decreased the spray-drive lessened, and now, with the full coming of day, some reflection of the golden morning sky crept through the spray. Yet neither to right nor left could they see shore or anything save that long, swift, sliding wall of brine, foam- tossed and terrible.

"To work!" said he again. "If we're going to save ourselves out of this inferno we've got to make some kind of preparation. We can't just swim and trust to luck. We shall have to make a float of some sort or other, I think."

"Yes, but what with?" asked she.

"With what remains of the yawl!"

And even as he spoke he led the way to the crevice where the splintered boards and the torn sail had been wedged fast.

"A slim hope, I know," he admitted, "but it's all we've got now."

Driven home as the wreckage was by the terrific impact of the blow, Stern had a man's work cut out for him to get it clear; but his was as the strength of ten, and before half an hour had passed he had, with the girl's help, freed all the planks and laid them out along the rock-shelf, the most sheltered spot of the ledge.

Soon the planks had been lashed into a rough sort of float with what cordage remained and with platted strips of the mat sail.

"It's not half big enough to hold us up altogether," judged the man, "but if we merely use it to keep our heads out of water it will serve, and it's got the merit of being unsinkable, anyhow. God knows how long we may have to be in the water, little girl. But whatever comes we've got to face it. There's no other chance at all!"

They waited now calmly, with the resignation of those who have no alternative to hardship. And steadily the flood mounted up, up, toward the ledge, and now the seethe was very near. Now already the leaping froth of the plunge was dashing up against their rock. In a few moments the shelter would be submerged.

He put his lips close to her ear, for now his voice could not carry.

"Let's jump for it!" he cried. "If we wait till the flood reaches us here we'll be crushed against the rock. Come on, Beatrice, we've got to plunge!"

She answered with her eyes; he knew the girl was ready. To him he drew her and their kiss was one that spoke eternal farewell. But of this thought no word passed their lips.

"Come!" bade the man once more.

How they leaped into that vortex of mad waters, how they vanished in that thunderous welter, rose, sank, fought, strangled, rose again and caught the air, and once more were whirled down and buried in that crushing avalanche; how they clung to the lashed planks and with these spiraled in mad sarabands among the whirlpools and green eddies; how they were flung out into smoother water, blinded and deafened, yet with still the spark of life and consciousness within them, and how they let the frail raft bear them, fainting and dazed, all their senses concentrated just on gripping this support -- all this they never could have told.

Stern knew at last, with something of clarity, that he was float-ing easily along an oily current which ran, undulating, beneath a slate-gray mist; he realized that with one hand he was grasping the planks, with the other arm upbearing the girl.

Pale and with closed eyes, she lay there in the hollow of his arm, her face free from water, her long hair floating out upon the tide.

He saw her lids twitch and knew she lived. Yet even as he thanked God and took a firmer hold on her, consciousness lapsed again, and with it all realization of time or of events.

Yet though the moments -- or were they hours? -- which followed left no impress on his brain, some intelligence must have directed Stern. For when once more he knew, he found the mist and fog all gone; he saw a golden sun that weltered all across the heaving flood in a brave splendor; and, off to northward, a wooded line of hills, blue in the distance, yet beautiful with their promise of salvation.

Stern understood, then, what must have happened. He saw that the upfilling of the abyss, whatever might have caused it, had flung them forth; he perceived that the temporary flood which had taken place before once more another terrific down-draft should pour into the gaping chasm, had cast them out, floated by their raft of planks, even as match-straws might be flung and floated on the outburst of a geyser.

He understood; he knew that, fortune favoring, life still beck-oned there ahead.

And in his heart resolve leaped up.

"Life! Life!" he cried. "Oh, Beatrice, look! See! There's land ahead, there -- land!"

But the girl, still circled by his arm, lay senseless. Allan knew he could make no progress in that manner. So by dint of great labor, he managed to draw her somewhat onto the float and there to lash her with a loose end of cordage in such wise that she could breathe with no danger of drowning.

Himself he summoned all his forces, and now began to swim through the smooth tides, which, warm with some grateful heat, vastly unlike the usual ocean chill, stretched lazily rolling away and away to that far off shore.

That day was long and bitter, an agony of toil, hope, despair, labor and struggle, and the girl, reviving, shared it toward the end. Only their frail raft fenced death away, but so long as the buoyant planks held together they could not drown.

Thirst and exhaustion tortured them, but there was no hope of appeal to any help. In this manless world there could be no rescue. Here, there, a few gulls wheeled and screamed above the flood; and once a school of porpoises, glistening as they curved their shining backs in long leaps through the brine, played past. Allan and the girl envied the creatures, and renewed their fight for life.

The south wind favored, and what seemed a landward current drew them on. Their own strength, too, in spite of the long fast and the incredible hardships, held out well. For now that civilization was a thing of the oblivious past, they shared the vital forces and the very powers of Mother Nature herself. And, like two favored children of that all-mother, they slowly made their way to land.

Night found them utterly exhausted and soaked to the marrow, yet alive, stretched out at full length, inert, upon the warm sands of a virgin beach. There they lay, supine, above high tide, whither they had dragged themselves with terrible exertion. And the stars wheeled overhead; and down upon them the strange-featured moon wondered with her pallid gleam.

Fireless, foodless and without shelter, unprotected in every way, possessing nothing now save just their own bodies and the draggled garments that they wore, they lay and slept. In their supreme exhaustion they risked attack from wild beasts and from anthropoids. Sleep to them was now the one vital, inevitable necessity.

Thus the long night hours passed and strength revived in them, up-welling like fresh tides of life; and once more a new day grayed the east, then transmuted to bright gold and blazoned its insignia all up the eastern sky.

Stern woke first, dazed with the long sleep, toward mid-morning.

A little while he lay as though adream, trying to realize what had happened; but soon remembrance knitted up the fabric of the peril and the close escape. And, arising stiffly from the sand, he stretched his splendid muscles, rubbed his eyes, and stared about him.

A burning thirst was tormenting him. His tongue clave to the roof of his mouth; he found, by trial, that he could scarcely swallow.

"Water!" gasped he, and peered at the deep green woods, which promised abundant brooks and streams.

But before he started on that quest he looked to see that Beatrice was safe and sound. The girl still slept. Bending above her he made sure that she was resting easily and that she had taken no harm. But the sun, he saw, was shining in her face.

"That won't do at all!" he thought; and now with a double motive he strode off up the beach, toward the dense forest that grew down to the line of shifting sands.

Ten minutes and he had discovered a spring that bubbled out beneath a moss-hung rock, a spring whereof he drank till renewed life ran through his vigorous body. And after that he sought and found with no great labor a tree of the same species of breadfruit that grew all about their bungalow on the Hudson.

Then, bearing branches of fruit, and a huge, fronded tuft of the giant fern-trees that abounded there, he came back down the beach to the sleeping girl, who still lay unconscious in her tigerskin, her heavy hair spread drying on the sands, her face buried in the warm, soft hollow of her arm.

He thrust the stalk of the fern-tree branch far down into the sand, bending it so that the thick leaves shaded her. He ate plentifully of the fruit and left much for her. Then he knelt and kissed her forehead lightly, and with a smile upon his lips set off along the beach.

A rocky point that rose boldly against the morning, a quarter-mile to southward, was his objective.

"Whatever's to be seen round here can be seen from there," said he. "I've got my job cut out for me, all right -- here we are, stranded, without a thing to serve us, no tools, weapons or implements or supplies of any kind -- nothing but our bare hands to

85

work with, and hundreds of miles between us and the place we call home. No boat, no conveyance at all. Unknown country, full of God knows what perils!"

Thinking, he strode along the fine, smooth, even sands, where never yet a human foot had trodden. For the first time he seemed to realize just what this world now meant -- a world devoid of others of his kind. While the girl and he had been among the ruins of Manhattan, or even on the Hudson, they had felt some contact with the past; but here, Stern's eye looked out over a world as virgin as on the primal morn. And a vast loneliness assailed him, a yearning almost insupportable. that made him clench his fists and raise them to the impassive, empty sky that mocked him with its deep and azure calm.

But from the rocky point, when he had scaled its height, he saw far off to westward a rising column of vapor which for a while diverted his thoughts. He recognized the column, even though he could not hear the distant roaring of the cataract he knew lay under it. And, standing erect and tall on the topmost pinnacle, eyes shaded under his level hand, he studied the strange sight.

"Yes, the flood's rushing in again, down that vast chasm," he exclaimed. "The chasm that nearly proved a grave to us! And every day the same thing happens -- but how and why? By Jove, here's a problem worthy a bigger brain than mine!

"Well, I can't solve it now. And there's enough to do, without bothering about the maelstrom -- except to avoid it!"

He swept the sea with his gaze. Far off to southward lay a dim, dark line, which at one time must have been Long Island; but it was irregular now and faint, and showed that the island had been practically submerged or swept away by the vast geodetic changes of the age since the catastrophe.

A broken shore-line, heavily wooded, stretched to east and west. Stern sought in vain for any landmark which might give him position on a shore once so familiar to him. Whether he now stood near the former site of New Haven, whether he was in the vicinity of the one-time mouth of the Connecticut River, or whether the shore where he now stood had once been Rhode Island, there was no means of telling. Even the far line of land on the horizon could not guide him.

"If that is some remnant of Long Island," he mused, "it would indicate that we're no further east than the Connecticut; but there's no way to be sure. Other islands may have been heaved up from the ocean floor. There's nothing definite or certain about anything now, except that we're both alive, without a thing to help us but our wits and that I'm starving for something more substantial than that breadfruit!"

Wherewith he went back to Beatrice.

He found her, awake at last, sitting on the beach under the shadow of the fern-tree branch, shaking out her hair and braiding it in two thick plaits. He brought her water in a cup deftly fashioned from a huge leaf; and when she had drunk and eaten some of the fruit they sat and talked a while in the grateful warmth of the sun.

She seemed depressed and disheartened, at last, as they discussed what had happened and spoke of the future.

"This last misfortune, Allan," said she, "is too much. There's nothing now except life --"

"Which is everything!" he interrupted, laughing. "If we can weather a time like that, nothing in store for us can have any terrors!" His own spirits rose fast while he cheered the girl.

He drew his arm about her as they sat together on the beach.

"Just be patient, that's all," bade he. "Just give me a day or so to find out our location, and I'll get things going again, never fear. A week from now we may be sailing into Boston Harbor -- who knows?,'

And, shipwrecked and destitute though they were, alone in the vast emptiness of that deserted world, yet with his optimism and his faith he coaxed her back to cheerfulness and smiles again.

"The whole earth is ours, and the fulness thereof!" he cried, and flung his arms defiantly outward. "This is no time for hesitance or fear. Victory lies all before us yet. To work! To work!"

14. A Fresh Start

Indomitably the human spirit, temporarily beaten down and crushed by misfortunes beyond all calculation, once more rose in renewed strength to the tremendous task ahead. And, first of all, Stern and the girl made a camping place in the edge of the forest, close by the spring under the big rock.

"We've got to have a base of supplies, or something of that sort," the man declared. "We can't start trekking away into the wilderness at once, without consideration and at least some definite place where we can store a few necessaries and to which we can retreat, in case of need. A camp, and -- if possible -- a fire, these are our first requisites."

Their camp they built (regardless of the protests of birds and squirrels and many little woodland folk) roughly, yet strongly enough to offer protection from the rain, under a thick- leaved oak, which in itself gave shelter. This oak, through whose branches darted many a gay- plumaged bird of species unknown to Stern, grew up along the overhanging face of Spring Rock, as they christened it.

By filling in the space between the rock and the bole of the oak with moss and stones, and then by building a heavy lean-to roof of leafy branches, thatched with lashed bundles of marsh- grass, they constructed in two days a fairly comfortable shack, hard by an abundant, never- failing supply of the finest water ever a human set lip to.

Here Stern piled fragrant grasses in great quantity for the girl's bed. He himself volunteered to sleep at the doorway, on guard with his only weapon -- a jagged boulder lashed with leather thongs to a four-foot heft, even in the; very fashion of the neolithic ancestors of man.

Their food supply reverted to such berries and fruits as they could gather in the fringes of the forest, for as yet they dared not penetrate far from the shore. To these they added a plentiful supply of clams, which they dug with sharp sticks, at low tide, far out across the sand-flats -- toiling for all the world like two of the identical savages who in the long ago, a thousand or five thousand years before the white man came to America, had left shell-heap middens along the north Atlantic coast.

This shell-fish gathering brought the action of the tides to their careful attention. The tide, they found, behaved in an erratic manner. Instead of two regular flows a day there was but one. And at the ebb more than two miles of beach and sea-bottom lay exposed below the spot where they had landed at the flood. Stern analyzed the probable cause of this phenomenon.

"There must be two regular tides," he said, "only they're lost in the far larger flux and reflux caused by the vortex we escaped from. Any marine geyser like that, able to, suck down water enough from the sea to lay bare two miles of beach every day and capable of throwing a column of mist and spray like that across the sky, is worth investigating. Some day you and I are going to know more about it -- a lot more!"

And that was truth; but little the engineer suspected how soon, or under what surpassingly strange circumstances, the girl and he were destined to behold once more the workings of that terrible and mighty force.

On the third day Stern set himself to work on the problem of making fire. He had not even flint-and-steel now; nor any firearm. Had he possessed a pistol he could have collected a little birch-bark, sought out a rotten pine-stump, and discharged his weapon into the "punk," then blown the glow to a flame, and almost certainly have got a blaze. But he lacked everything, and so was forced back to primitive man's one simplest resource -- friction.

As an assistant instructor in anthropology at Harvard University, he had now and then produced fire for his class of expectant students by using the Peruvian fire-drill; but even this simple expedient required a head-strap and a jade bearing, a well-formed spindle and a bow. Stern had none of these things, neither could he fashion them without tools. He had, therefore, to resort to the still more primitive method of "fire-sawing," such as long, long ago the Australian bushmen had been wont to practice.

He was a strong man, determined and persistent; but two days more had passed, and many blisters covered his palms ere -- after innumerable experiments with different kinds of woods and varying strokes -- the first tiny glow fell into the carefully scraped sawdust. And it was with a fast-beating heart and tremulous breath that he blew his spark to a larger one, then laid on his shredded strips of bark and blew again, and so at last, with a great up-welling triumph in his soul, beheld the flicker of a flame once more.

Exhausted, he carefully fed that precious fire, while the girl clapped her hands with joy. In a few moments more the evening air in the dim forest aisles was gladdened by the ruddy blaze of a camp-fire at the door of the lean-to, and for the first time smoke went wafting up among the branches of that primeval wood.

"Now for some real meat!" cried Stern with exultation. "Tomorrow I go hunting!"

That evening they sat for hours feeding their fire with deadfalls, listening to the trickle of the little spring and to the night sounds of the forest, watching the bats flicker among the dusky spaces, and gazing at the slow and solemn march of the stars beyond the leafy fretwork overhead. Stern slept but little that night, in his anxiety to keep the fire fed; and morning found him eager to be at his work with throwing-sticks among the vistas of the wilderness.

Together they hunted that day. She carried what his skilful aim brought down from the tangled greenery above. Birds, squirrels, chipmunks, all were welcome. Noon found them in possession of more than thirty pieces of small game, including two hedgehogs. And for the first time in almost a week they tasted flesh again, roasted on a sharp stick over the glowing coals.

Stern hunted all that day and the next. He dressed the game with an extraordinarily large and sharp clamshell, which he whetted from time to time on a rock beside the spring. And soon the fire was overhung with much meat, being smoked with a pinecone smudge in preparation for the journey into the unknown.

"Inside of a week, at this rate," he judged, "we'll be able to start again. You must set to work platting a couple of sacks. The grass along the brook is tough and long. We can carry fifty or seventy-five pounds of meat, for emergencies. Fruits we can gather on the way."

"And fire? Can we carry that?"

"We can take a supply of properly dried-out woods with punk. I've already had practice enough, so I ought to be able to get fire at any time inside of half an hour."

"Weapons?"

"I'll make you a battle-ax like my own, only lighter. That's the best we can do for the present, till we strike some ruin or other where a city used to be."

"And you're still bent on reaching Boston?"

"Yes. I reckon we're more than half-way there by now. It's the nearest big ruin, the nearest place where we can refit and recoup the damage done, get supplies and arms and tools, build another boat, and in general take a fresh start. If we can make ten miles a day, we can reach it in; ten days or less. I think, all things considered, the Boston plan's the wisest possible one."

She gazed into the fire a moment before replying. Then, stirring the coals with a stick, said she:

"All right, boy; but I've got a suggestion to make."

"What is it?"

"We'll do better to follow the shore all the way round."

"And double the distance?"

"Yes, even so. You know, this shore is -- or used to be -- flat and sandy most of the way. We can make better progress along beaches and levels than we can through the forest. And there's the matter of shell-fish to consider; and most important of all --"

"Well, what?"

"The sea will guide us. We can't get lost, you understand. With the exception of cutting across the shank of Cape Cod, if the cape still exists, we needn't ever get out of sight of salt water. And it will bring us surely to the Hub."

"By Jove, you're right!" he cried enthusiastically. "The shore-line has it! And tomorrow morning at sunup we begin preparations in earnest. You'll weave the knapsacks while I go after still more meat. Gad! Now that everything's decided, the quicker we're on our way the better. I'm keen to see old Tremont Hill again, and get my hands on a good stock of arms and ammunition once more!"

That night, long after Beatrice was sleeping soundly on her bed of odorous grasses, Allan lay musing by the lean-to door, in the red glow of the fire. He was thinking of the long and painful history of man, of the great catastrophe and of the terrible responsibility that now lay on his own shoulders.

As in a panorama, he saw the emergence of humanity from the animal stage, the primitive savagery of his kind; then the beginnings of the family, the nomadic epoch, the stone age, and the bronze age, and the age of iron; the struggle up to agriculturalism, and communism, and the beginnings of the village groups, with all their petty tribal wars.

He saw the slow formation of small states, the era of slavery, then feudalism and serfdom, and at last the birth of modern nations, the development of machinery, and the vast nexus of exploitation known as capitalism -- the stage which at one blow had been utterly destroyed just as it had been transmuting into collectivism.

And at thought of this Stern felt a pang of infinite regret.

"The whole evolutionary process wiped out," mused he, "just as it was about to pass into its perfect form, toward which the history of all the ages had conspired, for which oceans of blood had been spilled and millions of men and women -- billions! -- lived and toiled and died!

"All gone, all vanished -- it's all been in vain, the woe and travail of the world since time began, unless she and I, just we two, preserve the memory and the knowledge of the world's long, bitter fight, and hand them down to strong descendants.

"Our problem is to bridge this gap, to keep the fires of science and of truth alive, and, if that be possible, to start the world again on a higher plane, where all the harsh and terrible phases will no longer have to be lived through again. Our problem and our task! Were ever two beings weighed by such a one?"

And as he pondered, in the firelight, his thoughts and dreams and hopes all centered in the sleeping girl, there in the lean-to sheltered by his watchful care. But what those dreams were, what his visions of the future -- who shall set forth or fully understand?

15. Labor and Comradeship

Four days later, having hastened all their preparations and worked with untiring energy, they broke camp for the long, perilous trek in quest of the ruins of a dead and buried city.

It was at daylight that they started from the little shack in the edge of the forest. Both were refreshed by a long sleep and by a plunge in the curling breakers that now, at high tide, were driven up the beach by a stiff sea-breeze.

The morning, which must have been toward the end of September -- Stern had lost accurate count but reckoned the day at about the twenty-fifth -- dawned clear and bracing, with just a tang of winelike exhilaration in the air. Before them the beach spread away and away to eastward, beyond the line of vision, a broad and yellow road to bid them travel on.

"Come, girl, *en marche!*" cried the man cheerily, as he adjusted Beta's knapsack so that the platted cord should not chafe her shoulders, then swung his own across his back. And with a buoyant sense of conquest, yet a regret at leaving the little camp which, though crude and rough, had yet been a home to them for a week, they turned their faces to the rising sun and set out on the journey into the unexplored.

Much altered were they now from those days at Hope Villa, when they had been able to restore most of the necessities and even some of the refinements of civilization. Now the girl's hair hung in two thick braids down over her worn tiger-skin, each braid as big as a strong man's wrist, for she lacked any means to do it up; she had not so much as a comb, nor could Stern, without a knife, fashion one for her. Their sandals hung in tatters. Stern had tried to repair them with strips of squirrel-skin clumsily hacked out with the sharp clam-shell, but the result was crude.

Long were his hair and beard, untrimmed now, unkempt

and red. Clad in his ragged fur garment, bare legged and bare armed, with the grass-cloth sack slung over his sinewy shoulder and the heavy stone-ax in his hand, he looked the very image of prehistoric man -- as she, too, seemed the woman of that distant age.

But though their outward guise was that of savages far cruder than the North American Indian was when Columbus first beheld him, yet in their brains lay all the splendid inheritance of a world-civilization. And as the fire-materials in Stern's sack contained, in germ, all the mechanic arts, so their joint intelligence presaged everything that yet might be.

They traveled at an easy pace, like voyagers who foresee many hard days of journeying and who are cautious not at first to drain their strength. Five hours they walked, with now and then a pause. Stern calculated they had made twelve miles or more before they camped beside a stream that flowing thinly from the wood, sank into the sand and was lost before it reached the sea.

Here they ate and rested till the sun began to pass its meridian, when once more they started on their pilgrimage. That night, after a day wherein they had met no other sign of life than gulls and crows ravaging the mussel-beds, they slept on piles of sun-dried kelp which they heaped into some crevices under an overhanging brow of low cliffs on a rocky point. And dawn found them again, traveling steadily eastward, battle-axes swinging, hopes high, in perfect comradeship and faith.

Toward what must have been about ten o'clock of that morning they reached the mouth of a river, something like half a mile wide where it joined the sea. By following this up a mile or so they reached a narrow point; but even here, burdened as they were, swimming was out of the question.

"The only thing to do," said Stern, "will be to wait till the tide backs up and gives us quiet water, then make our way across on a log or two " -- a plan they put into effect with good success. Mid-afternoon, and they were on their way again, east-bound

"Was that the Connecticut?" asked Beatrice. "Or do you think we've passed that already?"

"More likely to be the Thames," he answered. "I figure that what used be New London is less than five miles from here."

"Why not visit the ruins? There might be something there."

"Not enough to bother with. We mustn't be diverted from the main issue, Boston! Forward, march!"

Next day Stern descried a point jutting far out to sea, which he declared was none other than Watch Hill Point, on the Rhode Island boundary. And on the afternoon of the following day they reached what was indisputably Point Judith and Narragansett Bay.

Here they were forced to turn northward; and when camping time came, after they had dug their due allowance of clams and gathered their breadfruit and made their fire in the edge of the woods, they held conclave about their future course.

The bay was, indeed, a factor neither Stern nor she had reckoned on. To follow its detours all the way around would add seventy to a hundred miles to their journey, according as they hugged the shore or made straight cuts across some of the wooded promontories.

"And from Providence, at the head of the bay, to Boston, is only forty miles in a direct line northwest-by-north," said he, poking the fire contemplatively.

"But if we miss our way?"

"How can we, if we follow the remains of the railroad? The cuts and embankments will guide us all the way."

"I know; but the forest is so thick!"

"Not so thick but we can make at least five miles a day. That is, inside of eight days we can reach the Hub. And we shall have the help of tools and guns, remember. In a place the size of Providence there must be a few ruins still containing something of value. Yes, by all means the overland route is best, from now on. It means forty miles instead of probably two hundred."

Thus they agreed upon it; and, having settled matters, gave them no more thought, but prepared for rest. And sunset came down once more; it faded, smoldering along the forest-line to westward; it burned to dull ambers and vague purples, then went out. And "the wind that runs after the sun awoke and sang softly among the tree-tops, a while, like the intoning of a choir invisible, and was silent again."

There by the firelight he half saw, half sensed her presence, vague and beautiful despite the travel-worn, tattered skin that clothed her. He felt her warm, vital nearness; his hand sought hers and pressed it, and the pressure was returned. And with a thrill of overwhelming tenderness he realized what this girl was to him and what his love meant and what it all portended.

Until long after dark they sat and talked of the future, and of life and death, and of the soul and of the great mystery that had swept the earth clean of all of their kind and had left them, alone, of all those fifteen hundred million human creatures.

And overhead, blotting out a patch of sky and stars, moved slowly the dark object which had so puzzled Stern since the first time he had observed it -- the thing he meant to know about and solve, once he could reach the Cambridge Observatory. And of this, too, they talked; but neither he nor she could solve the riddle of its nature.

Their talk together, that night, was typical of the relationship that had grown up between them in the long weeks since their awakening in the Tower. Almost all, if not quite all, the old-time idea of sex had faded -- the old, false assumption on the part of the man that he was by his very nature the superior of woman.

Stern and Beatrice now stood on a different footing; their friendship, comradeship and love were based on the tacit recognition of absolute equality, save for Stern's accidental physical superiority. It was as though they had been two men, one a little stronger and larger than the other, so far as the notion of equality went; though this by no means destroyed that magnetic sex-emotion which, in other aspects, thrilled and attracted and infused them both.

Their love never for a moment obscured Stern's recognition of the girl as primarily a human being, his associate on even terms in this great game that they were playing together, this tremendous problem they were laboring to solve -- the vastest and most vital problem that ever yet had confronted the human race, now represented in its totality by these two living creatures.

And as Beatrice recalled the world of other times, with all its false conventions, limitations and pettily stupid gallantries, she shuddered with repulsion. In her heart she knew that, had the choice been hers, she would not have gone back to that former state of half-chattel patronage, half-hypocritical homage and total misconception.

Contrasting her present state with her past one, and comparing this man -- all ragged, unshaven and long-haired as he was, yet a true man in every inch of his lithe, virile body -- with others she remembered, she found up-welling in her a love so deep and powerful, grounded on such broad bases of respect and gratitude, mutual interest and latent passion, that she herself could not yet understand it in all its phases and its moods.

The relation which had grown up between them, comrades and partners in all things, partook of a fine tolerance, an exquisite and never-failing tenderness, a wealth of all intimate, yet respectful adoration. It held elements of brotherhood and parenthood; it was the love of co-workers striving toward a common goal, of companions in life and in learning, in striving, doing, accomplishing, even failing. Failure mattered nothing; for still the comradeship was there.

And on this soil was growing daily and hourly a love such as never since the world began had been equaled in purity and power, faith, hope, integrity. It purified all things, made easy all things, braved all things, pardoned all things; it was long-suffering and very kind.

They had no need to speak of it; it showed in every word and look and act, even in the humblest and most commonplace of services each for each. Their love was lived, not talked about.

All their trials and tremendous hardships, their narrow passes with death, and their hard-won escapes, the vicissitudes of a savage life in the open, with every imaginable difficulty and hard expedient, could not destroy their illusions or do aught than bind them in closer bonds of unity.

And each realized when the time should ripen for another and a more vital love, that, too, would circle them with deeper tenderness, binding them in still more intense and poignant bonds of joy.

16. Finding the Biplane

The way up the shores of Narragansett Bay was full of experiences for them both. Animal life revealed itself far more abundantly here than along the open sea.

"Some strange blight or other must lie in the proximity of that terrific maelstrom," judged Stern, "something that repels all the larger animals. But skirting this bay, there's life and to spare. How many deer have we seen today? Three? And one bull-buffalo -- With any kind of a gun, or even a revolver, I could have had them all. And that big-muzzled, shaggy old moose we saw drinking at the pool, back there, would have been meat for us if we had had a rifle. No danger of starving here, Beatrice, once we get our hands on something that'll shoot again!"

The night they camped on the way, Stern kept constant guard by the fire, in case of possible attack by wolves or other beasts. He slept only an hour, when the girl insisted on taking his place; but when the sun arose, red and huge through the mists upon the bay, he started out again on the difficult trail as strong and confident as though he had not kept nine hours of vigil.

Everywhere was change and desolation. As the travelers came into a region which had at one time been more densely populated, they began to find here and there mournful relics of the life that once had been -- traces of man, dim and all but obliterated, but now and then puissant in their revocation of the distant past.

Twice they found the ruins of villages -- a few vague hollows in the earth, where cellars had been, hollows in which huge trees were rooted, and where, perhaps, a grass-grown crumble of disintegrated brick indicated the one-time presence of a chimney. They discovered several farms, with a few stunted apple-trees, the distant descendants of orchard growths, struggling against the larger forest strength, and with perhaps a dismantled well-curb, a moss-covered fireplace or a few bits of iron that had possibly been a stove, for all were relics of the other age. Mournful were the long stone walls, crumbling down yet still discernible in places -- walls that had cost the labor of generations of farmers and yet now lay useless and forgotten in the universal ruin of the world.

On the afternoon of the fifth day since having left their lean-to by the shore of Long Island Sound, they came upon a canyon which split the hills north of the site of Greenwich, a gigantic "fault "in the rocks, richly striated and stratified with rose and red and umber, a great cleft on the other side of which the forest lay somber and repellent in the slanting rays of the September sun.

"By Jove, whatever it was that struck the earth," said Stern, "must have been good and plenty. The whole planet seems to be ripped up and broken and shattered. No wonder it knocked down New York and killed everybody and put an end to civilization. Why, there's ten cubic miles of material gouged out right here in sight; here's a regular Panama Canal, or bigger, all scooped out in one piece! What the devil could have happened?"

There was no answer to the question. After an hour spent in studying the formations along the lip of the cleft they made a detour eastward to the shore, crossed the fjord that ran into the canyon, and again kept to the north. Soon after this they struck a railroad embankment, and this they followed now, both because it afforded easier travel than the shore, which now had grown rocky and broken, and also because it promised to guide them surely to the place they sought.

It was on the sixth day of their exploration that they at last penetrated the ruins of Providence. Here, as in New York, pavements and streets and squares were all grassed over and covered with pines and elms and oaks, rooting among the stones and shattered brickwork that lay prone upon the earth. Only here or there a steel or concrete building still defied the ravages of time.

"The wreckage is even more complete here than on Manhattan Island," Stern judged as he and the girl stood in front of the ruins of the post-office surveying the debris. The smaller area, of course, would naturally be covered sooner with the inroads of the forest. I doubt whether there's enough left in the whole place to be of any real service to us."

"Tomorrow will be time enough to see," answered the girl. "It's too late now for any more work today."

They camped that night in an upper story of the Pequot National Bank Building on Hampstead Street. Here, having cleared out the bats and spiders, they made themselves an eerie secure from attack, and slept long and soundly. Dawn found them at work among the overgrown ruins, much as -- three months before -- they had labored in the Metropolitan Tower and about it. Less, however, remained to salvage here. For the smaller and lighter types of buildings had preserved far less of the relics of civilization than had been left in the vast and solid structures of New York.

In a few places, none the less, they still came upon the little piles of the gray ash that marked where men and women had fallen and died; but these occurred only in the most sheltered spots. Stern paid no attention to them. His energies and his attention were now fixed on the one task of getting skins, arms, ammunition and supplies. And before nightfall, by a systematic looting of such shops as remained -- perhaps not above a score in all could even be entered -- the girl and he had gathered more than enough to last them on their way to Boston. One find which pleased him immensely was a dozen sealed glass jars of tobacco.

"As for a pipe," said he, "I can make that easily enough. What's more I will!" More still, he did, that very evening, and the gloom was redolent again of good smoke. Thereafter he slept as not for a long, long time.

They spent the next day in fashioning new garments and sandals; in putting to rights the two rifles Stern had chosen from the basement of the State armory, and in making bandoliers to carry their supply of cartridges. The possession of a knife once more, and of steel wherewith readily to strike fire, delighted the man enormously. The scissors they found in a hardware- shop, though rusty, enabled him to trim his beard and hair. Beatrice hailed a warped hard-rubber comb with joy.

But the great discovery still awaited them, the one supreme find which in a moment changed every plan of travel, opened the world to them, and at a single stroke increased their hopes ten thousandfold -- the discovery of the old Pauillac biplane!

They came upon this machine, pregnant with such vast possibilities, in a concrete hangar back of the Federal courthouse on Anderson Street. The building attracted Stern's attention by its unusual state of preservation. He burst in one of the rusted iron shutters and climbed through the window to see what might be inside.

A moment later Beatrice heard a cry of astonishment and joy.

"Great Heavens!" the man exclaimed, appearing at the window. "Come in! Come in -- see what I've found!"

And he stretched out his hands to help her up and through the aperture.

"What is it, boy? More arms? More --"

"An aeroplane! Good God, think o' that, will you?"

"An aeroplane? But it's all to pieces, of course, and --"

"Come on in and look at it, I say!" Excitedly he lifted her through the window. "See there, will you? Isn't that the eternal limit? And to think I never even thought of trying to find one in New York!"

He gestured at the dust-laden old machine that, forlorn and in sovereign disrepair, stood at the other end of the hangar. Together they approached it.

"If it will work," the man exclaimed thickly; "if it will only work --"

"But will it?" the girl exclaimed, her eyes lighting with the excitement of the find, heart beating fast at thought of what it might portend. "Can you put it in shape, boy? Or --"

"I don't know. Let me look! Who knows? Maybe --"

And already he was kneeling, peering at the mechanism, feeling the frame, the gear, the stays, with hands that trembled more than ever they had trembled since their great adventure had begun.

As he examined the machine, while Beatrice stood by, he talked to himself.

"Good thing the framework is aluminum," said he, "or it wouldn't be worth a tinker's dam after all this time. But as it is, it's taken no harm that I can see. Wire braces all gone, rusted out and disappeared. Have to be rewired throughout, if I can find steel wire; if not, I'll use braided leather thongs. Petrol tank and feed pipe O. K. Girder boom needs a little attention. Steering and control column intact -- they'll do!"

Part by part he handled the machine, his skilled eye leaping from detail to detail.

"Canvas planes all gone, of course. Not a rag left; only the frame. But, no matter, we can remedy that. Wooden levers, skids, and so on, gone. Easily replaced. Main thing is the engine. Looks as though it had been carefully covered, but, of course, the covering has rotted away. No matter, we'll soon see. Now, this carbureter --"

His inspection lasted half an hour, while the girl, lost among so many technicalities, sat down on the dusty concrete floor beside the machine and listened in a kind of dazed admiration.

He gave her, finally, his opinion.

"This machine will go if properly handled," said he, rising triumphantly and slapping the dust off his palms. "The chassis needs truing up, the equilibrator has sagged out of plumb, and the ailerons have got to be readjusted, but it's only a matter of a few days at the outside before she'll be in shape.

"The main thing is the engine, and so far as I can judge, that's pretty nearly O. K. The magneto may have to be gone over, but that's a mere trifle. Odd, I never thought of either finding one of these machines in New York, or building one! When I think of all the weary miles we've tramped it makes me sick!"

"I know," she answered; "but how about fuel? And another thing -- have you ever operated one? Could you --"

"Run one?" He laughed aloud. "I'm the man who first taught

Carlton Holmes to fly -- you know Holmes, who won the Gordon-Craig cup for altitude record in 1916. I built the first --"

"I know, dear; but Holmes was killed at Schenectady, you remember, and this machine is different from anything you're used to, isn't it?" Beatrice asked.

"It won't be when I'm through with it! I tell you, Beatrice, we're going to fly. No more hiking through the woods or along beaches for us. From now on we travel in the air -- and the world opens out to us as though by magic.

"Distance ceases to mean anything. The whole continent is ours. If there's another human creature on it we find him! And if there isn't then, perhaps we may find some in Asia or in Europe, who knows?"

"You mean you'd dare to attack the Atlantic with a patched-up machine more than a thousand years old?"

"I mean that eventually I can and will build one that'll take us to Alaska, and so across the fifty-mile gap from Cape Prince of Wales to East Cape. The whole world lies at our feet, girl, with this new idea, this new possibility in mind!"

She smiled at his enthusiasm.

"But fuel?" asked she, practical even in her joy. "I don't imagine there's any gasoline left now, do you? A stuff as volatile as that, after all these centuries? What metal could contain it for a thousand years?"

"There's alcohol," he answered. "A raid on the ruins of a few saloons and drug-stores will give me all I need to carry me to Boston, where there's plenty, never fear. A few slight adjustments of the engine will fit it for burning alcohol. And as for the planes, good stout buckskin, well sewn together and stretched on the frames, will do the trick as well as canvas -- better, maybe."

"But --"

"Oh, what a little pessimist it is today!" he interrupted. "Always coming at me with objections, eh?" He took her in his arms and kissed her. "I tell you Beta, this is no pipe-dream at all, or anything like it; the thing's reality -- we're going to fly! But it'll mean the most tremendous lot of sewing and stitching for you!"

"You're a dear!" she answered inconsequentially. "I do believe if the whole world fell apart you could put it together again."

"With your help, yes," said he. "What's more, I'm going to -- and a better world at that than ever yet was dreamed of. Wait and see!"

Laughing, he released her.

"Well, now, we'll go to work," he concluded. "Nothing's accomplished by mere words. Just lay hold of that lateral there, will you? And we'll haul this old machine out where we can have a real good look at her, what do you say? Now, then, one, two, three --"

17. All Aboard for Boston!

Nineteen days from the discovery of the biplane, a singular happening for a desolate world took place on the broad beach that now edged the city where once the sluggish Providence River had flowed seaward.

For here, clad in a double suit of leather that Beatrice had made for him, Allan Stern was preparing to give the rehabilitated Pauillac a try-out.

Day by day, working incessantly when not occupied in hunting or fishing, the man had rebuilt and overhauled the entire mechanism. Tools he had found a-plenty in the ruins, tools which he had ground and readjusted with consummate care and skill. Alcohol he had gathered together from a score of sources. All the wooden parts, such as skids and levers and propellers, long since vanished and gone, he had cleverly rebuilt.

And now the machine, its planes and rudders covered with strongly sewn buckskin, stretched as tight as drum heads, its polished screw of the Chauviere type gleaming in the morning sun, stood waiting on the sands, while Stern gave it a painstaking inspection.

"I think," he judged, as he tested the last stay and gave the engine its final adjustment. "I think, upon my word, this machine's better today than when she was first built. If I'm not mistaken, buckskin's a better material for planes than ever canvas was -- it's far stronger and less porous, for one thing -- and as for the stays, I prefer the braided hide. Wire's so liable to snap.

"This compass I've rigged on gimbals here, beats anything Pauillac himself ever had. What's the matter with my home-made gyrostat and anemometer? And hasn't this aneroid barometer got cards and spades over the old-style models?"

Enthusiastic as a boy, Stern shook his head and smiled delightedly at Beatrice as he expounded the merits of the biplane and its fittings. She, half glad, half anxious at the possible outcome of the venture, stood by and listened and nodded as though she understood all the minutiae he explained.

"So then, you're ready to go up this morning?" she asked, with just a quiver of nervousness in her voice. "You're quite certain everything's all right -- no chance of accident? For if anything happened --"

"There, there, nothing can happen, nothing will!" he reassured her. "This motor's been run three hours in succession already without skipping an explosion. Everything's in absolute order, I tell you. And as for the human, personal equation, I can vouch for that myself!"

Stern walked around to the back of the machine, picked up a long, stout stake he had prepared, took his ax, and at a distance of about twelve feet behind the biplane drove the stake very deep into the hard sand.

He knotted a strong leather cord to the stake, brought it forward and secured it to the frame of the machine.

"Now, Beatrice," he directed, "when I'm ready you cut the cord. I haven't any corps of assistants to hold me back till the right moment and then give me a shove, so the best I can do is this. Give a quick slash right here when I shout. And whatever happens don't be alarmed. I'll come back to you safe and sound, never fear. And this afternoon it's 'All Aboard for Boston!'"

Smiling and confident, he cranked the motor. It caught, and now a chattering tumult filled the air, rising, falling, as Stern manipulated throttle and spark to test them once again.

Into the driver's seat he climbed, strapped himself in and turned to smile at Beatrice.

Then with a practiced hand he threw the lever operating the friction-clutch on the propeller-shaft. And now the great blades began to twirl, faster, faster, till they twinkled and buzzed in the sunlight with a hum like that of a gigantic electric fan.

The machine, yielding to the urge, tugged forward, straining at its bonds like a whippet eager for a race. Beatrice, her face flushed with excitement, stood ready with the knife.

Louder, faster whirled the blades, making a shiny blur; a breeze sprang out behind them; it became a wind, blowing the girl's hair back from her beautiful face.

Stern settled himself more firmly into the seat and gripped the wheel.

The engine was roaring like a battery of Northrup looms. Stern felt the pull, the power, the life of the machine. And his heart leaped within him at his victory over the dead past, his triumph still to be!

"All right!" he cried. "Let go -- let go!"

The knife fell. The parted rope jerked back, writhing, like a wounded serpent.

Gently at first, then with greater and greater speed, shaking and bouncing a little on the broad, flat wheels that Stern had fitted to the alighting gear, the plane rolled off along the firm-beaten sands.

Stern advanced the spark and now the screw sang a louder, higher threnody. With ever-accelerating velocity the machine tooled forward down the long stretch, while Beatrice stood gazing after it in rapt attention.

Then all at once, when it had sped some three hundred feet, Stern rotated the rising plane; and suddenly the machine lifted. In a long smooth curve, she slid away up the air as though it had been a solid hill -- up, up, up -- swifter and swifter now, till a suddenly accelerated rush cleared the altitude of the tallest pines in the forest edging the beach, and Stern knew his dream was true!

With a great shout of joy, he leaped the plane aloft! Its rise had all the exhilarating suddenness of a seagull flinging up from the foam-streaked surface of the breakers. And in that moment Stern felt the bliss of conquest.

Behind him, the spruce propellers were making a misty haze of humming energy. In front, the engine spat and clattered. The vast spread of the leather wings, sewn, stretched and tested, crackled and boomed as the wind got under them and heaved them skyward.

Stern shouted again. The machine, he felt, was a thing of life, friendly and true. Not since that time in the tower, months ago, when he had repaired the big steam-engine and actually made it run, had he enjoyed so real a sense of mastery over the world as now; had he sensed so definite a connection with the mechanical powers of the world that was, the world that still should be.

No longer now was he fighting the forces of nature, all bare-handed and alone. Now back of him lay the energy of a machine, a metal heart, throbbing and inexhaustible and full of life! Now he had tapped the vein of Power! And in his ears the ripping volley of the exhaust sounded as sweetly as might the voice of a long-absent and beloved girl returning to her sweetheart.

For a moment he felt a choking in his throat, a mist before his eyes. This triumph stirred him emotionally, practical and cool and keen though he was. His hand trembled a second; his heart leaped, throbbing like the motor itself.

But almost immediately he was himself once more. The weakness passed. And with a sweep of his clear eyes, he saw the speeding landscape, woods, hills, streams, that now were running there beneath him like a fluid map.

"My God, it's grand, though!" he exclaimed, swerving the plane in a long, ascending spiral. All the art, the knack of flight came back to him, at the touch of the wheel, as readily as swimming to an expert in the water. Fear? The thought no more occurred to him than to you, reading these words.

Higher he mounted, higher still, his hair whipping out behind in the wild wind, till he could see the sparkle of Narragansett Bay, there in the distance where the river broadened into it. At him the wind tore, louder even than the spitting crackle of the motor. He only laughed, and soared again.

But now he thought of Beatrice; and, as he banked and came about, he peered far down for sight of her.

Yes, there she stood, a tiny dot upon the distant sand. And though he knew she could not hear, in sheer animal spirits and overwhelming joy he shouted once again, a wild, mad triumphant hurrah that lost itself in empty space.

The test he gave the Pauillac convinced him she would carry all the load they would need put upon her, and more. He climbed, swooped, spiraled, volplaned, and rose again, executing a series of evolutions that would have won him fame at any aero meet. And when, after half an hour's exhaustive trial, he swooped down toward the beach again, he found the plane alighted as easily as she had risen.

Like a sea-bird sinking with flat, outstretched wings, coming to rest with perfect ease and beauty on the surface of the deep, the Pauillac slid down the long hill of air. Stern cut off power. The machine took the sand with no more than vigorous bound, and, running forward perhaps fifty yards, came to a stand.

Stern had no sooner leaped from the seat than Beatrice was with him.

"Oh, glorious!" she cried, her face alight with joy and fine enthusiasm. All her spontaneity, her love and admiration were aroused. And she kissed him with so frank and glad a love that Stern felt his heart jump wildly. He thought she never yet had been so beautiful.

But all he said was:

"Couldn't run finer, little girl! Barring a little stiffness here and there, she's perfect. So, then, when do we start, eh? Tomorrow morning, early?"

"Why not this afternoon? I'm sure we can get ready by then."

"Afternoon it is, if you say so! But we've got to work, to do it!"

By noon they had gathered together all the freight they meant to carry, and -- though the sun had dimmed behind dull clouds of a peculiar slaty gray, that drifted in from eastward -- had prepared for the flight to Boston. After a plentiful dinner of venison, berries and breadfruit, they loaded the machine.

Stern calculated that, with Beatrice as a passenger, he could carry seventy-five or eighty pounds of freight. The two rifles, ammunition, knives, ax, tools and provisions they packed into the skin sack Beatrice had prepared, weighed no more than sixty. Thus Stern reckoned there would be a fair "coefficient of safety "and more than enough power to carry them with safety and speed.

It was at 1:15 that the girl took her place in the passenger's seat and let Stern strap her in.

"Your first flight, little girl?" he asked smiling, yet a trifle grave. The barking motor almost drowned his voice.

She nodded but did not speak. He noted the pulse in her throat, a little quick, yet firm.

"You're positive you're not going to be afraid?"

"How could I, with you?"

He made all secure, climbed up beside her, and strapped himself in his seat.

Then he threw in the clutch and released the brake.

"Hold fast!" cried he. "All aboard for Boston! Hold fast!"

18. The Hurricane

Soaring strongly even under the additional weight, humming with the rush of air, the plane made the last turn of her spiral and straightened out at the height of twelve hundred feet for her long northward run across the unbroken wilderness.

Stern preferred to fly a bit high, believing the air-currents more dependable there. Even as he rose above the forest-level, his experienced eye saw possible trouble in the wind-clouds banked to eastward and in the fall of the barometer. But with the thought, "At this rate we'll make Boston in three-quarters of an hour at the outside, and the storm can't strike so soon," he pushed the motor to still greater speed and settled to the urgent business of steering a straight course for Massachusetts Bay.

Only once did he dare turn aside his eyes even so much as to glance at Beatrice. She, magnificently unafraid on the quivering back of this huge airdragon, showed the splendid excitement of the moment by the sparkle of her glance, the rush of eloquent blood to her cheeks.

Stern's achievement, typical of the invincible conquest of the human soul over matter, time and space, thrilled her with unspeakable pride. And as she breathed for the first time the pure, thin air of those upper regions, her strong heart leaped within her breast, and she knew that this man was worthy of her most profound, indissoluble love.

Far down beneath them now the forest sped away to southward. The gleam of the river, dulled by the sunless sky, showed here and there through the woods, which spread their unbroken carpet to the horizon, impenetrable and filled with nameless perils. At thought of how he was cheating them all, Stern smiled to himself with grim satisfaction.

"Good old engine!" he was thinking, as he let her out another notch. "Some day I'll put you in a boat, and we'll go cruising. With you, there's no limit to the possibilities. The world is really ours now, with your help!"

Behind them now lay the debris of Pawtucket. Stern caught a glimpse of a ruined building, a crumpled-in gas-tank with an elm growing up through the stark ribs of it, a jumble of wreckage, all small and toylike, there below; then the plane swooped onward, and all lay deep buried in the wilderness again.

"A few minutes now," he said to himself, "and we'll be across what used to be the line, and be spinning over Massachusetts. This certainly beats walking all hollow! Whew!" as the machine lurched forward and took an ugly drop. He jerked the rising-plane lever savagely. "Still the same kind of unreliable air, I see, that we used to have a thousand years ago!"

For a few minutes the biplane hummed on and on in long rising and falling slants, like a swallow skimming the surface of a lake. The even staccato of the exhaust, echoless in that height and vacancy, rippled with cadences like a monster mowing-machine. And Stem was beginning to consider himself as good as in Boston already -- was beginning to wonder where the best place might be to land, whether along the shore or on the Common, where, perhaps, some open space still remained -- when another formidable air-pocket dropped him with sickening speed.

He righted the plane with a wrench that made her creak and tremble.

"I've got to take a higher level, or a lower," he thought. "Something's wrong here, that's certain!"

But as he shot the biplane sharply upward, hoping to find a calmer lane, a glance at the sky showed trouble impending.

Over the gray background of wind-clouds, a fine-shredded cloud was beginning to scud. The whole east had grown black. Only far off to westward did a little patch of dull blue show; and even this was closing up with singular rapidity. And, though the motion of the machine made this hard to estimate, Stern thought to see by the lateral drift of the country below, that they were being carried westward by what -- to judge from the agitation of the tree-tops far below -- must already be a considerable gale.

For a moment the engineer cursed his foolhardiness in having started in face of such a storm as now every moment threatened to break upon them.

"I should have known," he told himself, "that it was suicidal to attempt a flight when every indication showed a high wind coming. My infernal impatience, as usual! We should have stayed safe in Providence and let this blow itself out, before starting. But now -- well, it's too late."

But was it? Had he not time enough left to make a wide sweep and circle back whence he had come? He glanced at the girl. If she showed fear he would return. But on her face he saw no signs of aught but confidence and joy and courage. And at sight of her, his own resolution strengthened once again.

"Why retreat?" he pondered, holding the machine to her long soaring rise. "We must have made a good third of the distance already -- perhaps a half. In ten or fifteen minutes more we ought to sight the blue of the big bay. No use in turning back now. And as for alighting and letting the storm blow over, that's impossible. Among these forests it would mean only total wreckage. Even if we could land, we never could start again. No; the only thing to do is to hold her to it and plow through, storm or no storm. I guess the good old Pauillac can stand the racket, right enough!"

Thus for a few moments longer he held the plane with her nose to the northeast-by-north, his compass giving him direction, while far, far below, the world slid back and away in a vast green carpet of swaying trees that stretched to the dim, dun horizon.

Stern could never afterward recall exactly how or when the hurricane struck them. So stunning was the blow that hurled itself, shrieking, in a tumult of mad cross-currents, air maelstroms and frenzied whirls, all across the sky; so overpowering the chill tempest that burst from those inky clouds; so sudden the darkness that fell, the slinging hail volleys that lashed and pelted them, that any clear perception of their plight became impossible.

All the man knew was that direction and control had been knocked clean from his hands; that the world had suddenly vanished in a black drive of cloud and hail and wild-whipping vapor; that he no longer knew north from south, or east from west; but that -- struggling now even to breathe, filled with sick fears for the safety of the girl beside him -- he was fighting, wrenching, wrestling with the motor and the planes and rudders, to keep the machine from up-ending, from turning turtle in mid-air, from sticking her nose under an air-layer and swooping, hurtling over and over, down, down, like a shattered rocket, to dash herself to pieces on the waiting earth below.

The first furious onset showed the engineer he could not hope to head up into that cyclone and live. He swung with it, therefore; and now, driving across the sky like a filament of cloud-wrack, rode on the crest of the great storm, his motor screaming its defiance at the shrieking wind.

Did Beatrice shout out to him? Did she try to make him hear? He could not tell. No human voice could have been audible in such a turmoil. Stern had no time to think even of her at such a moment of deadly peril.

As a driver with a runaway stallion jerks and saws and strains upon the leather to regain control, so now the man wrestled with his storm-buffeted machine. A less expert aeronaut must have gone down to death in that mad nexus of conflicting currents; but Stern was cool and full of craft and science. Against the blows of the huge tempest he pitted his own skill, the strength of the stout mechanism, the trained instincts of the born mechanician.

And, storm-driven, the biplane hurtled westward, ever westward, through the gloom. Nor could its two passengers by any sight or sound determine what speed they traveled at, whither they went, what lay behind, or what ahead.

Concepts of time, too, vanished. Did it last one hour or three? Five hours, or even more? Who could tell? Lacking any point of contact with reality, merged and whelmed in that stupendous chill nightmare, all wrought of savage gale, rain, hail-blasts, cloud and scudding vapor, they sensed nothing but the fight for life itself, the struggle to keep aloft till the cyclone should have blown itself out, and they could seek the shelter of the earth once more.

Reality came back with a rift in the jetty sky, the faint shine of a little pale blue there, and -- a while later -- a glimpse of water, or what seemed to be such, very far below.

More steady now the currents grew. Stern volplaned again; and as the machine slid down toward earth, came into a calmer and more peaceful stratum.

Down, down through clouds that shifted, shredded and reassembled, he let the plane coast, now under control once more; and all at once there below him, less than three thousand feet beneath, he saw, dim and vague as though in the light of evening, a vast sheet of water that stretched away, away, till the sight lost it in a bank of low-hung vapors on the horizon.

"The sea?" thought Stern, with sudden terror. Who could tell? Perhaps the storm, westbound, had veered; perhaps it might have carried them off the Atlantic coast! This might be the ocean, a hundred or two hundred miles from land. And if so, then good-by!

Checking the descent, he drove forward on level wings, peering below with wide eyes, while far above him the remnants of the storm fled, routed, and let a shaft of pallid sunlight through.

Stern's eye caught the light of that setting beam, which still reached that height, though all below, on earth, was dusk; and now he knew the west again and found his sense of direction.

The wind, he perceived, still blew to westward; and with a thrill of relief he felt, as though by intuition, that its course had not varied enough to drive him out to sea.

Though he knew the ripping clatter of the engine drowned his voice, he shouted to the girl:

"Don't be alarmed! Only a lake down there!" and with fresh courage gave the motor all that she would stand.

A lake! But what lake? What sheet of water, of this size, lay in New England? And if not in New England, then where were they?

A lake? One of the Great Lakes? Could that be? Could they have been driven clear across Massachusetts, its whole length, and over New York State, four hundred miles or more from the sea, and now be speeding over Erie or Ontario?

Stern shuddered at the thought. Almost as well be lost over the sea as over any one of these tremendous bodies! Were not the land near, nothing but death now faced them; for already the fuel-gage showed but a scant two gallons, and who could say how long the way might be to shore?

For a moment the engineer lost heart, but only for a moment.

His eye, sweeping the distance, caught sight of a long, dull, dark line on the horizon.

A cloud-bank, was it? Land, was it? He could not tell.

"I'll chance it, anyhow," thought he, "for it's our only hope now. When I don't know where I am, one direction's as good as any other. We've got no other chance but that! Here goes!"

Skilfully banking, he hauled the plane about, and settled on a long, swift slant toward the dark line.

"If only the alcohol holds out, and nothing breaks!" his thought was. "If only that's the shore, and we can reach it in time!"

19. Westward Ho!

Fate meant that they should live, those two lone wanderers on the face of the great desolation; and, though night had gathered now and all was cloaked in gloom, they landed with no worse than a hard shake-up on a level strip of beach that edged the confines of the unknown lake.

Exhausted by the strain and the long fight with death, chilled by that sojourn in the upper air, drenched and stiffened and half dead, they had no strength to make a camp.

The most that they could do was drag themselves down to the water's edge and -- finding the water fresh, not salt -- drink deeply from hollowed palms. Then, too worn-out even to eat, they crawled under the shelter of the biplane's ample wings, and dropped instantly into the long and dreamless sleep of utter weariness.

Mid-morning found them, still lame and stiff but rested, cooking breakfast over a cheery fire on the beach near the machine. Save for here and there a tree that had blown down in the forest, some dead branches scattered on the sands, and a few washed-out places where the torrent of yesterday's rain had gullied the earth, nature once more seemed fair and calm.

The full force of the terrific wind-storm had probably passed to northward; this land where they now found themselves -- whatever it might be -- had doubtless borne only a small part of the attack. But even so, and even through the sky gleamed clear and blue and sunlit once again, Stern and the girl knew the hurricane had been no ordinary tempest.

"It must have been a cyclone, nothing less," judged the engineer, as he finished his meal and reached for his comforting pipe. "And God knows where it's driven us to! So far as judging distances goes, in a hurricane like that it's impossible. This may be any one of the Great Lakes; and, again, it may not. For all we know, we may be up in the Hudson Bay region somewhere. This may be Winnipeg, Athabasca, or Great Slave. With the kind of storms that happen nowadays, anything's possible."

"Nothing matters, after all," the girl assured him, "except that we're alive and unhurt; and the machine can still travel, for --"

"Travel!" cried Stern. "With about a quart of fuel or less! How far, I'd like to know?"

"That's so; I never thought of that!" the girl replied, dismayed. "Oh, dear, what shall we do now?"

Stern laughed.

"Hunt for a town, of course," he reassured her. "There, there, don't worry! If we find alcohol, we're all right, anyhow. If not, we're better off than we were after the maelstrom almost got us, at any rate. Then we had no arms, ammunition, tools, or means to make fire, while now we've got them all. Forgive my speaking as I did, little girl. Don't worry -- everything will come right in the end."

Reassured, she sat before the fire, and for an hour or more they drew maps and diagrams in the sand, made plans, and laid out their next step in this long campaign against the savage power of a deserted world.

At last, their minds made up, they wheeled the plane back to the forest, where Stern cut out among the trees a space for its protection. And, leaving it here, covered with branches of the thick-topped fern-tree, they took provisions and once more set out on their exploration.

But this time they had an ax and their two rifles, and as they strode northward along the shore they felt a match for any peril.

An hour's walk brought them to the ruins of a steel recreation-pier, with numerous traces of a town along the lake behind it.

"That settles the Hudson Bay theory," Stern rejoiced, as they wandered among the debris. "This is certainly one of the Great Lakes, though which one, of course, we can't tell as yet. And now if we can round up some alcohol we'll be on our way before very long."

They found no alcohol, for the only ruin where drugs or liquors had evidently been sold had caved in, a mass of shattered brickwork, smashing every bottle in the place. Stern found many splintered shards of glass; but that was all, so far as fuel was concerned. He discovered something else, however, that proved of tremendous value -- the wreck of a printing-office.

Presses and iron of all kind had gone to pieces, but some of the larger lead types and quads still were recognizable. And, the crucial thing, he turned up a jagged bit of stereotype-sheet from under the protection of a concrete plinth that had fallen into the cellar.

All corroded and discolored though it was, he still could make out a few letters.

"A newspaper head, so help me!" he exclaimed, as with a trembling finger he pointed the letters out to Beatrice: "Here's an 'H' -- here's 'mbur ' -- here's 'ally,' and 'ronicl'! Eh, what? 'Chronicle,' it must have been! By Jove, you're right! And the whole thing used to spell 'Hamburg Daily Chronicle,' or I'm a liar!"

He thought a moment -- thought hard -- then burst out:

"Hamburg, eh? Hamburg, by a big lake? Well, the only Hamburg by a lake that I know of used to be Hamburg, New York. I ought to remember. I drew the plans for the New York Central bridge, just north of here, over the Spring Creek ravine.

"Yes, sir, this certainly is Hamburg, New York. And this lake must be Erie. Now, if I'm correct, just back up there on that hill we'll find the remains of the railway cut, and less than ten miles north of here lies all that's left of Buffalo. Some luck, eh? Cast away, only fifteen miles or so from a place like that. And we might have gone to Great Bear Lake, or to -- h-m! -- to any other place, for all the cyclone cared.

"Well, come on now, let's see if the railway cut is still there, and my old bridge; and if so, it's Buffalo for ours!"

It was all as he had said. The right-of-way of the railroad still showed distinctly, in spite of the fact that ties and rails had long since vanished. Of the bridge nothing was left but some rusted steel stringers lying entangled about the disintegrated concrete piers. But Stern viewed them with a melancholy pride and interest -- his own handiwork in the very long ago.

They had no time, however, for retrospection; but, once more taking the shore, kept steadily northward. And before noon they reached the debris of Buffalo, stark and deserted by the lake where once its busy commerce and its noisy life had thronged. By four o'clock that afternoon they had collected fuel enough for the plane to do that distance on, and more. Late that night they were again back at the spot where they had landed the night before.

And here, in high spirits and with every hope of better fortune now to follow evil, they cooked their meal and spent an hour in planning their next move, then slept the sleep of well-earned rest.

They had now decided to abandon the idea of visiting Boston. This seeming change of front was not without its good reasons.

"We're half-way to Chicago as it is," Stern summed up next morning. "Conditions are probably similar all along the Atlantic coast; there's no life to be found there: On the other hand, if we strike for the West there's at least a chance of running across survivors. If we don't find them there, then we probably sha'n't find them anywhere. In Chicago we can live and restock for further explorations, and as for locating a telescope, the University of Chicago ruins are as promising as those of Harvard. Chicago, by all means!"

They set out at nine o'clock, and, having made a good start, reached Buffalo by twenty minutes past, flying easily along the shore at not more than five hundred feet elevation.

Gaily the lake sparkled and wimpled in the morning sun, unvexed now by any steamer's prow, unshaded by any smoke from cities or roaring mills along its banks.

Despite the lateness of the season, the morning was warm; a mild breeze swayed the treetops and set the little whitecaps foaming here and there over the broad expanse of blue. Beatrice and Stern felt the joy of life reborn in them at that sight.

"Magnificent!" cried the engineer. "Now for a swing up past Niagara, and we're off!"

The river, they found as the plane swept onward, had dwindled to a brook that they could almost leap across. The rapids now were but a dreary waste of blackened rocks, and the Falls themselves, dry save for a desolate trickle down past Goat Island, presented a spectacle of death -- the death of the world as Beatrice and Stern had known it, which depressed them both.

That this tremendous cataract could vanish thus; that the gorge and the great Falls which for uncounted centuries had thundered to the rush and tumult of the mighty waters could now lie mute and dry and lifeless, saddened them both beyond measure.

And they were glad when, with a wide sweep of her wings, the Pauillac veered to westward again along the north shore of Lake Erie and settled into the long run of close on two hundred and fifty miles to Detroit, where Stern counted on making his first stop.

Without mishap, yet without sighting a single indication of the presence of man, they coasted down the shore and ate their dinner on the banks of Lake Saint Clair, near the ruins of Windsor, with those of Detroit on the opposite side. For some reason or other, impossible to solve, the current now ran northward toward Huron, instead of south to Erie. But this phenomenon they could do little more than merely note, for time lacked to give it any serious study.

Mid-afternoon found them getting under way again westbound.

"Chicago next," said Stern, making some slight but necessary adjustment of the air-feed in the carburetor. "And here's hoping there'll be some natives to greet us!"

"Amen to that!" answered the girl. "If any life has survived at all, it ought to be on the great central plain of the country, say from Indiana out through Nebraska. But do you know, Allan, if it should come right down to meeting any of our own kind of people -- savages, of course, I mean, but white -- I really believe I'd be awfully afraid of them. Imagine white savages dressed in skins --"

"Like us!" interrupted Stern, laughing.

"And painted with woad, whatever woad is; I remember reading about it in the histories of England; all the early Britons used it. And carrying nice, knobby stone clubs to stave in our heads!

It would be nice to meet a hundred or a thousand of them, eh? Rather a different matter from dealing with a horde of those anthropoid creatures, I imagine."

Stern only smiled, then answered:

"Well, I'll take my chances with 'em. Better a fight, say I, with my own kind, than solitude like this -- you and I all alone, girl, getting old some time and dying with never a hand-clasp save perhaps such as it may please fate to give us from whatever children are to be. But come, come, girl. No time for gloomy speculations of trouble. In you get now, and off we go -- westward bound again."

Only half an hour out of Detroit it was that they first became aware of some strange disturbance of the horizon, some inexplicable appearance such as neither of them had ever seen, a phenomenon so peculiar that, though both observed it at about the same time, neither Stern could believe his own senses nor Beatrice hers.

For all at once it seemed to them the sky-line was drawing suddenly nearer; it seemed that the horizon was approaching at high speed.

The dark, untrodden forest mass still stretched away, away, until it vanished against the dim blue of the sky; but now, instead of that meeting-line being forty miles off, it seemed no farther than twenty, and minute by minute it indubitably was rushing toward them with a speed equal to their own.

Stern, puzzled and alarmed at this unusual sight, felt an impulse to slow, to swerve, to test the apparition in some way; but second thought convinced him it must be deception of some sort.

"Some peculiar state of the atmosphere," thought he, "or perhaps we're approaching a high ridge, on the other side of which lie clouds that cut away the farther view. Or else -- no, hang it! the world seems to end right there, with no clouds to veil it -- nothing, only -- what?"

He saw the girl pointing in alarm. She, too, was clearly stirred by the appearance.

What to do? Stern felt indecision for the first time since he had started on this long, adventurous journey. Shut off and descend?

Impossible among those forests. Swing about and return? Not to be thought of. Keep on and meet perils perhaps undreamed of? Yes -- at all hazards he would keep on.

And with a tightening of the jaw he drove the Pauillac onward, ever onward -- toward the empty space that yawned ahead.

"End o' the world?" thought he. "All right, the old machine is good for it, and so are we. Here goes!"

20. On the Lip of the Chasm

Very near, now, was the strange apparition. On, on, swift as a falcon, the plane hurtled. Stern glanced at Beatrice. Never had he seen her more beautiful. About her face, rosy and full of life, the luxuriant loose hair was whipping. Her eyes sparkled with this new excitement, and on her full red lips a smile betrayed her keen enjoyment. No trace of fear was there -- nothing but confidence and strength and joy in the adventure.

The phenomenon of the world's end -- for nothing else describes it adequately -- now appeared distinctly as a jagged line, beyond which nothing showed. It differed from the horizon, line, inasmuch as it was close at hand. Already the adventurers could peer down upon it at an acute angle.

Plainly could they see the outlines of trees growing along the verge. But beyond them, nothing.

It differed essentially from a canyon, because there was no other side at all. Strain his eye as he might, Stern could detect no opposite wall. And now, realizing something of the possibilities of such a chasm, he swung the Pauillac southward. Flying parallel to the edge of this tremendous barrier, he sought to solve the mystery of its true nature.

"If I go higher, perhaps I may be able to get some notion of it," thought he, and swinging up-wind, he spiraled till the barometer showed he had gained another thousand feet.

But even this additional view profited him nothing. Half a mile to westward the ragged tree-line still showed as before, with vacancy behind it, and as far as Stern could see to north, to south, it stretched away till the dim blue of distance swallowed it. Yet, straight across the gulf, no land appeared. Only the sky itself was visible there, as calm and as unbroken as in the zenith, yet extending far below where the horizon-line should have been -- down, in fact, to where the tree-line cut it off from Stern's vision.

The effect was precisely that of coming to the edge of a vast plain, beyond which nothing lay, save space.

"The end of the world, indeed!" thought the engineer, despite himself. "But what can it mean? What can have happened to the sphere to have changed it like this? Good Heavens, what a marvel -- what a catastrophe!"

Determined at all hazards to know more of this titanic break or "fault," or whatsoever it might be, he banked again, and now, on a descending slant, veered down toward the lip of the chasm.

"Going out over it?" cried Beatrice.

He nodded.

"It may be miles deep!"

"You can't get killed any deader falling a hundred miles than you can a hundred feet!" he shouted back, above the droning racket of the motor.

And with a fresh grip on the wheel, head well forward, every sense alert and keen to meet whatever conditions might arise, to battle with cross-currents, "air-holes," or any other vortices swirling up out of those unknown depths, he skimmed the Pauillac fair toward the lip of the monstrous vacancy.

Now as they rushed almost above the verge he could see conclusively they were not dealing here with a canyon like the Yosemite or like any other he had ever seen or heard of in the old days.

There was positively no bottom to the terrific thing!

Just a sheer edge and beyond that -- nothing.

Nowhere any sign of an opposite bank; nowhere the faintest trace of land. Far, far below, even a few faint clouds showed floating there as if in mid-heaven.

The effect was ghastly, unnerving and altogether terrible. Not that Stern feared height. No, it was the unreality of the experience, the inexplicable character of this yawning edge of the world that almost overcame him.

Only by a strong exercise of will-power could he hold the biplane to her course. His every instinct was to veer, to retreat back to solid earth, and land somewhere, and once more, at all hazards, get the contact of reality.

But Stern resisted all these impulses, and now already had driven the Pauillac right to the lip of the vast nothingness.

Now they were over!

"My God!" he cried, stunned by the realization of this thing. "Sheer space! No bottom anywhere!"

For all at once they had shot, as it were, out into a void which seemed to hold no connection at all with the earth they now were quitting.

Stern caught a glimpse of the tall forest growing up to within a hundred yards of the edge, then of smaller trees, dwindling to bushes and grasses, and strange red sand that bordered the gap -- sand and rocks, barren as though some up-draft from the void had killed off vegetable growth along the very brink.

Then all slid back and away. The red-ribbed wall of the great chasm, shattered and broken as by some inconceivable disaster, some cosmic cataclysm, fell away and away, downward, dimmer and more dim, until it faded gradually into a blue haze, then vanished utterly.

And there below lay nothingness -- and nothingness stretched out in front to where the sight lost itself in pearly vapors that over-dimmed the sky.

Beatrice glanced at Stern as the Pauillac sped true as an arrow in its flight, out into this strange and incomprehensible vacuity.

Just a shade paler now he seemed. Despite the keen wind, a Blister of sweat-drops studded his forehead. His jaw was set, set hard; she could see the powerful maxillary muscles knotted there where the throat-cords met the angle of the bone. And she understood that, for the first time since their tremendous adventure had begun, the man felt shaken by this latest and greatest of all the mysteries they had been called upon to face.

Already the verge lay far behind; and now the sense of empty space above and on all sides and there below was overpowering.

Stern gasped with a peculiar choking sound. Then all at once, throwing the front steering plane at an angle, he brought the machine about and headed for the distant land.

He spoke no word, nor did she; but they both swept the edge of the chasm with anxious eyes, seeking a place to light.

It was with tremendous relief that they both saw the solid earth once more below them. And when, five minutes later, having chosen a clear and sand-barren on the verge, some two miles southward along the abyss, Stern brought the machine to earth, they felt a gratitude and a relief not to be voiced in words.

"By Jove!" exclaimed the man, lifting Beatrice from the seat, "if that isn't enough to shake a man's nerve and upset all his ideas, geological or otherwise, I'd like to know what is!"

"Going to try to cross it?" she asked anxiously; "that is, if there is any other side? I know, of course, that if there is you'll find out, some way or other!"

"You overestimate me," he replied. "All I can do, for now, is to camp down here and try to figure the problem out -- with your help. Whatever this thing is, it's evident it stands between us and our plan. Either Chicago lies on the other side -- (provided, of course, as you say, that there is one) -- or else it's been swallowed up, ages ago, by whatever catastrophe produced this yawning gulf.

"In either event we've got to try to discover the truth, and act accordingly. But for now, there's nothing we can do. It's getting late already. We've had enough for one day, little girl. Come on, let's make the machine ready for the night, and camp down here and have a bite to eat. Perhaps by tomorrow we may know just what we're up against!"

The moon had risen, flooding the world with spectral light, before the two adventurers had finished their meal. All during it they had kept an unusual silence. The presence of that terrible gulf, there not two hundred feet away to westward of them, imposed its awe upon their thoughts.

And after the meal was done, by tacit understanding they refrained from trying to approach it or to peer over. Too great the risks by night. They spoke but little, and presently exhausted by the trying events of the day -- sought sleep under the vanes of the Pauillac.

But for an hour, tired as he was, the engineer lay thinking of the chasm, trying in vain to solve its problem or to understand how they were to follow any further the search for the ruins of Chicago, where fuel was to be had, or carry on the work of trying to find some living members of the human race.

Morning found them revived and strengthened. Even before they made their fire or prepared their breakfast they were exploring along the edge of the gigantic cleft.

Going first to make sure no rock should crumble under the girl's tread, no danger threaten, Stern tested every foot of the way to the very edge of the sheer chasm.

"Slowly, now!" he cautioned, taking her hand. "We've got to be careful here. My God, what a drop!"

Awed, despite themselves, they stood there on a flat slab of schist that projected boldly over the void. Seen from this point, the immense nothingness opened out below them even more terrible than it had seemed from the biplane.

The fact is common knowledge that a height, viewed from a balloon or aeroplane, is always far less dizzying than from a lofty building or a monument. Giddiness vanishes when no solid support lies under the feet. This fact Stern and the girl appreciated to the full as they peered over the edge. Ten times more ominous and frightful the vast blue mystery beneath them now appeared than it had seemed before.

"Let's look sheer down," said the girl. "By lying flat and peering over, there can't be any danger."

"All right, but only on condition that I keep tight hold of you!"

Cautiously they lay down and worked their way to the edge. The engineer circled Beta's supple waist with his arm.

"Steady, now!" he warned. "When you feel giddy, let me know, and we'll go back."

The effect of the chasm, from the very edge of the rock, was terrifying. It was like nothing ever seen by human eyes. Peering down into the Grand Canyon of the Colorado would have been child's play beside it. For this was no question of looking down a half-mile, a mile, or even five, to some solid bottom.

Bottom there was none -- nothing save dull purple haze, shifting vapors, and an unearthly dim light which seemed to radiate upward as though the sun's rays, reflected, were striving to beat up again.

"There must be miles and miles of air below us," said Stern, "to account for this curious light-effect. Air, of course, will eventually cut off the vision. Given a sufficiently thick layer, say a few hundred miles, it couldn't be seen through. So if there is a bottom to this place, be it one hundred or even five hundred miles down, of course we couldn't see it. All we could see would be the air, which would give this sort of blue effect."

"Yes; but in that case how can we see the sun, or the moon, or stars?"

"Light from above only has to pierce forty or fifty miles of really dense air. Above that height it's excessively rarified. While down below earth-level, of course, it would get more and more dense all the time, till at the bottom of a five-hundred-mile drop the density and pressure would be tremendous."

Beatrice made no answer. The spectacle she was gazing at filled her with solemn thoughts. Jagged, rent and riven, the rock extended downward. Here vast and broken ledges ran along its flanks -- red, yellow, black, all seared and burned and vitrified as by the fire of Hell; there huge masses, up-piled, seemed about to fall into the abyss.

A quarter-mile to southward, a rivulet had found its way over a projecting ledge. Spraying and silvery it fell, till, dissipated by the up-draft from the abyss, it dissolved in mist.

The ledge on which they were lying extended downward perhaps three hundred yards, then sloped backward, leaving sheer empty space beneath them. They seemed to be poised in mid-heaven. It was totally unlike the sensation on a mountain-top, or even floating among the clouds; for a moment it seemed to Stern that he was looking up toward an unfathomable, infinite dome above him.

He shuddered, despite his cool and scientific spirit of observation.

"Some chemical action going on somewhere down there," said

he, half to divert his own attention from his thoughts. "Smell that sulphur? If this place wasn't once the scene of volcanic activities, I'm no judge!"

A moderate yet very steady wind blew upward from the chasm, freighted with a scent of sulphur and some other substance new to Stern.

Beatrice, all at once overcome by sudden giddiness, drew back and hid her face in both hands.

"No bottom to it -- no end!" she said in a scared tone. "Here's the end of the world, right here, and beyond this very rock -- nothing!"

Stern, puzzled, shook his head.

"That's really impossible, absurd and ridiculous, of course," he answered. "There must be something beyond. The way this stone falls proves that."

He pitched a two-pound lump of granite far out into the air. It fell vertically, whirling, and vanished with the speed of a meteor.

"If a whole side of the earth had split off, and what we see down below there were really sky, of course the earth's center of gravity would have shifted," he explained, "and that rock would have fallen in toward the cliff below us, not straight down."

"How can you be sure it doesn't fall that way after the impulse you gave it has been lost?"

"I shall have to make some close scientific tests here, lasting a day or two, before I'm positive; but my impression is that this, after all, is only a canyon -- a split in the surface -- rather than an actual end of the crust."

"But if it were a canyon, why should blue sky show down there at an angle of forty-five degrees?"

"I'll have to think that out, later," he replied. "Directly under us, you see all seems deep purple. That's another fact to consider. I tell you, Beatrice, there's more to be figured out here than can be done in half an hour.

"As I see it, some vast catastrophe must have rent the earth, a thousand or fifteen hundred years ago, as a result of which everybody was killed except you and me. We're standing now on the edge of the scar left by that explosion, or whatever it was. How deep or how wide that scar is, I don't know. Everything depends on our finding out, or at least on our guessing it with some degree of accuracy."

"How so?"

"Because, don't you see, this chasm stands between us and Chicago and the West, and all our hopes of finding human life there. And --"

"Why not coast south along the edge here, and see if we can't run across some ruined city or other where we can refill the tanks?"

"I'll think it over," the engineer answered. "In the meantime we can camp down here a couple of days or so, and rest; and I can make some calculations with a pendulum and so on.

"And if you decide there's probably another side to this gulf, what then?"

"We cross," he said; then for a while stood silent, musing as he peered down into the bottomless abyss that stretched there hungrily beneath their narrow observation-rock.

"We cross, that's all!"

21. Lost in the Great Abyss

For two days they camped beside the chasm, resting, planning, discussing, while Stern, with improvised transits, pendulums and other apparatus, made tests and observations to determine, if possible, the properties of the great gap.

During this time they developed some theories regarding the catastrophe which had swept the world a thousand years ago.

"It seems highly and increasingly probable to me," the engineer said, after long thought, "that we have here the actual cause of the vast blight of death that left us two alone in the world. I rather think that at the time of the great explosion which produced this rent, certain highly poisonous gases were thrown off, to impregnate the entire atmosphere of the world. Everybody must have been killed at once. The poison must have swept the earth clean of human life."

"But how did we escape?" asked the girl.

"That's hard telling. I figure it this way: The mephitic gas probably was heavy and dense, thus keeping to the lower air-strata, following them, over plain and hill and mountain, like a blanket of death.

"Just what happened to us, who can tell? Probably, tightly housed up there in the tower, the very highest inhabited spot in the world, only a very slight infiltration of the gas reached us. If my theory won't work, can you suggest a better one? Frankly, I can't; and until we have more facts, we've got to take what we have. No matter, the condition remains -- we're alive and all the rest are dead: and I'm positive this cleft here is the cause of it."

"But if everybody's dead, as you say, why hunt for men?"

"Perhaps a handful may have survived among the highlands of the Rockies. I imagine that after the first great explosion there followed a series of terrible storms, tornadoes, volcanic eruptions, tidal waves and so on. You remember how I found the bones of a whale in lower Broadway; and many of the ruins in New York show the action of the sea -- they're laid flat in such a manner as to indicate that the island was washed on one or two occasions by monster waves.

"Well, all these disturbances probably finished up what few survivors escaped, except possibly among the mountains of the West. A few scattered colonies may have survived a while -- mining camps, for instance, or isolated prospectors, or what-not. They may all have died out, or again, they may have come together and re-established some primitive form of barbarous or even savage life by this time. There's no telling. Our imperative problem is to reach that section and explore it thoroughly. For there, if anywhere, we'll find survivors of our race."

"How about that great maelstrom that nearly got us?" asked the girl. "Can you connect that with the catastrophe?"

"I think so. My idea is that, in some way or other, the sea is being sucked down into the interior of the earth and then hurled out again; maybe there's a gradual residue being left; maybe a great central lake or sea has formed. Who knows? At any rate all the drainage system of the country seems to have been changed and reversed in the most curious and unaccountable manner. I think we should find, if we could investigate everything thoroughly, that this vast chasm here is intimately connected with the whole thing."

These and many other questions perplexed the travelers, but most of all they sought to know the breadth of the vast gap and to determine if it had, as they hoped, another side, or if it were indeed the edge of an enormous mass split bodily off the earth.

Stern believed he had an answer to this problem on the afternoon of the second day. For many hours he had hung his pendulums over the cliff, noted deflections, taken triangulations, and covered the surface of the smooth stone with X's, Y's, Z's, sines and cosines and abstruse formulae -- all scrawled with charcoal, his only means of writing.

At last he finished the final equation, and, with a smile of triumph and relief, got to his feet again.

Back to the girl, who was cooking over an odorous fire of cedar, he made his way, rejoicing.

"I've got it!" he shouted gladly. "Making reasonable allowances for depth, I've got it!"

"Got what?"

"The probable width!"

"Oh!" And she stood gazing at him in admiration, beautiful and strong and graceful. "You mean to say --"

"I'm giving the chasm a hundred miles' depth. That's more than anybody could believe possible -- twice as much. On that assumption, my tests show the distance to the other side -- and there is another side, by the way! -- can't be over --"

"Five hundred miles?"

"Nonsense! Not over one hundred to one-fifty. I'm going on a liberal allowance for error, too. It may not be over seventy-five. The --"

"But if that's as far as it is, why can't we see the other side?"

"With all that chemicalized vapor rising constantly? Who knows what elements may be in it? Or what polarization may be taking place?"

"Polarization?"

"I mean, what deflection and alteration of light? No wonder we can't see! But we can fly! And we're going to, what's more!"

"Going to make a try for Chicago, then?" she asked, her eyes lighting up joyfully at thought of the adventure.

"Tomorrow morning, sure!"

"But the alcohol?"

"We've still got what we started with from Detroit, minus only what we've burned reaching this place. And we reckoned when we set out that it would far more than be enough. Oh, that part of it's all right!"

"Well, you know best," she answered. "I trust you in all things, Allan. But now just look at this roast partridge; come, dear, let tomorrow take care of itself. It's supper-time now!"

After the meal they went to the flat rock and sat for an hour while the sun went down beyond the void. Its disappearance seemed to substantiate the polarization theory. There was no sudden obliteration of the disk by a horizon. Rather the sun faded away, redder and duller; then slowly losing form and so becoming a mere blur of crimson, which in turn grew purple and so gradually died away to nothing.

For a long time they sat in the deepening gloom, their rifles close at hand, saying little, but thinking much. The coming of night had sobered them to a sense of what now inevitably lay ahead. The solemn purple pall that adumbrated the world and the huge nothingness before them, so silent, so immutable and pregnant with terrible mysteries, brought them close together.

The vague, untrodden forest behind them, where the night-sounds of the wild dimly reechoed now and then, filled them with indefinable emotions. And that night sleep was slow in coming.

Each realized that, despite all calculations and all skill, the morrow might be their last day of life. But the morning light, golden and clear above the eastern sky-line of tall conifers, dispelled all brooding fears. They were both up early and astir, in preparation for the crucial flight. Stern went over the edge of the chasm, while Beatrice prepared breakfast, and made some final observations of wind, air currents and atmosphere density.

An eagle which he saw soaring over the abyss, more than half a mile from its edge, convinced him a strong upward current existed today, as on the day when they had made their short flight over the void. The bird soared and circled and finally shot away to northward, without a wing-flap, almost in the manner of a vulture. Stern knew an eagle could not imitate the feat without some aid in the way of an up-draft.

"And if that draft is steady and constant all the way across," thought he, "it will result in a big saving of fuel. Given a sufficient rising current, we could volplane all the way across with a very slight expenditure of alcohol. It looks now as though everything were coming on first-rate. Couldn't be better. And what a day for an excursion!"

By nine o'clock all was ready. Along the land a mild south wind was blowing. Though the day was probably the 5th of October or thereabout, no signs of autumn yet were blazoned in the forest. The morning was perfect, and the travelers' spirits rose in unison with the abounding beauty of the day.

Stern had given the Pauillac another final going over, tightening the stays and laterals, screwing up here a loosened nut, there a bolt, making certain all was in perfect order.

At nine-fifteen, after he had had a comforting pipe, they made a clean getaway, rising along the edge of the chasm, then soaring in huge spirals.

"I want all the altitude I can get," Stern shouted at the girl as they climbed steadily higher. "We may need it to coast on. And from a mile or two up maybe we can get a glimpse of the other side."

But though they ascended till the aneroid showed eight thousand five hundred feet, nothing met their gaze but the same pearly blue vapor which veiled the mystery before them. And Stern, satisfied now that nothing could be gained by any further ascent, turned the machine due west, and sent her skimming like a swallow out over the tremendous nothingness below.

As the earth faded behind them they began to feel distinctly a warm and pungent wind that rose beneath -- a steady current, as from some huge chimney that lazily was pouring out its monstrous volume of hot vapors.

Away and away behind them slid the lip of this gigantic gash across the world; and now already with the swift rush of the plane the solid earth had begun to fade and to grow dim.

Stern only cast a glance at the sun and at his compass, hung there in gimbals before him, and with firm hand steadied the machine for the long problematical flight to westward. Behind them the sun kept even with their swift pace; and very far below and ahead, at times they thought to see the fleeing shadow of the biplane cast now and then on masses of formless vapor that rose from the unsounded deeps.

Definitely committed now to this tremendous venture, both Stern and the girl settled themselves more firmly in their seats. No time to feel alarm, no time for introspection, or for thoughts of what might lie below, what fate theirs must be if the old Pauillac failed them now!

No time save for confidence in the stout mechanism and in the skill of hand and brain that was driving the great planes, with a roaring rush like a gigantic gull, a swooping rise and fall in long arcs over the hills of air, across the vast enigma of that space!

Stern's whole attention was fixed on driving, just on the manipulation of the swift machine. Exhaust and interplay, the rhythm of each whirling cam and shaft, the chatter of the cylinders, the droning diapason of the blades, all blent into one intricate yet perfect harmony of mechanism; and as a leader knows each instrument in the great orchestra and follows each, even as his eye reads the score, so Stern's keen ear analyzed each sound and action and reaction and knew all were in perfect tune and resonance.

The machine -- no early and experimental model, such as were used in the first days of flying, from 1900 to 1915, but one of the perfected and self-balancing types developed about 1920, the year when the Great Death had struck the world -- responded nobly to his skill and care. From her landing-skids to the farthest tip of her ailerons she seemed alive, instinct with conscious and eager intelligence.

Stern blessed her mentally with special pride and confidence in her mercury equalizing balances. Proud of his machine and of his skill, superb like Phaeton whirling the sun-chariot across the heavens, he gave her more and still more speed.

Below nothing, nothing save vapors, with here and there an open space where showed the strange dull purple of the abyss. Above, to right, to left, nothing -- absolute vacant space.

Gone now was all sight of the land that they had left. Unlike balloonists who always see dense clouds or else the earth, they now saw nothing. All alone with the sun that rushed behind them in their skimming flight, they fled like wraiths across the emptiness of the great void.

Stern glanced at the barometer, and grunted with surprise.

"H'm! Twelve thousand four hundred and fifty feet -- and I've been jockeying to come down at least five hundred feet already!" thought he. "How the devil can that be?"

The explanation came to him. But it surprised him almost as much as the noted fact.

"Must be one devil of a wind blowing up out of that place," he pondered, "to carry us up nearly four thousand feet, when I've been trying to descend. Well, it's all right, anyhow -- it all helps."

He looked at the spinning anemometer. It registered a speed of ninety-seven miles an hour. Yet now that they were out of sight of any land, only the rush of the wind and the enormous vibration of the plane conveyed an idea of motion. They might as well have been hung in mid-space, like Mohammed's tomb, as have been rushing forward; there was no visible means of judging what their motion really might be.

"Unique experience in the history of mankind!" shouted Stern to the girl. "The world's invisible to us."

She nodded and smiled back at him, her white teeth gleaming in the strange, bluish light that now enveloped them.

Stern, keenly attentive to the engine, advanced the spark another notch, and now the needle crept to 102½.

"We'll be across before we know it," thought he. "At this rate, I shouldn't be surprised to sight land any minute now."

A quarter-hour more the Pauillac swooped along, cradling in her swift flight to westward.

But all at once the man started violently. Forward he bent, staring with widened eyes at the tube of the fuel-gage.

He blinked, as though to convince himself he had not seen aright, then stared again; and as he looked a sudden grayness overspread his face.

"What?" he exclaimed, then raised his head and for a moment sniffed, as though to catch some odor, elusive yet ominous, which he had for some time half sensed yet paid no heed to.

Then suddenly he knew the truth; and with a cry of fear bent, peering at the fuel-tank.

There, quivering suspended from the metal edge of the aluminum tank, hung a single clear white drop -- alcohol!

Even as Stern looked it fell, and at once another took its place, and was shaken off only to be succeeded by a third, a fourth, a fifth!

The man understood. The ancient metal, corroded almost through from the inside, had been eaten away. That very morning a hole had formed in the tank. And now a leak -- existing since what moment he could not tell -- was draining the very life-blood of the machine.

"The alcohol!" cried Stern in a hoarse, terrible voice, his wide eyes denoting his agitation. With a quivering hand he pointed.

"My God! It's all leaked out -- there's not a quart left in the tank! We're lost -- lost in the bottomless abyss!"

22. Lights!

At realization of the ghastly situation that confronted them, Stern's heart stopped beating for a moment. Despite his courage, a sick terror gripped his soul; he felt a sudden weakness, and in his ears the rushing wind seemed shouting mockeries of death.

As in a dream he felt the girl's hand close in fear upon his arm, he heard her crying something -- but what, he knew not.

Then all at once he fought off the deadly horror. He realized that now, if ever, he needed all his strength, resource, intelligence. And, with a violent effort, he flung off his weakness. Again he gripped the wheel. Thought returned. Though the end might be at hand, thank God for even a minute's respite!

Again he looked at the indicator.

Yes, only too truly it showed the terrible fact! No hallucination, this. Not much more than a pint of the precious fluid now lay in the fuel tank. And though the engine still roared, he knew that in a minute or two it must slacken, stop and die.

What then?

Even as the question flashed to him, the engine barked its protest. It skipped, coughed, stuttered. Too well he knew the symptoms, the imperative cry: "More fuel!"

But he had none to give. In vain for him to open wide the supply valve. Vain to adjust the carburetor. Even as he made a despairing, instinctive motion to perform these useless acts -- while Beatrice, deathly pale and shaking with terror, clutched at him -- the engine spat forth a last, convulsive bark, and grew silent.

The whirling screws hummed a lower note, then ceased their song and came to rest.

The machine lurched forward, swooped, spiraled, and with a

141

sickening rush, a flailing tumult of the stays and planes, plunged into nothingness!

Had Stern and the girl not been securely strapped to their seats, they must have been precipitated into space by the violent, erratic dashes, drops, swerves and rushes of the uncontrolled Pauillac.

For a moment or two, instinctively despite the knowledge that it could do no good, Stern wrenched at the levers. A thousand confused, wild, terrible impressions surged upon his consciousness.

Swifter, swifter dropped the plane; and now the wind that seemed to rise had grown to be a hurricane! Its roaring in their ears was deafening. They had to fight even for breath itself.

Beatrice was leaning forward now, sheltering her face in the hollow of her arm. Had she fainted? Stern could not tell. He still was fighting with the mechanism, striving to bring it into some control. But, without headway, it defied him. And like a wounded hawk, dying even as it struggled, the Pauillac staggered wildly down the unplumbed abyss.

How long did the first wild drop last? Stern knew not. He realized only that, after a certain time, he felt a warm sensation; and, looking, perceived that they were now plunging through vapors that sped upward -- so it seemed -- with vertiginous rapidity.

No sensation now was there of falling. All motion seemed to lie in the uprushing vapors, dense and warm and pale violet in hue. A vast and rhythmic spiraling had possessed the Pauillac. As you have seen a falling leaf turn in air, so the plane circled, boring with terrific speed down, down, down through the mists, down into the unknown!

Nothing to be seen but vapors. No solid body, no land, no earth to mark their fall and gauge it. Yet slowly, steadily, darkness was shrouding them. And Stern, breathing with great difficulty even in the shelter of his arms, could now hardly more than see as a pale blur the white face of the girl beside him.

The vast wings of the machine, swirling, swooping, plunging down, loomed hugely vague in the deepening shadows. Dizzy, sick with the monstrous caroming through space, deafened by the thunderous roaring of the up-draft, Stern was still able to retain enough of his scientific curiosity to peer upward. The sun! Could he still see it?

Vanished utterly was now the glorious orb! There, seeming to circle round and round in drunken spirals, he beheld a weird, diffused, angry-looking blotch of light, tinted a hue different from any ever seen on earth by men. And involuntarily, at sight of this, he shuddered.

Already with the prescience of death full upon him, with a numb despair clutching his soul, he shrank from that ghastly, hideous aspect of what he knew must be his last sight of the sun.

Around the girl he drew his right arm; she felt his muscles tauten as he clasped her to him. Useless now, he knew, any further struggles with the aeroplane. Its speed, its plummetlike drop checked only by the huge sweep of its parachute wings, Stern knew now it must fall clear to the bottom of the abyss -- if bottom there were. And if not -- what then?

Stern dared not think. All human concepts had been shattered by this stupendous catastrophe. The sickly and unnatural hue of the rushing vapors that tore and slatted the planes, confused his senses; and, added to this, a stifling, numbing gas seemed diffused through the inchoate void. He tried to speak, but could not. Against the girl's cheek he pressed his own. Hers was cold!

In vain he struggled to cry out. Even had his parched tongue been able to voice a sound, the howling tempest they themselves were creating as they fell, would have whipped the shout away and drowned it in the gloom.

In Stern's ears roared a droning as of a billion hornets. He felt a vast, tremendous lassitude. Inside his head it seemed as though a huge, merciless pressure were grinding at his very brain. His breath came only slowly and with great difficulty.

"My God!" he panted. "Oh, for a little fuel! Oh, for a chance -- a chance to fight -- for life!"

But chance there was none, now. Before his eyes there seemed to darken, to dazzle, a strange and moving curtain. Through it, piercing it with a supreme effort of the will, he caught dim sight of the dial of the chronometer. Subconsciously he noted that it marked 11.25.

How long had they been falling? In vain his wavering intelligence battered at the problem. Now, as in a delirium, he fancied it had been only minutes; then it seemed hours. Like an insane man he laughed -- he tried to scream -- he raved. And only the stout straps that had held them both prevented him from leaping free of the hurtling machine.

"Crack!"

A lashing had given way! Part of the left hand plane had broken loose. Drunkenly, whirling head over like an albatross shot in mid-air, the Pauillac plunged.

It righted, swerved, shot far ahead, then once again somersaulted.

Stern had disjointed, crazy thoughts of air-pressure, condensation and compression, resistance, abstruse formulae. To him it seemed that some gigantic problem in stress-calculation were being hurled at him, to solve -- it seemed that, blind, deaf, dumb, some sinister and ghoul-like demon were flailing him until he answered -- and that he could not answer!

He had a dim realization of straining madly at his straps till the veins started big and swollen in his hammering brows. Then consciousness lapsed.

Lapsed, yet came again -- and with it pain. An awful pain in the ear-drums, that roared and crackled without cease.

Breath! He was fighting for breath!

It was a nightmare -- a horrible dream of darkness and a mighty booming wind -- a dream of stifling vapors and an endless void that sucked them down, down, down, eternally!

Delusions came, and mocking visions of safety. Both hands flung out as though to clutch the roaring gale, he fought the intangible.

Again he lost all knowledge.

And once again -- how long after, how could he know? -- he came to some partial realization of tortured existence.

In one of the mad downward rushes -- rushes which ended in

144

a long spiral slant-his staring, bloodshot eyes that sought to pierce the murk, seemed to behold a glimmer, a dull gleam of light.

The engineer screamed imprecations, mingled with wild, demoniac laughter.

"Another hallucination!" was his thought. "But if it's not -- if it's Hell -- then welcome, Hell! Welcome even that, for a chance to stop!"

A sweep of the Pauillac hid the light from view. Even that faintest ray vanished. But -- what? It came again! Much nearer now, and brighter! And -- another gleam! Another still! Three of them -- and they were real!

With a tremendous effort, Stern fixed his fevered eyes upon the lights.

Up, up at a tremendous rate they seemed speeding. Blue and ghastly through the dense vapors, spinning in giddy gyrations, as the machine wheeled, catapulted and slid from one long slant to another, their relative positions still remained fixed.

And, with a final flicker of intelligence, Stern knew they were no figment of his brain.

"Lights, Beatrice! Lights, lights, real lights!" he sought to scream.

But even as he fought to shake her from the swoon that wrapped her senses, his own last fragment of strength deserted him.

He had one final sense impression of a swift upshooting of the lights, a sudden brightening of those three radiant points.

Then came a sudden gleam as though of waters, black and still.

A gleam, blue and uncanny, across the inky surface of some vast, mysterious, hidden sea.

Up rushed the lights at him; up rushed the sea of jetty black!

Stern shouted some wild, incoherent thing.

Crash!

A shock! A frightful impact, swift, sudden, annihilating!

Then in a mad and lashing struggle, all knowledge and all feeling vanished utterly. And the blackness of oblivion received him into its insensate bosom.

23. The White Barbarians

Warmth, wetness, and a knowledge of great weakness -- these, joined with a singular lassitude, oppression of the lungs and stifling of the breath, were Allan Stern's sensations when conscious life returned.

Pain there was as well. His body felt sorely bruised and shaken. His first thought, his intense yearning wonder for the girl's welfare and his sickening fear lest she be dead, mingled with some attempt to analyze his own suffering; to learn, if possible, what damage he had taken in flesh and bone.

He tried to move, but found he could not. Even lying inert, as he now found himself, so great was the exertion to breathe that only by a fight could he keep the breath of life in his shaken frame.

He opened his eyes.

Light! Could it be? Light in that place?

Yes, the light was real, and it was shining directly in his face.

At first all that his disturbed, half-delirious vision could make out was a confused bluish glare. But in a moment this resolved itself into a smoking, blazing cressets. Stern could now distinctly see the metal bands of the fire-basket in which it lay, as well as a supporting staff, about five feet long, that seemed to vanish downward in the gloom.

And, understanding nothing, filled with vague, half-insane hallucinations and wild wonders, he tried to struggle upward with a babbling cry:

"Beatrice! Oh, Beatrice -- where are you?"

To his intense astonishment, a human hand, bluish in the strange glare, laid itself upon his breast and pushed him down again.

Above him he saw a face, wrinkled, bearded and ghastly blue. And as he struggled still he perceived by the unearthly light that a figure was bending over him.

"A man!" he gulped. "Man! Man! Oh, my God! At last -- a man!"

He tried to raise himself upon his elbow, for his whole soul was flooded with a sudden gratitude and love and joy in presence of that long-sought goal. But instantly, as soon as his dazed senses could convey the terrible impression to his brain, his joy was curdled into blank astonishment and fear and grief.

For to his intense chagrin, strive as he might, he could move neither hand nor foot!

During his unconsciousness, which had lasted he could not tell how long, he had been securely bound. And now, awakening slowly, once more, fighting his way up into consciousness, he found himself a prisoner!

A prisoner! With whom? Among what people -- with what purpose? After the long quest, the frightful hardships and the tremendous fall into the abyss, a prisoner!

"Merciful God!" groaned Stern, and in his sudden anguish, strained against the bonds, that drawn tight and fast, were already cutting painfully into his swollen, water sodden flesh.

In vain did he struggle. Terrible thoughts that Beatrice, too, might be subjected to this peril and humiliation branded themselves upon his brain. He shouted wildly, calling her name, with all the force of his spent lungs; but naught availed. There came no answer but the shrouding fogs.

The strange man bent above him, peering from beneath wrinkled brows. Stern heard a few words in a singular, guttural tone -- words rendered dull by the high compression of the air. What the words might be he could not tell, yet their general sound seemed strangely familiar and their command was indubitable.

But, still half-delirious, Stern tried again to stretch up his arms, to greet this singular being, even as a sick man recovering from etherization raves and half sees the nurses and doctors, yet dreams wild visions in the midst of pain.

The man, however, only shook his head, and with a broad, firm hand, again held the engineer from trying to sit up. Stern, understanding nothing clearly, relapsed to quietude. To him the thought came: "This is only another delusion after all!" And then a vast and poignant woe possessed him -- a wonder where the girl might be. But under the compulsion of that powerful hand, he lay quite still.

Half consciously he seemed to realize that he was lying prone in the bottom of some strange kind of boat, rude and clumsy, strangely formed of singular materials, yet safe and dry and ample.

To his laboring nostrils penetrated a rank and pungent odor of fish, with another the like of which he never had known -- an odor not unpleasant, yet keenly penetrant and all-pervading. Wet through, the engineer lay reeking in heat and steam, wrapped in his suit of heavy furs. Then he heard a ripple of water and felt the motion of the craft as it was driven forward.

Another voice spoke now and the strange man answered briefly. Again the engineer half seemed to comprehend the meaning, though no word was intelligible.

"Where's the girl, you?" he shouted with all his might. "What have you done with her? If you hurt her, damn you, you'll be sorry! Where -- where is she?"

No answer. It was evident that English speech conveyed no meaning to his captors. Stern relapsed with a groan of anguish and sheer pain.

The boat rocked. Another man came creeping forward, holding to the gunwale to steady himself. Stern saw him vaguely through the drifting vapor by the blue-green light of the cressets at the bow.

He was clad in a coarse kind of brownish stuff, like the first, roughly and loosely woven. His long hair, pure white, was twisted up in a kind of topknot and fastened there by pins of dull gold. Bearded he was, but not one hair upon his head or chin was other than silvery white -- a color common to all these folk, as Stern was soon to know.

This man, evidently seeing with perfect clarity by a light which permitted the engineer only partial vision, also examined Stern and made speech thereto and nodded with satisfaction.

Then he put half a dozen questions to the prisoner with evident slowness and an attempt to speak each word distinctly, but nothing came of this. And with a contemptuous grunt he went back to his paddle.

"Hold on, there!" cried Stern. "Can't you understand? There were two of us, in a -- machine, you know! We fell. Fell from the surface of the earth -- fell all the way down into this pit of hell, whatever it is. Where's the girl? For God's sake, tell me!"

Neither man paid any heed, but the elder suddenly set hollowed palms to his lips and hailed; and from across the waters dully drifted another answering cry.

He shouted a sentence or two with a volume of noise at which the engineer marveled, for so compressed was the air that Stern's best effort could hardly throw a sound fifty feet. This characteristic of the atmosphere he well recognized from work he had often done in bridge and tunnel caissons. And a wonder possessed him, despite his keen anxiety, how any race of men could live and grow and develop the evident physical force of these people under conditions so unnatural.

Turning his head and wrenching his neck sidewise, he was able to catch a glimpse of the water, over the low gunwale -- a gunwale made, like the framework of the boat itself, of thin metallic strips cleverly riveted.

There, approaching through the mists, he got sight of another boat, also provided with its cressets that flung an uncanny shaft of blue across the jetty expanse -- a boat now drawing near under the urge of half-seen oarsmen. And farther still another torch was visible; and beyond that a dozen, a score or more, all moving with dim and ghostly slowness, through the blind abyss of fog and heat and drifting vapors.

Stern gathered strength for another appeal.

"Who are you people?" cried he passionately. "What are you going to do with us? Where are we -- and what kind of a place are we in? Any way to get out, out to the world again? And the girl -- that girl! Oh, great God! Can't you answer something?"

No reply. Only that same slow, strong paddling, awful in its purposeful deliberation. Stern questioned in French, Spanish and German, but got not even the satisfaction of attracting their attention. He flung what few phrases of Latin and Esperanto he had at them. No result. And a huge despair filled his soul, a feeling of utter and absolute helplessness.

For the first time in his life -- that life which had covered a thousand years or more -- he found himself unable to make himself intelligible. He had not now even recourse to gestures, to sign language. Bound hand and foot, trussed like a fowl, ignored by his captors (who, by all rules, should have been his hosts and shown him every courtesy), he felt a profound and terrible anger growing in his heart.

A sudden rage, unreasoning and insensate, blazed within him. His fists clenched; once more he tugged, straining at his stout bonds. He called down maledictions on those two strange, impassive, wraithlike forms hardly more than half seen in the darkness and fog.

Then, as delirium won again over his tortured senses and disjointed thoughts, he shouted the name of Beatrice time after time out into the echoing dark that brooded over the great waters. All at once he heard her voice, trembling and faint and weak, but still hers!

From the other boat it came, the boat now drawing very near. And as the craft loomed up through the vapors that rose incessantly from that Stygian sea, he made a mighty effort, raised himself a little and suddenly beheld her -- dim, vague, uncertain in the shuddering bluish glare, yet still alive!

She was crouching midships of the canoe and, seemingly, was not bound. At his hail she stretched forth a hand and answered with his name.

"Oh, Allan! Allan!" Her voice was tremulous and very weak.

"Beatrice! You're safe? Thank God!"

"Hurt? Are you hurt?"

"No -- nothing to speak of. These demons haven't done you any damage, have they? If so --"

"Demons? Why, Allan! They've rescued us, haven't they?"

"Yes -- and now they've got me tied here, hand and foot! I

can't more than just move about two or three inches, blast them! They haven't tied you, have they?"

"No," she answered. "Not yet! But -- what an outrage! I'll free you, never fear. You and I together --"

"Can't do anything, now, girl. There may be hundreds of these people. Thousands, perhaps. And we're only two -- two captives, and -- well -- hang it, Beatrice! I don't mean to be pessimistic or anything like that, but it certainly looks bad!"

"But who are they, boy? Who can they be? And where are we?"

"Hanged if I know! This certainly beats any dream I ever had. For sheer outrageous improbability --"

He broke off short. Beatrice had leaned her head upon her arms, along the gunwale of the other canoe which now was running parallel to Stern's, and he knew the girl was weeping.

"There, there!" he cried to her. "Don't you be afraid, little girl! I've got my automatic yet; I can feel it under me, as I lie here in this infernal boat. They haven't taken yours away?"

"No!" she answered, raising her head again. "And before they ever do, I'll use it, that's all!"

"Good girl!" he cheered her, across the space of water. "That's the way to talk! Whatever happens, shoot straight if you have to shoot at all -- and remember, at worst, the last cartridge is for yourself!"

24. The Land of the Merucaans

"I'll remember," she answered simply, and for a little space there came silence between them.

A vast longing possessed the man to take her in his arms and hold her tight, tight to his fast-throbbing heart. But he lay bound and helpless. All he could do was call to her again, as the two canoes now drew on, side by side and as still others, joining them, made a little fleet of strange, flare-lighted craft.

"Beatrice!"

"Yes -- what is it?"

"Don't worry, whatever happens. Maybe there's no great harm done, after all. We're still alive and sound -- that's ninety-nine per cent of the battle."

"How could we have fallen like that and not been killed? A miracle!"

"The machine must have struck the surface on one of its long slants. If it had plunged straight down -- well, we shouldn't be here, that's all. These infernal pirates, whoever they are, must have been close by, in their boats, and cut us loose from our straps before the machine sank, and got us into their canoes. But --"

"Without the machine, how are we ever going to get out of here again?"

"Don't bother about that now! We've got other more important things to think of. It's all a vast and complex problem, but we'll meet it, never fear. You and I, together, are going to win! We've got to -- for the sake of the world!"

"Oh, if they'd only take us for gods, as the Horde did!"

"Gods nothing! They're as white as we are -- whiter, even. People that can make boats like these, out of iron bars covered with pitched fabric, and weave cloth like this they're wearing, and use oil-flares in metal baskets, aren't mistaking us for gods. The way they've handled me proves it. Might be a good thing if they weren't so devilish intelligent!"

He relapsed into silence, and for a while there came no sound but the cadenced dipping of many paddles as the boats, now perhaps a score in number, all slowly moved across the unfathomed black as though toward some objective common point. Each craft bore at its bow a fire-basket filled with some spongy substance, which, oil-soaked, blazed smokily with that peculiar blue-green light so ghostly in its wavering reflections.

Many of the folk sat in these boats, among their brown fiber nets and long, iron-tipped lances. All alike were pale and anemic-looking, though well-muscled and of vigorous build. Even the youngest were white-haired. All wore their hair twisted in a knot upon the crown of the head; none boasted anything even suggesting a hat or cap.

By contrast with their chalky skins, white eyebrows and lashes, their pinkish eyes -- for all the world like those of an albino -- blinked oddly as they squinted ahead, as though to catch some sign of land. Every one wore a kind of cassock of the brown coarse material; a few were girdled with belts of skin, having well-wrought metal buckles. Their paddles were not of wood. Not one trace of wood, in fact, was anywhere to be seen. Light metal blades, well-shaped and riveted to iron handles, served for propulsion.

Stern lay back, still faint and sick with the shock of the fall and with the pain, humiliation and excitement of the capture. Yet through it all he rejoiced that the girl and he had escaped with life and were both still sound of limb and faculty.

Even the loss of the machine could not destroy all his natural enthusiasm, or kill his satisfaction in this great adventuring, his joy at having found after all, a remnant of the human race once more.

"Men, by the Almighty!" thought he, peering keenly at such as he could see through the coiling, spiraling wreaths of mist that arose from the black water into the dun air. "Men! White men, too! Given such stock to work with -- provided I get the chance -- who shall say anything's impossible? If only there's some way out of this infernal hole, what may not happen?"

And, as he watched, he thrilled with nascent pride, with consciousness of a tremendous mission to perform; a sense that here -- here in the actual living flesh -- dwelt the potentialities of all his dreams, of all the many deep and noble plans which he and Beatrice had laid for a regenerated world!

Men they certainly were, white men, Caucasians, even like himself. Despite all changes of superficial character, their build and cast of features bore witness that these incredible folk, dwellers upon that nameless and buried sea, were the long-distant descendants of Americans!

"Americans, so help me!" he pondered as the boats drew onward toward what goal he knew not. "Barbarians, yet Americans, still. And with half a chance at them, God! we'll work miracles yet, she and I!"

Again he raised his voice, calling to Beatrice:

"Don't be afraid, little girl! They're our own people, after all -- Americans!"

At sound of that word a startled cry broke from the lips of Stern's elder boatman, a cry which, taken up from boat to boat, drifted dully through the fog, traversed the whole fleet of strange, slow-moving craft, and lost itself in the vague gloom.

"Merucaans! Merucaans!" the shout arose, with other words whereof Stern knew not the meaning; and closer pressed the outlying boats. The engineer felt a thrill run through the strange, mysterious folk.

"They knew their name, anyhow! Hurrah!" he exulted. "God! If we had the Stars and Stripes here, I wager a million they'd go mad about it! Remember? You bet they'll remember, when I learn their lingo and tell them a few things! Just wait till I get a chance at 'em, that's all!"

Forgotten now his bonds and all his pain. Forgotten even the perilous situation. Stern's great vision of a reborn race had swallowed minor evils. And with a sudden glow of pride that some of his own race had still survived the vast world catastrophe, he cheered again, eager as any schoolboy.

Suddenly he heard the girl's voice calling to him:

"Something ahead, Allan -- land, maybe. A big light through the mist!"

He wrenched his head a trifle up and now perceived that through the vapors a dim yet steady glow was beginning to shine, and on each side of it there stretched a line of other, smaller, blue-green lights. These, haloed by the vapor with the most beautiful prismatic rings, extended in an irregular row high above water level.

Lower down other lights were moving slowly to and fro, gathering for the most part at a point toward which the boats were headed.

"A settlement, Beatrice! A town, maybe! At last -- men, men!" he cried.

Forward the boats moved, faster now, as the rowers bent to their tasks; and all at once, spontaneously, a song rose up. First from one boat, then another, that weird, strange melody drifted through the dark air. It blended into a spectral chorus, a vague, tremulous, eerie chant, ghostlike and awful, as though on the black stream of Acheron the lost souls of a better world had joined in song.

Nothing could Stern catch of the words; but like some faint and far re-echoing of a half-heard melody, dream-music perhaps, a vaguely reminiscent undertone struck to his heart with an irresistible, melancholy, penetrant appeal.

"That tune! I know it -- if I could only think!" the engineer exclaimed. "Those words! I almost seem to know them!"

Then, with the suddenness characteristic of all that drew near in the fog, the shore-lights grew rapidly bigger and more bright.

The rowers lay back on their paddles at a sharp word of command from one of the oarsmen in Stern's boat.

Came a grating, a sliding of keels on pebbles. The boat stopped. Others came up to land. From them men began clambering.

The song died. A sound of many voices rose, as the boatmen mingled with those who, bearing torches, now began gathering about the two canoes where Stern and Beatrice still were.

"Well, we're here, anyhow, wherever here is!" exclaimed the engineer. "Hey, you fellows, let me loose, will you? What kind of a way is this to treat a stranger, I'd like to know?"

Two of the men waded through the water, tepid as new milk, to where Stern lay fast-bound, lifted him easily and carried him ashore. Black though the water was, Stern saw that it was clear. As the torch-light struck down through it, he could distinguish the clean and sandy bottom shining with metallic luster.

A strange hissing sound pervaded all the air, now sinking to a dull roar, now rising shrill as a vast jet of escaping steam.

As the tone lowered, darkness seemed to gain, through the mists; its rising brought a clearer light. But what the phenomenon was, Stern could not tell. For the source of the faint, diffused illumination that verberated through the vapor was hidden; it seemed to be a huge and fluctuating glow, off there somewhere beyond the fog-curtain that veiled whatever land this strange weird place might be.

Vague, silent, dim, the wraithlike men stood by, peering with bent brows, just as Dante described the lost souls in Hell peering at Virgil in the eternal night. A dream-crew they seemed. Even though Stern felt the vigorous muscles of the pair who now had borne him up to land, he could scarce realize their living entity.

"Beatrice! Beatrice!" he called. "Are you all right? Don't mind about me -- just look out for yourself! If they hurt you in any way, shoot!"

"I'm all right, I'm coming!" He heard her voice, and then he saw the girl herself. Unaided she had clambered from her boat; and now, breaking through the throng, she sought to reach him. But hands held her back, and words of hard command rose from a score of lips.

Stern had only time to see that she was as yet unharmed when with a quick slash of a blade somebody cut the thongs that bound his feet.

Then he was pushed forward, away from the dim and ghostly sea up an acclivity of smooth black pebbles all wet with mist.

Limping stiffly, by reason of his cramped muscles, he stumbled onward, while all about him and behind him -- as about the girl, who followed -- came the throng of these strange people.

Their squinting, pinkish eyes and pallid faces showed ghastly by the torch-glare, as, murmuring among themselves in their incomprehensible yet strangely familiar tongue, they climbed the slope. Even then, even there on that unknown beach beside an uncharted sea at the bottom of the fathomless abyss, Stern thought with joy of his revolver which still swung on his hip.

"God knows how we're going to talk to these people," reflected he, "or what sort of trouble they've got ready to hand out to us. But, once I get my right hand free -- I'm ready for whatever comes!"

25. The Dungeon of the Skeletons

As the two interlopers from the outer world moved up the slippery beach toward the great, mist-dimmed flare, escorted by the strange and spectral throng, Stern had time to analyze some factors of the situation.

It was evident that diplomacy was now -- unless in a sharp crisis -- the only role to play. How many of these people there might be he could not tell. The present gathering he estimated at about a hundred and fifty or a hundred and seventy-five; and moment by moment more were coming down the slope, looming through the vapor, each carrying a cresset on a staff or a swinging light attached to a chain.

"The village or settlement, or whatever it is," thought he, "may contain hundreds of them, thousands perhaps. And we are only two! The last thing in the world we want is a fight. But if it comes to fighting, Beatrice and I with our backs to the wall could certainly make a mighty good showing against barbarians such as these.

"It's evident from the fact that they haven't taken our revolvers away they don't know the use of firearms. Ages ago they must have forgotten even the tradition of such weapons. Their culture status seems to be a kind of advanced barbarism. Some job, here, to bring them up to civilization again."

Slow-moving, unemotional, peering dimly through the hot fog, their wraithlike appearance (as more and more came crowding) depressed and saddened Stern beyond all telling. And at thought that these were the remnants of the race which once had conquered a vast continent, built tall cities and spanned abysses with steel -- the remnants of so many million keen, energetic, scientific people -- he groaned despairingly.

"What does all this mean?" he exclaimed in a kind of passionate outburst. "Where are we? How did you get here? Can't you understand me? We're Americans, I tell you -- Americans! For God's sake, can't you understand?"

Once more the word "Merucaans" passed round from mouth to mouth; but beyond this Stern got no sign of comprehension.

"Village! Houses!" shouted he. "Shelter! Rest, eat, sleep!"

They merely shoved him forward up the slope, together with the girl; and now Stern saw a curious kind of causeway, paved with slippery, wet, black stones that gleamed in the torchlight, a causeway slanting sharply upward, its further end hidden in the dense vapor behind which the great and unknown light shone with ever-clearer glowing.

This road was bordered on either hand by a wall of carefully cut stone about three and a half feet high; and into the wall, at equal distances of twenty feet or so, iron rods had been let. Each rod bore a fire-basket, some only dully flickering, some burning bright and blue.

Numbers of the strange folk were loitering on the causeway or coming down to join the throng which now ascended; many clambered lithely up onto the wall, and, holding to the rods or to each other -- for the stones, like everything here, were wet and glairy -- watched with those singular-hued and squinting eyes of theirs the passage of the strangers.

Stern and Beatrice, their breathing now oppressed by the thickening smoke which everywhere hung heavy, as well as by this fresh exertion in the densely compressed air, toiled, panting, up the steep incline.

The engineer was already bathed in a heavy sweat. The intense heat, well above a hundred degrees, added to the humidity, almost stifled him. His bound arms pained almost beyond endurance. Unable to balance himself, he slipped and staggered.

"Beatrice!" he called chokingly. "Try to make them understand I want my hands freed. It's bad enough trying to clamber up this infernal road, anyhow, without having to go at it all trussed up this way."

She, needing no second appeal, raised her free arms, pointed to her wrists and then at his, and made a gesture as of cutting. But the elder boatman of Stern's canoe -- seemingly a person of some authority -- only shook his head and urged the prisoners upward, ever upward toward the great and growing light.

Now they had reached the top of the ascent.

On either hand, vanishing in shadows and mist, heavy and high walls extended, all built of black, cut stone surmounted by cressets.

Through a gateway the throng passed, and the prisoners with them -- a gateway built of two massive monoliths of dressed stone, octagonal and highly polished, with a huge, straight plinth that Stern estimated at a glance never could have weighed less than ten tons.

"Ironwork, heavy stonework, weaving, fisheries -- a good beginning here to work on," thought the engineer. But there was little time for analysis. For now already they were passing through a complex series of inner gateways, passages, detours and labyrinthic defenses which -- all well lighted from above by fire-baskets -- spoke only too plainly the character of the enclosure within.

"A walled town, heavily fortified," Stern realized as he and Beatrice were thrust forward through the last gate. "Evidently these people are living here in constant fear of attack by formidable foes. I'll wager there's been some terrible fighting in these narrow ways -- and there may be some more, too, before we're through with it. God, what a place! Makes me think of the machicolations and posterns at old Carcassonne. So far as this is concerned, we're back again in the Dark Ages -- dark, dark as Erebus!"

Then, all at once, out they issued into so strange a scene that, involuntarily, the two captives stopped short, staring about them with wide eyes.

Stretching away before them till the fog swallowed it -- a fog now glowing with light from some source still mist-hidden -- an open plaza stretched. This plaza was all surrounded, so far as they could see, with singular huts, built of dressed stone, circular for the most part, and with conical roofs like monster beehives. Windows there were none, but each hut had an open door facing the source of the strange, blue-green light.

Stern could now see the inside of the wall, topped with torches; its crest rose some five feet above the level of the plaza; and, where he could catch a glimpse of its base between the huts and through the crowding folk, he noticed that huge quantities of boulders were piled as though for instant use in case of attack.

A singular dripping of warmish water, here a huge drop, there another, attracted his attention; but though he looked up to determine its source, if possible, he could see nothing except the glowing mist. The whole floor of the enclosure seemed to be wet and shining with this water; and all the roughly clad folk, now coming from the huts and concentrating toward the captives, from every direction, were wet as well, as though with this curious, constant, sparsely scattered rain.

Not a quadruped of any kind was to be seen. Neither cat nor dog was there, neither goat nor pig nor any other creature such as in the meanest savage villages of other times might have been found upon the surface of the earth. But, undisturbed and bold, numbers of a most extraordinary fowl -- a long-legged, red-necked fowl, wattled and huge of beak -- gravely waddled here and there or perched singly and in solemn rows upon the huts.

"Great Heavens, Beatrice," exclaimed the engineer, "what are we up against? Of all the incredible places! That light! That roaring!"

He had difficulty in making himself even heard. For now the hissing roar which they had perceived from afar off seemed to fill the place with a tremendous vibrant blur, rising, falling, as the light waxed and waned.

Terribly confusing all these new sense-impressions were to Stern and Beatrice in their unnerved and weakened state. And, staring about them as they went, they slowly moved along with the motion of their captors toward the great light.

All at once Stern stopped, with a startled cry.

"The infernal devils!" he exclaimed, and recoiled with an involuntary shudder from the sight that met his eyes.

The girl, too, cried out in fear.

Some air-current, some heated blast of vapor from the vast flame they now saw shooting upward from the stone flooring of the plaza, momently dispelled the thick, white vapors.

Stern got a glimpse of a circular row of stone posts, each about nine feet high -- he saw not the complete circle, but enough of it to judge its diameter as some fifty feet. In the center stood a round and massive building, and from each post to that building stretched a metal rod perhaps twenty feet in length.

"Look! Look!" gasped Beatrice, and pointed.

Then, deadly pale, she hid her face in both her hands and crouched away, as though to blot the sight from her perception.

Each metal bar was sagging with a hideous load -- a row of human skeletons, stark, fleshless, frightful in their ghastliness. All were headless. All, suspended by the cervical vertebrae, swayed lightly as the blue-green light glared on them with its weird, unearthly radiance.

Before either Stern or the girl had time even to struggle or so much as recover from the shock of this fell sight, they were both pushed roughly between two of the posts into the frightful circle.

Stern saw a door yawn black before them in the massive hut of stone.

Toward this the Folk of the Abyss were thrusting them.

"No, you don't, damn you!" he howled with sudden passion. "None o' that for us! Shoot, Beta! Shoot!"

But even as her hand jerked at the butt of the automatic, in its rawhide holster on her hip, an overmastering force flung them both forward into the foul dark of the round dungeon. A metal door clanged shut. Absolute darkness fell.

"My God!" cried Stern. "Beta! Where are you? Beta! Beta!"

But answer there was none. The girl had fainted.

26. "You Speak English!"

Even in his pain and rage and fear, Stern did not lose his wits. Too great the peril, he subconsciously realized, for any false step now. Despite the fact that the stone prison could measure no more than some ten feet in diameter, he knew that in its floors some pit or fissure might exist, frightfully deep, for their destruction. And other dangers, too, might lie hidden in this fearful place. So, restraining himself with a strong effort, he stood there motionless a few seconds, listening, trying to think. Severe now the pain from his lashed wrists had grown, but he no longer felt it. Strange visions seemed to dance before his eyes, for weakness and fever were at work upon him. In his ears still sounded, though muffled now, the constant hissing roar of the great flame, the mysterious and monstrous jet of fire which seemed to form the center of this unknown, incomprehensible life in the abyss.

"Merciful Heavens!" gasped he. "That fire -- those skeletons -- this black cell -- what can they mean?" He found no answer in his bewildered brain. Once more he called, "Beatrice! Beatrice!" but only the close echo of the prison replied.

He listened, holding his breath in sickening fear. Was there, in truth, some waiting, yawning chasm in the cell, and had she, thrust rudely forward, been hurled down it? At the thought he set his jaws with terrible menace and swore, to the last drop of his blood, vengeance on these inhuman captors.

But as he listened, standing there with bound hands in the thick gloom, he seemed to catch a slow and sighing sound, as of troubled breathing. Again he called. No answer. Then he understood the truth. And, unable to grope with his hands, he swung one foot slowly, gently, in the partial circumference of a circle.

At first he found nothing save the smooth and slippery stone of the floor, but, having shifted his position very cautiously and tried again, he experienced the great joy of feeling his sandaled foot come in contact with the girl's prostrate body.

Beside her on the floor he knelt. He could not free his hands, but he could call to her and kiss her face. And presently, even while the joy of this discovery was keen upon him, obscuring the hot rage he felt, she moved, she spoke a few vague words, and reached her hands up to him; she clasped him in her arms.

And there in the close, fetid dark, imprisoned, helpless, doomed, they kissed again, and once more -- though no word was spoken -- plighted their love and deep fidelity until the end.

"Hurt? Are you hurt?" he panted eagerly, as she sat up on the hard floor and with her hands smoothed back the hair from his hot, aching head.

"I feel so weak and dizzy," she answered. "And I'm afraid -- oh, Allan, I'm afraid! But, no, I'm not hurt."

"Thank God for that!" he breathed fervently. "Can you untie these infernal knots? They're almost cutting my hands off!"

"Here, let me try!"

And presently the girl set to work; but even though she labored till her fingers ached, she could not start the tight and water-soaked ligatures.

"Hold on, wait a minute," directed he. "Feel in my right-hand pocket. Maybe they forgot to take my knife."

She obeyed.

"They've got it," she announced. "Even if they don't know the meaning of revolvers, they understand knives all right. It's gone."

"Pest!" he ejaculated hotly. Then for a moment he sat thinking, while the girl again tried vainly to loosen the hard-drawn knots.

"Can you find the iron door they shoved us through?" asked he at length.

"I'll see!"

He heard her creeping cautiously along the walls of stone, feeling as she went.

"Look out!" he warned. "Keep testing the floor as you go. There may be a crevice or pit or something of that kind."

All at once she cried: "Here it is! I've found it!"

"Good! Now, then, feel it all over and see if there's any rough place on it. Any sharp edge of a plate, or anything of that kind, that I could rub the cords on."

Another silence. Then the girl spoke.

"Nothing of that kind here," she answered depairingly. "The door's as smooth as if it had been filed and polished. There's not even a lock of any kind. It must be fastened from the outside in some way."

"By Heaven, this is certainly a hard proposition!" exclaimed the engineer, groaning despite himself. "What the deuce are we going to do now?"

For a moment he remained sunk in a kind of dull and apathetic despair.

But suddenly he gave a cry of joy.

"I've got it!" he exclaimed. "Your revolver, quick! Aim at the opposite wall, there, and fire!"

"Shoot, in here?" she queried, astonished. "Why -- what for?"

"Never mind! Shoot!"

Amazed, she did his bidding. The crash of the report almost deafened them in that narrow room. By the stabbing flare of the discharge they glimpsed the black and shining walls, a deadly circle all about them.

"Again?" asked she.

"No. That's enough. Now, find the bullet. It's somewhere on the floor. There's no pit; it's all solid. The bullet -- find the bullet!"

Questioning no more, yet still not understanding, she groped on hands and knees in the impenetrable blackness. The search lasted more than five minutes before her hand fell on the jagged bit of metal.

"Ah!" cried she. "Here it is!"

"Good! Tell me, is the steel jacket burst in any such way as to make a jagged edge?"

A moment's silence, while her deft fingers examined the metal. Then said she:

"I think so. It's a terribly small bit to saw with, but --"

"To work, then! I can't stand this much longer."

With splendid energy the girl attacked the tough and water-soaked bonds. She worked half an hour before the first one, thread by thread yielding, gave way. The second followed soon after; and now, with torn and bleeding fingers, she released the final bond.

"Thank Heaven!" he breathed as she began chafing his numb wrists and arms to bring the circulation back again; and presently, when he had regained some use of his own hands, he also rubbed his arms.

"No great damage done, after all," he judged, "so far as this is concerned. But, by the Almighty, we're in one frightful fix every other way! Hark! Hear those demons outside there? God knows what they're up to now!"

Both prisoners listened.

Even through the massive walls of the circular dungeon they could hear a dull and gruesome chant that rose, fell, died, and then resumed, seemingly in unison with the variant roaring of the flame.

Thereto, also, an irregular metallic sound, as of blows struck on iron, and now and then a shrill, high-pitched cry. The effect of these strange sounds, rendered vague and unreal by the density of the walls, and faintly penetrating the dreadful darkness, surpassed all efforts of the imagination.

Beatrice and Stern, bold as they were, hardened to rough adventurings, felt their hearts sink with bodings, and for a while they spoke no word. They sat there together on the floor of polished stone -- perceptibly warm to the touch and greasy with a peculiarly repellent substance -- and thought long thoughts which neither one dared voice.

But at length the engineer, now much recovered from his pain and from the oppression of the lungs caused by the compressed air, reached for the girl's hand in the dark.

"Without you where should I be?" he exclaimed. "My good angel now, as always!"

She made no answer, but returned the pressure of his hand. And for a while silence fell between them there -- silence broken only by their troubled breathing and the cadenced roaring of the huge gas-well flame outside the prison wall.

At last Stern spoke.

"Let's get some better idea of this place," said he. "Maybe if we know just what we're up against we'll understand better what to do."

And slowly, cautiously, with every sense alert, he began exploring the dungeon. Floor and walls he felt with minute care, reaching as high as he could and eagerly seeking some possible crevice, some promise -- no matter how remote -- of ultimate escape.

But the examination ended only in discouragement. Smooth almost as glass the walls were, and the floor as well, perhaps worn down by countless prisoners.

The iron door, cleverly let into the wall, lay flush with it, and offered not the slightest irregularity to the touch. So nicely was it fitted that not even Stern's finger-nail could penetrate the joint.

"Nothing doing in the escape line," he passed judgment unwillingly. "Barbarians these people certainly are, in some ways, but they've got the arts of stone and iron working down fine. I, as an engineer, have to appreciate that, and give the remote descendants of our race credit for it, even if it works our ruin. Gad, but they're clever, though!"

Discouraged, in spite of all his attempted optimism, he sought the girl again, there in the deep and velvet dark. To himself he drew her; and, his arm about her sinuous, supple body, tried to comfort her with cheering speech.

"Well, Beatrice, they haven't got us yet! We're better off, on the whole, than we had any right to hope for, after having fallen one or two hundred miles -- maybe five hundred, who knows? If I can manage to get a word or two with these confounded barbarians, I'll maybe save our bacon yet! And, at worst -- well, we're in a mighty good little fort here. I pity anybody that tries to come in that door and get us."

"Oh, Allan -- those skeletons, those headless skeletons!" she whispered; and in his arms he felt her shudder with unconquerable fear.

"I know; but they aren't going to add us to their little collection, you mark my words! These men are white; they're our own kind, even though they have slid back into barbarism. They'll listen to reason, once I get a chance at them."

Thus, talking of the abyss and of their fall -- now of one phase, now another, of their frightful position -- they passed an hour in the stifling dark.

And, joining their observations and ideas, they were able to get some general idea of the conditions under which these incredible folk were dwelling.

From the warmth of the sea and the immense quantities of vapor that filled the abyss, they concluded that it must be at a tremendous depth in the earth -- perhaps as far down as Stern's extreme guess of five hundred miles -- and also that it must be of very large extent.

Beatrice had noted also that the water was salt. This led them to the conclusion that in some way or other, perhaps intermittently, the oceans on the surface were supplying the subterranean sea.

"If I'm not much mistaken," judged the engineer, "that tremendous maelstrom near the site of New Haven -- the cataract that almost got us, just after we started out -- has something very vital to do with this situation.

"In that case, and if there's a way for water to come down, why mayn't there be a way for us to climb up? Who knows?"

"But if there were," she answered, "wouldn't these people have found it, in all these hundreds and hundreds of years?"

They discussed the question, pro and con, with many another that bore on the folk -- this strange and inexplicable imprisonment, the huge flame at the center of the community's life, the probable intentions of their captors, and the terrifying rows of headless skeletons.

"What those mean I don't know," said Stern. "There may be human sacrifice here, and offerings of blood to some outlandish god they've invented. Or these relics may be trophies of battle with other peoples of the abyss.

"To. judge from the way this place is fortified, I rather think there must be other tribes, with more or less constant warfare. The infernal fools! When the human race is all destroyed, as it is, except a few handfuls of albino survivors, to make war and kill each other! It's on a par with the old Maoris of New Zealand, who practically exterminated each other -- fought till most of the tribes were wiped clean out and only a remnant was left for the British to subdue!"

"I'm more interested in what they're going to do with us now," she answered, shuddering, "than in how many or how few survive! What are we going to do, Allan? What on earth can we do now?"

He thought a moment, while the strange chant, dimly heard, rose and fell outside, always in unison with the gigantic flame. Then said he:

"Do? Nothing, for the immediate present. Nothing, except wait, and keep all the nerve and strength we can. No use in our shouting and making a row. They'd only take that as an admission of fear and weakness, just as any barbarians would. No use hammering on the iron door with our revolver-butts, and annoying our white brothers by interrupting their song services.

"Positively the only thing I can see to do is just to make sure both automatics are crammed full of cartridges, keep our wits about us, and plug the first man that comes in through that door with the notion of making sacrifices of us. I certainly don't hanker after martyrdom of that sort, and, by God! the savage that lays hands on you, dies inside of one second by the stop-watch!"

"I know, boy; but against so many, what are two revolvers?"

"They're everything! My guess is that a little target practice would put the fear of God into their hearts in a most extraordinary manner!"

He tried to speak lightly and to cheer the girl, but in his breast his heart lay heavy as a lump of lead.

"Suppose they don't come in, what then?" suddenly resumed Beatrice. "What if they leave us here till --"

"There, there, little girl! Don't you go borrowing any trouble! We've got enough of the real article, without manufacturing any!"

Silence again, and a long, dark, interminable waiting. In the black cell the air grew close and frightfuly oppressive. Clad as they both were in fur garments suitable to outdoor life and to aeroplaning at great altitudes, they were suffering intensely from the heat.

Stern's wrists and arms, moreover, still pained considerably, for they had been very cruelly bruised with the ropes, which the barbarians had drawn tight with a force that bespoke both skill and deftness. His need of some occupation forced him to assure himself, a dozen times over, that both revolvers were completely filled. Fortunately, the captors had not known enough to rob either Beatrice or him of the cartridge-belts they wore.

How long a time passed? One hour, two, three?

They could not tell.

But, overcome by the vitiated air and the great heat, Beatrice slept at last, her head in the man's lap. He, utterly spent, leaned his back against the wall of black and polished stone, nodding with weariness and great exhaustion.

He, too, must have dropped off into a troubled sleep, for he did not hear the unbolting of the massive iron cell-door.

But all at once, with a quick start, he recovered consciousness. He found himself broad awake, with the girl clutching at his arm and pointing.

With dazzled eyes he stared -- stared at a strange figure standing framed in a rectangle of blue and foggy light.

Even as he shouted: "Hold on, there! Get back out o' that, you!" and jerked his ugly pistol at the old man's breast -- for very aged this man seemed, bent and feeble and trembling as he leaned upon an iron staff -- a voice spoke dully through the half-gloom, saying:

"Peace, friends! Peace be unto you!"

Stern started up in wild amaze.

From his nerveless fingers the pistol dropped. And, as it clattered on the floor, he cried:

"English? You speak English? Who are you? English! English! Oh, my God!"

27. Doomed!

The aged man stood for a moment as though tranced at sound of the engineer's voice. Then, tapping feebly with his staff, he advanced a pace or two into the dungeon. And Stern and Beatrice -- who now had sprung up, too, and was likewise staring at this singular apparition -- heard once again the words:

"Peace, friends! Peace!"

Stern snatched up the revolver and leveled it.

"Stop there!" he shouted. "Another step and I -- I --"

The old man hesitated, one hand holding the staff, the other groping out vacantly in front of him, as though to touch the prisoners. Behind him, the dull blue light cast its vague glow. Stern, seeing his bald and shaking head, lean, corded hand, and trembling body wrapped in its mantle of coarse brown stuff, could not finish the threat.

Instead, his pistol-hand dropped. He stood there for a moment as though paralyzed with utter astonishment. Outside, the chant had ceased. Through the doorway no living beings were visible--nothing but a thin and tenuous vapor, radiant in the gas-flare which droned its never-ending roar.

"In the name of Heaven, who -- what -- are you?" cried the engineer, at length. "A man who speaks English, here? Here?"

The aged one nodded slowly, and once again groped out toward Stern.

Then, in his strangely hollow voice, unreal and ghostly, and with uncertain hesitation, an accent that rendered the words all but unintelligible, he made answer:

"A man -- yea, a living man. Not a ghost. A man! and I speak the English. Verily, I am ancient. Blind, I go unto my fathers soon. But not until I have had speech with you. Oh, this miracle -- English speech with those to whom it still be a living tongue!"

171

He choked, and for a space could say no more. He trembled violently. Stern saw his frail body shake, heard sobs, and knew the ancient one was weeping.

"Well, great Scott! What d'you think of that?" exclaimed the engineer. "Say, Beatrice -- am I dreaming? Do you see it, too?"

"Of course! He's a survivor, don't you understand?" she answered, with quicker intuition than his. "He's one of an elder generation -- he remembers more! Perhaps he can help us!" she added eagerly. And without more ado, running to the old man, she seized his hand and pressed it to her bosom.

"Oh, father!" cried she. "We are Americans in terrible distress! You understand us -- you, alone, of all these people here. Save us, if you can!"

The patriarch shook his head, where still some sparse and feeble hairs clung, snowy-white.

"Alas!" he answered, intelligibly, yet still with that strange, hesitant accent of his -- "alas, what can I do? I am sent to you, verily, on a different mission. They do not understand, my people. They have forgotten all. They have fallen back into the night of ignorance. I alone remember; I only know. They mock me. But they fear me, also.

"Oh, woman!" -- and, dropping his staff a-clatter to the floor, he stretched out a quivering hand -- "oh, woman! and oh, man from above -- speak! Speak, that I may hear the English from living lips!"

Stern, blinking with astonishment there in the half-gloom, drew near.

"English?" he queried. "Haven't you ever heard it spoken?"

"Never! Yet, all my life, here in this lost place, have I studied and dreamed of that ancient tongue. Our race once spoke it. Now it is lost. That magnificent language, so rich and pure, all lost, forever lost! And we --"

"But what do you speak down here?" exclaimed the engineer, with eager interest. "It seemed to me I could almost catch something of it; but when it came down to the real meaning, I couldn't. If we could only talk with these people here, your people, they might give us some kind of a show! Tell me!"

"A -- a show?" queried the blind man, shaking his head and laying his other hand on Stern's shoulder. "Verily, I cannot comprehend. An entertainment, you mean? Alas, no, friends; they are not hospitable, my people. I fear me; I fear me greatly that -- that --"

He did not finish, but stood there blinking his sightless eyes, as though with some vast effort of the will he might gain knowledge of their features. Then, very deftly, he ran his fingers over Stern's bearded face. Upon the engineer's lips his digits paused a second.

"Living English!" he breathed in an awed voice. "These lips speak it as a living language! Oh, tell me, friends, are there now men of your race -- once our race -- still living, up yonder? Is there such a place -- is there a sky, a sun, moon, stars -- verily such things now? Or is this all, as my people say, deriding me, only the babbling of old wives' tales?"

A thousand swift, conflicting thoughts seemed struggling in Stern's mind. Here, there, he seemed to catch a lucid bit; but for the moment he could analyze nothing of these swarming impressions.

He seemed to see in this strange ancient-of-days some last and lingering relic of a former generation of the Folk of the Abyss, a relic to whom perhaps had been handed down, through countless generations, some vague and wildly distorted traditions of the days before the cataclysm. A relic who still remembered a little English, archaic, formal, mispronounced, but who, with the tenacious memory of the very aged, still treasured a few hundred words of what to him was but a dead and forgotten tongue. A relic, still longing for knowledge of the outer world-still striving to keep alive in the degenerated people some spark of memory of all that once had been!

And as this realization, not yet very clear, but seemingly certain in its general form, dawned on the engineer, a sudden interest in the problem and the tragedy of it all sprang up in him, so keen, so poignant in its appeal to his scientific sense, that for a moment it quite banished his distress and his desire for escape with Beatrice.

"Why, girl," he cried, "here's a case parallel, in real life, to the wildest imaginings of fiction! It's as though a couple of ancient

Romans had walked in upon some old archeologist who'd given his life to studying primitive Latin! Only you'd have to imagine he was the only man in the world who remembered a word of Latin at all! Can you grasp it? No wonder he's overcome!

"Gad! If we work this right," he added in a swift aside, "this will be good for a return ticket, all right!"

The old man withdrew his hand from the grasp of Beatrice and folded both arms across his breast with simple dignity.

"I rejoice that I have lived to this time," he stammered slowly, gropingly, as though each word, each distorted and mispronounced syllable had to be sought with difficulty. "I am glad that I have lived to touch you and to hear your voices. To know it is no mere tradition, but that, verily, there was such a race and such a language! The rest also, must be true -- the earth, and the sun, and everything. Oh, this is a wonder and a miracle! Now I can die in a great peace, and they will know I have spoken truth to their mocking!"

He kept silence a space, and the two captives looked fixedly at him, strangely moved. On his withered cheeks they could see, by the dull bluish glow through the doorway, tears still wet. The long and venerable beard of spotless white trembled as it fell freely over the coarse mantle.

"What a subject for a painter -- if there were any painters left!" thought Stern.

The old man's lips moved again.

"Now I can go in peace to my appointed place in the Great Vortex," said he, and bowed his head, and whispered something in that other speech they had already heard but could not understand.

Stern spoke first.

"What shall we call your name, father?" asked he.

"Call me J'hungaav," he answered, pronouncing a name which neither of them could correctly imitate. When they had tried he asked:

"And yours?"

Stern gave both the girl's and his own. The old man caught them both readily enough, though with a very different accent.

"Now, see here, father," the engineer resumed, "you'll pardon us, I know. There's a million things to talk about. A million we want to ask, and that we can tell you! But we're very tired. We're hungry. Thirsty. Understand? We've just been through a terrible experience. You can't grasp it yet; but I'll tell you we've fallen, God knows how far, in an aeroplane --"

"Fallen? In an -- an --"

"No matter. We've fallen from the surface. From the world where there's a sky, and sun, and stars, and all the rest of it. So far as we know, this woman and I are the only two people -- the original kind of people, I mean; the people of the time before -- er -- hang it! -- it's mighty hard to explain!"

"I understand. You are the only two now living of our former race? And you have come from above? Verily, this is strange!"

"You bet it is! I mean, verily. And now we're here, your people have thrown us into this prison, or whatever it is. And we don't like the look of those skeletons on the iron rods outside a little bit! We --"

"Oh, I pray! I pray!" exclaimed the patriarch, thrusting out both hands. "Speak not of those! Not yet!"

"All right, father. What we want to ask is for something to eat and drink, some other kind of clothes than the furs we're wearing, and a place to sleep -- a house, you know -- we've got to rest! We mean no harm to your people. Wouldn't hurt a hair of their heads! Overjoyed to find 'em! Now, I ask you, as man to man, can't you get us out of this, and manage things so that we shall have a chance to explain?

"I'll give you the whole story, once we've recuperated. You can translate it to your people. I ask some consideration for myself, and I demand it for this woman! Well?"

The old man stood in silent thought a moment. Plain to see, his distress was very keen. His face wrinkled still more, and on his breast he bowed his majestic head, so eloquent of pain and sorrow and long disappointment.

Stern, watching him narrowly, played his trump-card.

"Father," said he, "I don't know why you were sent here to talk

175

with us, or how they knew you could talk with us even. I don't know what any of this treatment means. But I do know that this girl and I are from the world of a thousand years ago -- the world in which your ancient forefathers used to dwell!

"She and I know all about that world. We know the language which to you is only a precious memory, to us a living fact. We can tell you hundreds, thousands of things! We can teach you everything you want to know! For a year -- if you people have years down here -- we can sit and talk to you, and instruct you, and make you far, far wiser than any of your Folk!

"More, we can teach your Folk the arts of peace and war -- a multitude of wonderful and useful things. We can raise them from barbarism to civilization again! We can save them -- save the world! And I appeal to you, in the name of all the great and mighty past which to you is still a memory, if not to them -- save us now!"

He ceased. The old man sighed deeply, and for a while kept silence. His face might have served as the living personification of intense and hopeless woe.

Stern had an idea.

"Father," he added -- "here, take this weapon in your hand!" He thrust the automatic into the patriarch's fingers. "This is a revolver. Have you ever heard that word? With this and other weapons even stronger, our race, your race, used to fight. It can kill men at a distance in a twinkling of an eye. It is swift and very powerful! Let this be the proof that we are what we say, survivors from the time that was! And in the name of that great day, and in the name of what we still can bring to pass for you and yours, save us from whatever evil threatens!"

A moment the old man held the revolver. Then, shuddering as with a sudden chill, he thrust it back at Stern.

"Alas!" cried he. "What am I against a thousand? A thousand, sunk in ignorance and fear and hate? A thousand who mock at me? Who believe you, verily, to be only some new and stronger kind of Lanskaarn, as we call our ancient enemies on the great islands in the sea.

"What can I do? They have let me have speech with you merely because they think me so old and so childish! Because they say my brain is soft! Whatever I may tell them, they will only mock. Woe upon me that I have known this hour! That I have heard this ancient tongue, only now forever to lose it! That I know the truth! That I know the world of old tradition was true and is true, only now to have no more, after this moment, any hope ever to learn about it!"

"The devil you say!" cried Stern, with sudden anger. "You mean they won't listen to reason? You mean they're planning to butcher us, and hang us up there along with the rest of the captured Lanskaarns, or whatever you call them? You mean they're going to take us -- us, the only chance they've got ever to get out of this, and stick us like a couple of pigs, eh? Well, by God! You tell them -- you tell --"

In the doorway appeared another form, armed with an iron spear. Came a quick word of command.

With a cry of utter hopelessness and heartbreak, a wail that seemed to pierce the very soul, the patriarch turned and stumbled to the door.

He paused. He turned, and, stretching out both feeble arms to them -- to them, who meant so infinitely much to him, so absolutely nothing to his barbarous race -- cried:

"Fare you well, O godlike people of that better time! Fare you well! Before another tide has risen on our accursed black beach, verily both of you, the last survivors --"

With a harsh word of anger, the spearsman thrust him back and away.

Stern leaped forward, revolver leveled.

But before he could pull trigger the iron door had clanged shut.

Once more darkness swallowed them.

Black though it was, it equaled not the blackness of their absolute despair,

28. The Battle in the Dark

For a time no word passed between them. Stern took the girl in his arms and comforted her as best he might; but his heart told him there was now no hope.

The old man had spoken only too truly. There existed no way of convincing these barbarians that their prisoners were not of some hated, hostile tribe. Evidently the tradition of the outer world had long since perished as a belief among them. The patriarch's faith in it had come to be considered a mere doting second childhood vagary, just as the tradition of the Golden Age was held to be by the later Greeks.

That Stern and Beatrice could in any way convince their captors of the truth of this outer world and establish their identity as real survivors of the other time, lay wholly outside the bounds of the probable.

And as the old man's prophecy of evil -- interrupted, yet frightfully ominous -- recurred to Stern's mind, he knew the end of everything was very close at hand.

"They won't get us, though, without a stiff fight, damn them!" thought he. "That's one satisfaction. If they insist on extermination -- if they want war -- they'll get it, all right enough! And it'll be what Sherman said war always was, too -- Hell!"

Came now a long, a seemingly interminable wait. The door remained fast-barred. Oppression, heat, thirst, hunger tortured them, but relief there was none.

And at length the merciful sleep of stupefaction overcame them; and all their pain, their anguish and forebodings were numbed into a welcome oblivion.

They were awakened by a confused noise -- the sound of cries and shouts, dulled by the thick walls, yet evidently many-voiced -- harsh commands, yells, and even some few sharp blows upon the prison stones.

The engineer started up, wide-eyed and all alert now in the gloom.

Gone were his lassitude, his pain. Every sense acute, pistol in hand, finger on trigger.

"Ready there, Beatrice!" cried he. "Something's started at last! Maybe it's our turn now. Here, get behind me -- but be ready to shoot when I tell you! Steady now, steady for the attack!"

Tense as coiled springs they waited. And all at once a bar slid, creaking. Around the edge of the metal door a thin blue line of light appeared.

"Stand back, you!" yelled Stern. "The first man through that door's a dead one!"

The line of light remained a moment narrow, then suddenly it broadened. From without a pandemonium of sound burst in -- howls, shrieks, imprecations, cries of pain.

Even in that perilous moment a quick wonder darted through Stern's brain, what the meaning of this infernal tumult might be, and just what ghastly fate was to be theirs -- what torments and indignities they might still have to face before the end.

"Remember, Beatrice," he commanded, "if I'm killed, use the revolver on yourself before you let them take you!"

"I know!" she cried. And, crouching beside him in the half light, she, too, awaited what seemed the inevitable.

The door swung open.

There stood the patriarch again, arms extended, face eager with a passionate hope and longing, a great pride even at that strange and pregnant moment.

"Peace, friends!" he cried. "I give you peace! Strike me not down with those terrible weapons of yours! For verily I bring you hope again!"

"Hope? What d'you mean?" shouted Stern.

Through the opened door he caught vague glimpses in the luminous fog of many spearmen gathered near -- of excited gestures and the wild waving of arms -- of other figures that, half seen, ran swiftly here and there.

"Speak up, you! What's the matter? What's wanted?" demand-

179

ed the engineer, keeping his automatic sighted at the doorway. "What's all this infernal row? If your people there think they're going to play horse with us, they're mightily mistaken! You tell them the first man that steps through that door to get us never'll take another step! Quick! What's up?"

"Come!" answered the aged man, his voice high and tremulous above the howling tumult and the roar of the great gas-well. "Come, now! The Lanskaarn -- they attack! Come! I have spoken of your weapons to my people. Come, fight for us! And verily, if we win --"

"What kind of a trick are you putting up on us, anyhow?" roared Stern with thrice-heated rage. "None o' that now! If your people want us, let 'em come in here and get us! But as for being fooled that way and tricked into coming out --"

"I swear the truth!" supplicated the patriarch, raising his withered hand on high." If you come not, you must verily die, oh, friends! But if you come --"

"Your own life's the first to pay for any falsehood now."

"I give it gladly! The truth, I swear it! Oh, listen, while there is still time, and come! Come!"

"What about it, girl?" cried Stern. "Are you with me? Will you take a chance on it?"

"There's nothing else to do, Allan. They've got us, anyway. And -- and I think the old man's telling the truth. Hear that, now --"

Off somewhere toward the fortification wall that edged the beach, sounds of indisputable conflict were arising. The howls, cries, shrieks, blows were not to be mistaken.

Stern's resolution was instant.

"I'm with you, old man!" he shouted. "But remember your promise. And if you fail me -- it's your finish!"

"Come, Beta! Stick close to me! If we fall, we'll go down together. It's both or neither. Come on -- come on!"

Out into the glare of the great flame they issued warily, out into the strangely glowing mist that covered the incredible village as with a virescent pall.

Blinking, they stared about them, not knowing for a moment whither to run or where to shoot.

But the patriarch had Stern by the arm now; and in the midst of a confused and shouting mass of the Folk -- all armed with spears and slings, knobbed clubs and battle-maces -- was pushing him out through the circle of those ghastly posts whence dangled the headless skeletons.

"Where? Which way?" cried Stern. "Show me -- I'll do the rest!"

"Thither!" the old man directed, pointing with one hand, while with the other he shoved the engineer forward. Blind though he was, he knew the right direction. "Thither -- to the wall!"

For a second Stern had the thought of leaving Beatrice in the cell, where she might at least be safe from the keen peril of battle; but greater dangers threatened her, he knew, in his absence.

At all hazards they must keep together. And with a cry: "Come! Come -- stick close to me!" once more he broke into a run toward the sea.

Through the mists, which grew darker as he neared the wall with Beatrice close beside him and the troop that followed them, he could catch glimpses of the battle.

Every hut seemed to have poured forth its inhabitants for now the plaza swarmed with life -- men, women, even children, running this way and that, some with weapons rushing towards the wall, others running wildly hither and yon with unintelligible cries.

A spear pierced the vapors; it fell clashing at Stern's feet and slid rattling away over the black stones, worn smooth and greasy by uncounted feet.

Past him as he ran a man staggered; the whole side of his head was bashed in, as though by a frightful blow from a mace. Up the wounded man flung both arms, and fell twitching.

The fog covered him with its drifting folds. Stern shuddered that Beatrice should see such hideous sights; but even now he almost fell over another prostrate body, hideously wounded in the back, and still kicking.

"Ready, now!" panted Stern. "Ready with the pistols!"

Where was the patriarch?

He no longer knew. About him the Folk pressed, but none molested either him or Beatrice.

In the confusion, the rush of the outskirts of battle, he could have shot down a score of them, but he was reserving his fire. It might, perhaps, be true, who could tell -- that safety lay in battling now against the Lanskaarn!

All at once the captives saw vague fire-lights in the gloom -- seemingly blazing comets of blue, that tossed and hurled and disappeared.

Then came the nearer sound of shouting and the clash of arms.

Stern, with the atavistic instincts of even the most civilized man, scented the kill. And with a roar he whirled into the confused and sweltering mass of men which now, emerging from the darkening mists, had suddenly become visible by the uncanny light of the cressets on the wall.

Beside him the girl, her face aglow, nostrils dilated, breath quick, held her revolver ready.

And then, quite suddenly, they found themselves at the wall.

"Shoot! Shoot!" bellowed Stern, and let drive, pointblank, at an ugly, grinning face that like a nightmare-vision all at once projected over the crest. His own revolver-fire was echoed by hers. The face vanished.

All down there, below him on the beach, he caught a dim, confused impression of the attacking swarm.

Subconsciously he realized that he -- he a man of the twentieth century -- was witnessing again a scene such as made the whole history of the Middle Ages sanguinary -- siege, by force of human strength and rage!

Even as he vaguely saw the swift and supple men, white-skinned yet larger than the Folk, which crowded the whole beach as far as he could pierce the mists with his straining sight, he knew that here was a battle of huge scope and terrible danger.

Up from the sea the attackers, the Lanskaarn, were swarming, from their dimly seen canoes. The place was alive with them.

At the base of the wall they were clotted in dense hordes; and siege-ladders were being raised; and now up the ladders the lithe men of darkness were running like so many ants.

Automatically as the mechanism of his own gun which he pumped into that dense mass as fast as he could pull trigger -- while beside him the girl was shooting hard and straight, as well -- he seemed to be recording these wonderful impressions.

Here he caught a glimpse of a siege-ladder hurled backward by the Folk, backward and down to the beach. Amid frightful yells and screams it fell; and a score of crushed and mangled men lay writhing there under the uncanny glare of the cressets.

There he saw fire-bales being hurled down from the walls - - these, the comet-like apparitions he had seen from a distance -- hurled, blazing, right into the mob.

Beyond, a party had scaled the wall, and there the fight was hand to hand -- with gruntings, thrustings of spears, slashings of long knives that dripped red and cut again and rose and fell with hideous regularity!

He jacked his pistol full of shells once more and thrust it into the girl's hand -- for she, excited beyond all control, was snapping the hammer of her weapon on empty steel.

"Give it to 'em! Shoot! Kill!" he yelled. "Our only chance now! If they -- get in -- we're dead!"

He snatched her weapon, reloaded, and again rained the steel-jacketed bolts of death against the attackers.

In the tumult and wild maelstrom of the fight the revolvers' crackling seemed to produce little effect. If Stern expected that this unknown weapon would at once bring panic and quick victory he reckoned without the berserker madness and the stern mettle of this horde of raging Lanskaarn.

White men, like himself, they yielded not; but with strange cries and frightful yells, pressed on and on, up to the walls, and up the ladders ever; and now came flights of spears, hissing through the dark air -- and now smooth black rocks from the beach, flung with terrible strength and skill by the slingers below, mowed down the defenders.

Here, there, men of the Folk were falling, pierced by the iron spears, shattered by the swift and heavy rocks.

The place was becoming a shambles where the blood of attackers and attacked mingled horribly in the gloom.

One ladder, pushed outward, dragged half a dozen of the Merucaans with it; and at the bottom of the wall a circling eddy of the Lanskaarn despatched the fighting Folkmen who had been hauled to their destruction by the grappling besiegers.

Blows, howls and screams, hurtling fire-bales and great rocks flung from above -- the rocks he had already noted laid along the inside of the wall -- these, and the smell of blood and fire, the horrid, sweaty contact of struggling bodies, the press and jam of the battle that surged round them, all gave Stern a kaleidoscopic picture of war -- war as it once was, in the long ago -- war, naked and terrible, such as he had never even dreamed!

But, mad with the lust of the kill, he heeded nothing now.

"Shoot! Shoot!" he kept howling, beside himself; and, tearing open the bandoliers where lay his cartridges, he crammed them with feverish fingers into the girl's weapon and his own -- weapons now burning hot with the quick, long-continued firing.

The battle seemed to dance, to waver there before his eyes, in the haze of mist and smoke and stifling air. The dark scene, blue-lit by the guttering torches, grew ever more sanguinary, more incredibly hideous. And still the attackers swarmed along the walls and up them, in front and on both sides, till the swirling mists hid them and the defenders from view.

He heard Beatrice cry out with pain. He saw her stagger and fall back.

To her he leaped.

"Wounded?" he gasped.

She answered nothing, but fell limp.

"God of Battles!" he howled. "Revenge!"

He snatched her automatic from beneath the trampling, crowding feet; he bore her back, away from the thick press. And in the shelter of a massive hut he laid her down.

Then, stark-mad, he turned and leaped into the battle-line that swayed and screamed along the wall.

Critical now the moment. In half a dozen places the besiegers had got their ladders planted. And, while dense masses of the Lanskaarn -- unminding fire-balls and boulders rained down upon them -- held these ladders firm, up the attackers came with a rush.

Stern saw the swing and crushing impact of the maces and iron clubs; he saw the stabbing of the spears on both sides.

Slippery and red the parapet became.

Men, killed there, crawled and struggled and fell both outward and inside, and were trampled in indiscriminate heaps, besieged and besiegers alike, still clawing, tearing, howling even in their death agony.

Now one of the ladders was down -- another fell, with horrid tumult -- a third!

An automatic in each hand, Stern scrambled to the glairy summit of the fortification.

A mace swung at him. He leaped sidewise, firing as he sprang. With a scream the ax-man doubled up and fell, and vanished in the gloom below the wall.

Raking the parapet with a hail of lead, he mowed down the attackers on top of the fourth ladder. With a mighty shout, those inside staved it away with iron grapples. It, too, swayed drunkenly, held below, pushed madly above. It reeled -- then fell with a horrible, grinding crash!

"Hurray, boys! One more down! Give 'em Hell!" he screamed. "One more!"

He turned. Subconsciously he felt that his right hand was wet, and hot, and dripping, but he felt no pain.

"One more! Now for another!"

And in the opposite direction along the wall he emptied his other revolver.

Before the stinging swarm of the steel-jacketed wasps of death the Lanskaarn writhed and melted down with screams such as Dante in his wildest vision never even dreamed.

Stern heard a great howl of triumph break from the mass of defenders fighting to overthrow the fifth ladder.

"Hold 'em! Hold 'em!" he bellowed. "Wait till I load up again -- I'll --"

185

A swift and crashing impact dashed sheaves of radiant fire through his brain.

Everything leaped and whirled.

He flung up both hands.

Clutching at empty air, then suddenly at the slippery parapet which seemed to have leaped up and struck him in the face, he fell.

Came a strange numbness, then a stabbing pain.

And darkness quenched all knowledge and all consciousness.

29. Shadows of War

A blue and flickering gleam of light, dim, yet persistent, seemed to enhalo a woman's face; and as Stern's weary eyes opened under languid lids, closed, then opened again, the wounded engineer smiled in his weakness.

"Beatrice!" he whispered, and tried to stretch a hand to her, as she sat beside his bed of seaweed covered with the coarse brown fabric. "Oh, Beatrice! Is this -- is this another -- hallucination?"

She took the hand and kissed it, then bent above him and kissed him again, this time fair upon the lips.

"No, boy," she answered. "No hallucination, but reality! You're all right now -- and I'm all right! You've had a little fever and -- and -- well, don't ask any questions, that's all. Here, drink this now and go to sleep!"

She set a massive golden bowl to his mouth, and very gently raised his head.

Unquestioningly he drank, as though he had been a child and she his mother. The liquid, warm and somewhat sweet, had just a tang of some new taste that he had never known. Singularly vitalizing it seemed, soothing yet full of life. With a sigh of contentment, despite the numb ache in his right temple, he lay back and once more closed his eyes. Never had he felt such utter weakness. All his forces seemed drained and spent; even to breathe was very difficult.

Feebly he raised his hand to his head.

"Bandaged?" he whispered. "What does that mean?"

"It means you're to go to sleep now!" she commanded. "That's all -- just go to sleep!"

He lay quiet a moment, but sleep would not come. A score, a hundred thoughts confusedly crowded his brain.

And once more looking up at her in the dim blue gloom of the hut where they were, he breathed a question:

"Were you badly hurt, dear, in -- in the battle?"

"No, Allan. Just stunned, that's all. Not even wounded. Be quiet now or I'll scold!"

He raised his arms to her and, weak though he was, took her to his breast and held her tight, tight.

"Thank God!" he whispered. "Oh, I love you! I love you so! If you'd been killed --"

She felt his tears hot upon his wasted cheeks, and unloosened his arms.

"There, there!" she soothed him. "You'll get into a fever again if you don't lie still and try not to think! You --"

"When was it? Yesterday?" he interrupted.

"Sh-h-h-h! No more questions now."

"But I want to know! And what happened to me? And the -- the Lanskaarn? What about them? And --"

"Heavens, but you're inquisitive for a man that's just missed -- I mean, that's been as sick as you have!" she exclaimed, taking his head in both hands and gazing down at him with eyes more deeply tender than he had ever seen them. "Now do be good, boy, and don't worry about all these things, but go to sleep -- there's a dear. And when you wake up next time --"

"No, no!" he insisted with passionate eagerness. "I'm not that kind! I'm not a child, Beta! I've got to know -- I can't go to sleep without knowing. Tell me a little about it, about what happened, and then -- then I'll sleep as long as you say!"

She pondered a moment, weighing matters, then made answer:

"All right, boy, only remember your promise!"

"I will."

"Good! Now listen. I'll tell you what the old man told me, for naturally I don't remember the last part of the fight any better than you do.

"I was struck by a flying stone, and -- well, it wasn't anything serious. It just stunned me for a while. I came to in a hut."

"Where I carried you, dearest, just before I --"

"Yes, I know, just before the battle-ax --"

"Was it an ax that hit me?"

"Yes. But it was only a glancing blow. Your long hair helped save you, too. But even so --"

"Skull cracked?"

"No, I guess concussion of the brain would be the right term for it." She took his groping hand in both her own warm, strong ones and kissed it tenderly. "But before you fell, your raking fire along the wall there -- you understand --"

"Cleaned 'em out, eh?" he queried eagerly.

"That's about it. It turned the tide against the Lanskaarn. And after that -- I guess it was just butchery. I don't know, of course, and the old man hasn't wanted to tell me much; but anyway, the ladders all went down, and the Folk here made a sortie from the gate, down the causeway, and -- and --"

"And they've got a lot more of those infernal skeletons hanging on the poles by the fire?" he concluded in a rasping whisper.

She nodded, then kept a minute's silence.

"Did any of 'em get away in their canoes?"

"A few. But in all their history the Folk never won such a victory. Oh, it was glorious, glorious! And all because of you!"

"And you, dear!"

"And now -- now," she went on, "we're not prisoners any more, but --"

"Everything coming our way? Is that it?"

"That's it. They dragged you out, after the battle, from under a big heap of bodies under the wall."

"Outside or inside?"

"Outside, on the beach. They brought you in, for dead, boy. And I guess they had an awful time about you, from what I've found out --"

"Big powwow, and all that?"

"Yes. If you'd died, they'd have gone on a huge war expedition out to the islands, wherever those are, and simply wiped out the rest of the Lanskaarn. But --"

"I'm glad I didn't," he interrupted. "No more killing from now

189

on! We want all the living humans we can get; we need 'em in our business!"

Stern was growing excited; the girl had to calm him once more.

"Be quiet, Allan, or I'll leave you this minute and you shan't know another thing!" she threatened.

"All right, I'll be good," he promised. "What next? I'm the Big Chief now, of course? What I say now goes?"

She answered nothing, but a troubled wrinkle drew between her perfect brows. For a moment there was silence, save for the dull and distant roaring of the flame.

By the glow of the bluish light in the hut, Stern looked up at her. Never had she seemed so beautiful. The heavy masses of her hair, parted in the middle and fastened with gold pins such as the Folk wore, framed her wonderful face with twilight shadows. He saw she was no longer clad in fur, but in a loose and flowing mantle of the brown fabric, caught up below the breast with a gold-clasped girdle.

"Oh, Beatrice," he breathed, "kiss me again!"

She kissed him; but even in the caress he sensed an unvoiced anxiety, a hidden fear.

"What's wrong?" asked he anxiously.

"Nothing, dear. Now you must be quiet! You're in the patriarch's house here. You're safe -- for the present, and --"

"For the present? What do you mean?"

"See here." the girl threatened, "if you don't stop asking questions, and go to sleep again, I'll leave you alone!"

"In that case I promise!"

And now obedient, he closed his eyes, relaxed, and let her soothingly caress him. But still another thought obtruded on his mind.

"Beatrice?"

"Yes, dearest."

"How long ago was that fight?"

"Oh, a little while. Never mind now!"

"Yes, but how long? Two days? Four? Five?"

"They don't have days down here," she evaded.

"I know. But reckoning our way -- five days?"

"Nearer ten, Allan."

"What? But then --"

The girl withdrew her hand from him and arose.

"I see it's no use, Allan," she said decisively. "So long as I stay with you you'll ask questions and excite yourself. I'm going! Then you'll have to keep still!"

"Beta! Beta!" he implored. "I'll be good! Don't leave me -- you mustn't!"

"All right; but if you ask me another question, a single one, mind, I'll truly go!"

"Just give me your hand, girlie, that's all! Come here -- sit down beside me again -- so!"

He turned on his side, on the rude couch of coarse brown fabric stuffed with dried seaweed, laid his hollow cheek upon her hand, and gave a deep sigh.

"Now, I'm off," he murmured. "Only, don't leave me, Beta!"

For half an hour after his deep, slow breathing told that the wounded man was sleeping soundly -- half an hour as time was measured where the sun shone, for down in the black depths of the abyss all such divisions were as naught, Beatrice sat lovingly and tenderly beside the primitive bed. Her right palm beneath his face, she stroked his long hair and his wan cheek with her other hand; and now she smiled with pride and reminiscence, now a grave, troubled look crossed her features.

The light, a fiber wick burning in a stone cup of oil upon a stone-slab table in the center of the hut, guttered unsteadily, casting huge and dancing shadows up the black walls.

"Oh, my beloved!" whispered the girl, and bent above him till the loosened sheaves of her hair swept his face. "My love! Only for you, where should I be now? With you, how could I be afraid? And yet --"

She turned at a sound from a narrow door opposite the larger one that gave upon the plaza, a door, like the other, closed by a heavy curtain platted of seaweed.

There, holding the curtain back, stood the blind patriarch. His hut, larger than most in the strange village, boasted two rooms.

191

Now from the inner one, where he had been resting, he came to speak with Beatrice.

"Peace, daughter!" said the old man. "Peace be unto you. He sleeps?"

"Yes, father. He's much better now, I think. His constitution is simply marvelous."

"Verily, he is strong. But far stronger are those terrible and wonderful weapons of yours! If our Folk only had such!"

"You're better off without them. But of course, if you want to understand them, he can explain them in due time. Those, and endless other things!"

"I believe that is truth." The patriarch advanced into the room, and for a minute stood by the bedside with venerable dignity. "The traditions, I remember, tell of so many strange matters. I shall know them, every one. All in time, all in time!"

"Your simple medicines, down here, are wonderful," said the girl admiringly. "What did you put into that draught I gave him to make him sleep this way?"

"Only the steeped root of our n'gahar plant, my daughter -- a simple weed brought up from the bottom of this sea by our strong divers. It is nothing, nothing."

Came silence again. The aged man sat down upon a curved stone bench that followed the contour of the farther wall. Presently he spoke once more.

"Daughter," said he, "it is now ten sleeping -- times -- nights, the English speech calls them, if I remember what my grandfather taught me -- since the battle. And my son, here, still lies weak and sick. I go soon to get still other plants for him. Stronger plants, to make him well and powerful again. For there is haste now -- haste!"

"You mean -- Kamrou?"

"Yea, Kamrou! I know the temper of that evil man better than any other. He and his boats may return from the great fisheries in the White Gulf beyond the vortex at any time, and --"

"But, father, after all we've done for the village here, and especially after what Allan's done? After this wonderful victory, I can't believe --"

"You do not know that man!" exclaimed the patriarch. "I know him! Rather would he and his slay every living thing in this community than yield one smallest atom of power to any other."

He arose wearily and gathered his mantle all about him, then reached for his staff that leaned beside the outer door.

"Peace!" he exclaimed. "Ah, when shall we have peace and learning and a better life again? The teaching and the learning of the English speech and all the arts you know, now lost to us -- to us, the abandoned Folk in the abyss? When? When?"

He raised the curtain to depart; but even then he paused once more, and turned to her.

"Verily, you have spoken truth," said he, "when you have said that all, all here are with us, with you and this wondrous man now lying weak and wounded in my house. But Kamrou -- is different. Alas, you know him not -- you know him not!"

"Watch well over my son, here! Soon must he grow strong again. Soon, soon! Soon, against the coming of Kamrou. For if the chief returns and my son be weak still, then woe to him, to you, to me! Woe to us all! Woe, Woe!"

The curtain fell. The patriarch was gone. Outside, Beatrice heard the click-click-click of his iron staff upon the smooth and flinty rock floor.

And to her ears, mingled with the far roaring of the flame, drifted the words:

"Woe, woe to him! Woe to us all -- woe -- woe!"

30. Exploration

Under the ministering care of Beatrice and the patriarch, Stern's convalescence was rapid. The old man, consumed with terror lest the dreaded chief, Kamrou, return ere the stranger should have wholly recovered, spent himself in efforts to hasten the cure. And with deft skill he brewed his potions, made his salves, and concocted revivifying medicines from minerals which only he -- despite his blindness -- knew how to compound.

The blow that had so shrewdly clipped Stern's skull must have inevitably killed, as an ox is dropped in the slaughter-house, a man less powerfully endowed with splendid energies and full vitality.

Even Stern's wonderful physique had a hard fight to regain its finely ripened forces. But day by day he gained -- we must speak of days, though there were only sleeping-times and waking- times -- until at length, upon the fifth, he was able for the first time to leave his seaweed bed and sit a while weakly on the patriarch's bench, with Beatrice beside him.

Hand in hand they sat, while Stern asked many questions, and the old man, smiling, answered such as he saw fit. But of Kamrou neither he nor the girl yet breathed one syllable.

Next day and the next, and so on every day, Stern was able to creep out of the hut, then walk a little, and finally -- sometimes alone, sometimes with one or both his nurses -- go all among the wondering and admiring Folk, eagerly watch their labors of all kinds, try to talk with them in the few halting words he was able to pick up, and learn many things of use and deepest interest. A grave and serious Folk they were, almost without games or sports, seemingly without religious rites of any kind, and lacking festivals such as on the surface every barbarous people had always had.

Their fisheries, netmaking, weaving, ironwork, sewing with

long iron needles and coarse fiber-thread keenly interested him. Accustomed now to the roaring of the flame, he seemed no longer to hear this sound which had at first so sorely disconcerted him.

He found out nothing concerning their gold and copper supply; but their oil, he discovered, they collected in pits below the southern wall of the village, where it accumulated from deep fissures in the rock. With joy he noted the large number of children, for this bespoke a race still vigorous and with all sorts of possibilities when trained.

Odd little, silent creatures the children were, white-faced and white-haired, playless and grave, laboring like their elders even from the age of five or six. They followed him about in little troops, watching him soberly; but when he turned and tried to talk with them they scurried off like frightened rabbits and vanished in the always-open huts of stone.

Thoroughly he explored every nook and corner of the village. As soon as his strength permitted, he even penetrated parts of the surrounding region. He thought at times to detect among the Folk who followed and surrounded him, unless he expressly waved them away, some hard looks here or there. Instinctively he felt that a few of the people, here one, there one, still held hate and bitterness against him as an alien and an interloper.

But the mass of them now outwardly seemed so eager to serve and care for him, so quick to obey, so grateful almost to adoration, that Stern felt ashamed of his own suspicions and of the revolver that he still always carried whenever outside the patriarch's hut.

And in his heart he buried his fears as unworthy delusions, as the imaginings of a brain still hurt. The occasional black looks of one or another of the people, or perchance some sullen, muttered word, he set down as the crude manners of a primitive and barbarous race.

How little, despite all his skill and wit, he could foresee the truth!

To Beatrice he spoke no word of his occasional uneasiness, nor yet to the old man. Yet one of the very first matters he attended to was the overhauling of the revolvers, which had been rescued out of the melee of the battle and been given to the patriarch, who had kept them with a kind of religious devotion.

Stern put in half a day cleaning and oiling the weapons. He found there still remained a hundred and six cartridges in his bandolier and the girl's. These he now looked upon as his most precious treasure. He divided them equally with Beatrice, and bade her never go out unless she had her weapon securely belted on.

Their life at home was simple in the extreme. Beatrice had the inner room of the hut for her own. Stern and the patriarch occupied the outer one. And there, often far into the hours of the sleeping-time, when Beatrice was resting within, he and the old man talked of the wonders of the past, of the outer world, of old traditions, of the abyss, and a thousand fascinating speculations.

Particularly did the old man seek to understand some notions of the lost machine on which the strangers had come from the outer world; but, though Stern tried most patiently to make him grasp the principle of the mechanism, he failed. This talk, however, set Stern thinking very seriously about the biplane; and he asked a score of questions relative to the qualities of the native oil, to currents in the sea, locations, depths, and so on.

All that he could learn he noted mentally with the precision of the trained engineer.

With accurate scientific observation he at once began to pile up information about the people and the village, the sea, the abyss -- everything, in fact, that he could possibly learn. He felt that everything depended on a sound understanding of the topography and nature of the incredible community where he and the girl now found themselves -- perhaps for a life stay.

Beatrice and he were clad now like the Folk; wore their hair twisted in similar fashion and fastened with heavy pins or spikes of gold, cleverly graven; were shod with sandals like theirs, made of the skin of a shark-like fish; and carried torches everywhere they went -- torches of dried weed, close-packed in a metal basket and impregnated with oil.

This oil particularly interested Stern. Its peculiar blue flame struck him as singular in the extreme. It had, moreover, the property of burning a very long time without being replenished. A wick immersed in it was never consumed or even charred, though the heat produced was intense.

"If I can't set up some kind of apparatus to distil that into gas-engine fuel, I'm no engineer, that's all," said Stern to himself. "All in time, all in time -- but first I must take thought how to raise the old Pauillac from the sea."

Already the newcomers' lungs had become absolutely accustomed to the condensed air, so that they breathed with entire ease and comfort. They even found this air unusually stimulating and revivifying, because of its greater amount of oxygen to the cubic unit; and thus they were able to endure greater exertions than formerly on the surface of the earth.

The air never grew foul. A steady current set in the direction that Stern's pocket-compass indicated as north. The heat no longer oppressed them; they were even getting used to the constant fog and to the darkness; and already could see far better than a fortnight previously, when they had arrived.

Stern never could have believed he could learn to do without sunlight and starlight and the free winds of heaven; but now he found that even these were not essential to human life.

Certain phenomena excited his scientific interest very keenly -- such as the source of the great gas-flare in the village, the rhythmic variations in the air-current, the small but well-marked tides on the sea, the diminished force of gravitation -- indicating a very great depth, indeed, toward the center of the earth -- the greater density of the seawater, the heavy vaporization, certain singular rock-strata of the cliffs near the village, and many other matters.

All these Stern promised himself he would investigate as soon as time and strength allowed.

The village itself, he soon determined, was about half a mile long and perhaps a quarter-mile across, measuring from the fortified gate directly back to the huge flame near the dungeon and the place of bones.

He found, incidentally, that more than one hundred and sixty freshly boiled and headless skeletons were now dangling from the iron rods, but wisely held his peace concerning them. Nor did the patriarch volunteer any information about the loss of life of the Folk in the battle. Stern estimated there were now some fifteen hundred people, men, women and children, still remaining in the community; but since he knew nothing of their number when he had arrived, he could not form more than a rough idea of the total slaughter.

He found, however, on one of his excursions outside the walls -- which at a distance of two hundred and fifty yards from the sea stretched in a vast irregular arc abutting at each end against the cliff -- the graveyard of the Folk.

This awesome and peculiar place consisted of heaps of smooth black boulders piled upon the dead, each heap surmounted by a stone with some crude emblem cut upon it, such as a circle, a square, a cluster of dots, even the rude figure of a bird, a fish, a tortoise, and so on.

Certain of the figures he could make nothing of; but he concluded rightly they were totem-signs, and that they represented all which still remained of the art of writing among those barbarous remnants of the once dominant, powerful and highly cultured race of Americans.

He counted more than two hundred freshly built piles of stone, but whether any of these contained more than one body of the Folk he could, of course, not tell. Allowing, however, that only two hundred of the Folk and one hundred and sixty of the Lanskaarn had fallen, he readily perceived that the battle had been, for intensity and high percentage of killing, sanguinary beyond all battles of his own time.

Under the walls, too, the vast numbers of boulders which had been thrown down, the debris of broken weapons, long and jaggedly barbed iron spear-points and so on, indicated the military ardor and the boldness of the fighting men he now had to dominate and master.

And in his soul he knew the problem of taming, civilizing, saving this rude and terrible people, was certainly the very greatest ever given into the hands of one man and one woman, since time began!

Along the beach he found a goodly number of empty revolver-shells. These he picked up, for possible reloading, in case he should be able at some later time to manufacture powder and some fulminating mixture.

He asked the patriarch to have search made for all such empty shells. The Folk eagerly and intelligently cooperated.

With interest he watched the weird sight of scores of men with torches rolling the great stones about, seeking for the precious cartridges. From the beach they tossed the shells up to him as he walked along the top of the fortifications so lately the scene of horrible combat; and despite him his heart swelled with pride in his breast, to be already directing them in some concerted labor, even so slight as this.

Save for some such interruption, the life of the community had now settled back into its accustomed routine.

With diminished numbers, but indomitable energy, the Folk went on with their daily tasks. Stern concluded the great funeral ceremony, which must have taken place over the fallen defenders, and the horrible rites attending the decapitation, boiling, and hanging up of the trophies of war, the Lanskaarn skeletons, certainly must have formed a series of barbaric pictures more ghastly than any drug-fiend's most diabolical nightmare. He thanked God that the girl had been spared these frightful scenes.

He could get the old man to tell him nothing concerning these terrific ceremonies. But he discovered, some thirty yards to southward of the circle of stone posts, a boiling geyserlike pool in the rock floor, whence the thick steam continually arose, and which at times burst up in terrific seething.

Here his keen eye detected traces of the recent rites. Here, he knew, the enemies' corpses -- and perhaps even some living captives -- had been boiled.

And as he stood on the sloping, slippery edge of the great natural caldron, a pit perhaps forty feet in diameter -- its margins all worn smooth and greasy by innumerable feet -- he shuddered in his soul.

"Good God!" thought he. "Imagine being flung in there!"

What was it, premonition or sheer repulsion, that caused him, brave as he was, to turn away with a peculiar and intense horror?

Try as he might, he could not banish from his mind the horrible picture of that boiling vat as it must have looked, crammed to the lip with the tumbling, crowding bodies of the dead.

He seemed still to hear the groans of the wounded, the shrieks of the prisoners being dragged thither, being hurled into the spumy, scalding water.

And in his heart he half despaired of ever bringing back to civilization a people so wild and warlike, so cruel, so barbarous as these abandoned People of the Abyss.

Could he have guessed what lay in store for Beatrice and himself should Kamrou, returning, find them still there, a keener and deadlier fear would have possessed his soul.

But of Kamrou he knew nothing yet. Even the chief's name he had not heard. And the patriarch, for reasons of his own, had not yet told the girl a tenth part of the threatening danger.

Even what he had told, he had forbidden her -- for Allan's own sake -- to let him know.

Thus in a false and fancied sense of peace and calm security, Stern made his observations, laid his plans, and day by day once more came back toward health and strength again.

And day by day the unknown peril drew upon them both.

31. Escape?

Who could, indeed, suspect aught of this threatening danger? Outwardly all now was peaceful. Each waking-time the fishers put forth in their long boats of metal strips covered with fish-skins. Every sleeping-time they returned laden with the fish that formed the principal staple of the community.

The weaving of seaweed fiber, the making of mats, blankets, nets and slings went on as probably for many centuries before.

At forges here and there, where gas-wells blazed, the smiths of the Folk shaped their iron implements or worked most skillfully in gold and copper; and the ringing of the hammers, through the dim-lit gloom around the strange blue fires, formed a chorus fit for Vulcan or the tempering of Siegfried's master-sword.

Stern took occasion to visit many of the huts. They were all similar. As yet he could not talk freely with the Folk but he took keen interest in examining their household arrangements, which were of the simplest. Stone benches and tables, beds of weed, and coarse blankets, utensils of metal or bone -- these completed the total.

Stern groaned inwardly at thought of all the arts he still must teach them before they should once more even approximate the civilization whence they had fallen since the great catastrophe.

Behind the village rose a gigantic black cliff, always dripping and running with water from the condensation of the fogs. This water the Folk very sensibly and cleverly drained down into large tanks cut in the rock floor. The tanks, always full, furnished their entire supply for drinking and cooking. Flat, warm and tasteless though it was, it seemed reasonably pure. None of this water was ever used for bathing. What little bathing the Folk ever indulged in took place at certain points along the shore, where the fine and jet-black sand made a good bottom.

Along the base of the vast cliff, which, broken and jagged, rose gleaming in the light of the great flame till it gradually faded in the luminous mist, they carried on their primitive cooking.

Over cracks in the stone, whence gas escaped steadily and burned with a blue flicker, hung copper pots fairly well fashioned, though of bizarre shapes. Here the communal cuisine went steadily forward, tended by the strange, white-haired, long-cloaked women; and odors of boiling and of frying, over hot iron plates, rose and mingled with the shifting, swirling vapors from the sea.

Beatrice tried, a few times, to take some part in this work. She was eager to teach the women better methods, but at last the patriarch told her to let them alone, as she was only irritating them. Unlike the men, who almost worshipped the revolvers, and would have handled them, and even quickly learned to shoot, if Stern had allowed, the women clung sternly to their old ways.

The patriarch had a special cooking place made for Beatrice, and got her a lot of the clumsy utensils. Here she busied herself preparing food for Allan and herself -- and a strange sight that was, the American girl, dressed in her long, brown robe, her thick hair full of gold pins, cooking over natural gas in the Abyss, with heavy copper pans and kettles of incredible forms!

Almost at once, the old man abandoned the native cookery and grew devoted to hers. Anything that told him of the other and better times, the days about which he dreamed continually in his blindness, was very dear to him.

The Merucaans were, truly, barbarously dull about their ways of preparing food. Day after day they never varied. The menu was limited in the extreme. Stern felt astonished that a race could maintain itself in such fine condition and keep so splendidly energetic, so keen and warlike, on such a miserable diet. The food must, he thought, possess nutritive qualities far beyond any expectation.

Fish was the basis of all -- a score of strange and unnatural-looking varieties, not one of which he had ever seen in surface waters. For the most part, they were gray or white; two or three species showed some rudiments of coloring. All were blind, with at most some faint vestigia of eye-structure, wholly degenerated and useless.

"Speaking of evolution," said the engineer, one day, to Beatrice, as they stood on the black boulder-beach and watched the fishermen toss their weird freight out upon the slippery stones -- "these fish here give a magnificent example of it. You see, where the use for an organ ceases, the organ itself eventually perishes. But take these creatures and put them back into the surface-ocean --"

"The eyes would develop again?" she queried.

"Precisely! And so with everything! Take the Folk themselves, for instance. Now that they've been living here a thousand or fifteen hundred years, away from the sunlight, all the protecting pigmentation that used to shield the human race from the actinic sun rays has gradually faded out. So they've got white hair, colorless skins, and pinkish eyes. Out in the world again, they'd gradually grow normal again. How I wish some of my old-time opponents to the evolutionary theory could stand here with me today in the Abyss! I bet a million I could mighty soon upset their nonsense!"

Such of the fish as were not eaten in their natural state were salted down in vats hollowed in the rock, at the far end of the village. Still others were dried, strung by the gills on long cords of seaweed fiber, and hung in rows near the great flame. There were certain days for this process.

At other times no fish were allowed anywhere near the fire. Why this was, Stern could not discover. Even the patriarch would not tell him.

Beside the fish, several seaweeds were cooked and eaten in the form of leaves, bulbs, and roots, which some of the Folk dived for or dragged from the bottom with iron grapples. All the weeds tasted alike to Stern and Beatrice; but the old man assured them there were really great differences, and that certain of them were rare delicacies.

A kind of huge, misshapen sea-turtle was the chief prize of all.

Three were taken during the strangers' first fortnight in the Abyss; but the fortunate boat-crews that brought them in devoured them, refusing to share even a morsel with any other of the people.

Stern and the girl were warned against tasting any weed, fish, or mussel on their own initiative. The patriarch told them certain deadly species existed -- species used only in preparing venoms in which to dip the spear and lance-points of the fighting men.

Beyond these foods the only others were the flesh and eggs of the highly singular birds the strangers had seen on their first entry into the village. These tasted rankly of fish, and were at first very disagreeable. But gradually the newcomers were able to tolerate them when cooked by Beatrice in as near an approximation to modern methods as she could manage.

The birds made a peculiar feature of this weird, uncanny life. Long of leg, wattled and web- footed, with ungainly bodies, sparsely feathered, and bare necks, they were, Stern thought, absolutely the most hideous and unreal-appearing creatures he had ever seen. In size they somewhat resembled an albatross. The folk called them kalamakee. They were so fully domesticated as to make free with all the refuse of the village and even to waddle into the huts in croaking search of plunder; yet they nested among the broken rocks along the cliff to northward of the place.

There they built clumsy structures of weed for their eggs and their incredibly ugly young. Every day at a certain time they took their flight out into the fog, with hoarse and mournful cries, and stayed the equivalent of some three hours.

Their number Stern could only estimate, but it must have mounted well toward five or six thousand. One of the most singular sights the newcomers had in the Abyss was the homecoming of the flight, the feeding of the young -- by discharging half-digested fish -- and the subsequent noisy powwow of the waddling multitude. All this, heard and seen by torch-light, produced a picture weirdly fascinating.

Fish, weeds, sea-fowl -- these constituted the sum total of food sources for the Folk. There existed neither bread, flesh -- meat, milk, fruit, sweets, or any of the abundant vegetables of the surface. Nor yet was there any plant which might be dried and smoked, like tobacco, nor any whence alcohol might be distilled. The folk had neither stimulants nor narcotics.

Stern blessed fate for this. If any such had existed, he knew human nature well enough to feel certain that, there in the eternal gloom and fog, the race would soon have given itself over to excesses and have miserably perished.

"To my mind," he said to Beatrice, one time, "the survival of our race under such conditions is one of the most marvelous things possibly to be conceived." Out toward the black and mist-hidden sea that rolled forever in the gloom he gestured from the wall where they were standing.

"Imagine!" he continued. "No sunlight -- for centuries! Without that, nothing containing chlorophyl can grow; and science has always maintained that human life must depend, at last analysis, on chlorophyl, on the green plants containing it. No grains, no soil, or agriculture, no mammals even! Why, the very Eskimo have to depend on mammals for their life!

"But these people here, and the Lanskaarn, and whatever other unknown tribes live in this vast Abyss, have to get their entire living from this tepid sea. They don't even possess wood to work with! If this doesn't prove the human race all but godlike in its skill and courage and adaptability, what does?"

She stood a while in thought, plainly much troubled. It was evident her mind was far from following his analysis. At last she spoke.

"Allan!" she suddenly exclaimed.

"Well?"

"It's still out there somewhere, isn't its Out there, in those black, unsounded depths -- the biplane?"

"You mean --"

"Why couldn't we raise it again, and --"

"Of course! You know I mean to try as soon as I have these people under some control so I can get them to cooperate with me -- get them to understand!"

"Not till then? No escape till then? But, Allan, it may be too late!" she burst out with passionate eagerness.

Puzzled, he turned and peered at her in the bluish gloom.

"Escape?" he queried. "Too late? Why, what do you mean? Escape from what? You mean that we should leave these people, here, before we've even begun to teach them? Before we've discovered some way out of the Abyss for them? Leave everything that means the regeneration of the human race, the world? Why --"

A touch upon his arm interrupted him.

He turned quickly to find the patriarch standing at his side. Silent and dim through the fog, he had come thither with sandaled feet, and now stood with a strange, inscrutable smile on his long-bearded lips.

"What keeps my children here," asked he, "when already it is long past the sleeping-hour? Verily, this should not be! Come," he commanded. "Come away! Tomorrow will be time for speech."

And, giving them no further opportunity to talk of this new problem, he spoke of other matters, and so led them back to his hospitable hut of stone.

But for a long time Allan could not sleep. Weird thoughts and new suspicions now aroused, he lay and pondered many things.

What if, after all, this seeming friendliness and homage of the savage Folk were but a mask?

A vision of the boiling geyser-pit rose to his memory. And the dreams he dreamed that night were filled with strange, confused, disquieting images.

32. Preparations

He woke to hear a drumming roar that seemed to fill the spaces of the Abyss with a wild tumult such as he had never known -- a steady thunder, wonderful and wild.

Starting up, he saw by the dim light that the patriarch was sitting there upon the stone, thoughtful and calm, apparently giving no heed to this singular tumult. But Stern, not understanding, put a hasty question.

"What's all this uproar, father? I never heard anything like that up in the surface-world!"

"That? Only the rain, my son," the old man answered. "Had you no rain there? Verily, traditions tell of rain among the people of that day!"

"Rain? Merciful Heavens!" exclaimed the engineer. Two minutes later he was at the fortifications, gazing out across the beach at the sea.

It would be hard to describe accurately the picture that met his eyes. The heaviest cloudburst that ever devastated a countryside was but a trickle compared with this monstrous, terrifying deluge.

Some five hundred miles of dense and saturated vapors, suddenly condensing, were precipitating the water, not in drops but in great solid masses, thundering, bellowing, crashing as they struck the sea, which, churned to a deep and raging froth, flung mighty waves even against the massive walls of the village itself.

The fog was gone now; but in its place the rushing walls of water blotted Out the scene. Yet not a drop was falling in the village itself. Stern wondered for a moment. But, looking up, he understood.

The vast cliff was now dimly visible in the glare of the great flame, the steady roar of which was drowned by the tumult of the rain.

Stern saw that the village was sheltered under a tremendous overhang of the black rock; he understood why the ancestors of the Folk, coming to these depths after incredible adventurings and long-forgotten struggles, had settled here. Any exposed location would have been fatal; no hut could have withstood the torrent, nor could any man, caught in it, have escaped drowning outright.

Amazed and full of wonder at this terrific storm, so different from those on the surface -- for there was neither wind nor lightning, but just that steady, frightful sluicing down of solid tons of rain -- Stern made his way back to the patriarch's house.

There he met Beatrice, just awakened.

"No chance to raise the machine today!" she called to: him as he entered. "He says this is apt to last for hours and hours!" She nodded toward the old man, much distressed.

"Patience!" he murmured. "Patience, friends -- and peace!"

Stern thought a moment.

"Well," said he, at last, making himself heard only with difficulty, "even so, we can spend the day in making ready."

And, after the simple meal that served for breakfast, he sat down to think out definitely some plan of campaign for the recovery of the lost Pauillac.

Though Stern by no means understood the girl's anxiety to leave the Abyss, nor yet had any intention of trying to do so until he had begun the education of the Folk and had perfected some means of trying to transplant this group -- and whatever other tribes he could find -- to the surface again, he realized the all-importance of getting the machine into his possession once more.

For more than an hour he pondered the question, now asking a question of the patriarch -- who seemed torn between desire to have the wonder-thing brought up, and fear lest he should lose the strangers -- now designing grapples, now formulating a definite line of procedure.

At last, all things settled in his mind, he bade the old man get for

208

him ten strong ropes, such as the largest nets were made of. These ropes which he had already seen coiled in huge masses along the wall at the northern end of the village, where they were twisted of the tough weed-fiber, averaged all of two hundred feet in length. When the patriarch had gone to see about having them brought to the hut, he himself went across the plaza, with Beatrice, to the communal smithy.

There he appropriated a forge, hammers, and a quantity of iron bars, and energetically set to work fashioning a huge three-pronged hook.

A couple of hours' hard labor at the anvil -- labor which proved that he was getting back his normal strength once more -- completed the task. Deftly he heated, shaped and reshaped the iron, while vast broken shadows danced and played along the titanic cliff behind him, cast by the wavering blue gas-flames of the forge. At length he found himself in possession of a drag weighing about forty pounds and provided with a stout ring at the top of the shank six inches in diameter.

"Now," said he to Beatrice, as he surveyed the finished product, while all about them the inquisitive yet silent Folk watched them by the unsteady light, "now I guess we're ready to get down to something practical. Just as soon as this infernal rain lets up a bit, we'll go angling for the biggest fish that ever came out of this sea!"

But the storm was very far from being at an end. The patriarch told Stern, when he brought the grapple to the hut -- followed by a silent, all-observant crowd -- that sometimes these torrential downpours lasted from three to ten sleep-times, with lulls between.

"And nobody can venture on the sea," he added, "till we know -- by certain signs we have that the great rain is verily at an end. To do that would mean to court death; and we are wise, from very long experience. So, my son, you must have patience in this as in all things, and wait!"

Part of that afternoon of forced inactivity Stern spent in his favorite habit of going about among the Folk, closely mingling with them and watching all their industrial processes and social life, and trying, as usual, to pick up words and phrases of the very far-degenerated speech that once had been English but was now a grammarless and formless jumble of strange words.

Only a few of the most common words he found retained anything like their original forms -- such as w'haata, water; fohdu, food; yernuh, iron; vlaak, black; gomu, come; ghaa, go; fysha, fish; and so on for about forty others.

Thousands upon thousands of terms, for which no longer any objects now existed among the Folk, had been of course utterly forgotten; and some hundreds of new words, relative to new conditions, had been invented.

The entire construction was altered; the language now bore no more resemblance to English than English had borne to the primitive Indo-Germanic of the Aryan forefathers. Now that writing had been lost, nothing retarded changes; and Stern realized that here -- were he a trained philologist -- lay a task incomparably interesting and difficult, to learn this Merucaan speech and trace its development from his own tongue.

But Stern's skill was all in other lines. The most that he could do was to make some rough vocabularies, learn a few common phrases, and here or there try to teach a little English. A deeper study and teaching, he knew, would come later, when more important matters had been attended to.

His attempts to learn and to talk with these people -- by pointing at objects and listening to their names -- were comparable to those, perhaps, of a prehistoric Goth turned loose in an American village of the twentieth century. Only the patriarch had retained the mother-tongue, and that in an archaic, imperfect manner, so that even his explanations often failed. Stern felt the baffling difficulties in his way; but his determination only grew.

The rain steadily continued to drum down, now lessened, now again in terrific deluges of solid black water churned to white as they struck the sea and flung the froth on high. The two Americans passed an hour that afternoon in the old man's hut, drawing up a calendar on which to check as accurately as possible, the passage of time as reckoned in the terms of life upon the surface.

They scratched this on a slab of slatelike rock, with a sharp iron awl; and, reckoning the present day as about October first, agreed that every waking-time they would cross off one square.

"For," said the engineer, "it's most important that we should keep track of the seasons up above. That may have much to do with our attempts to transplant this colony. It would never do to take a people like this, accustomed to heat and vapor, and carry them out into even the mild winter that now prevails in a present-day December. If we don't get them to the surface before the last of this month, at latest --"

"We'll have to wait until another spring?" asked she.

"Looks that way," he assented, putting a few final touches to the calendar. "So you see it's up to us to hurry -- and certainly nothing more inopportune than this devilish rain could possibly have happened! Haste, haste! We must make haste!"

"That's so'" exclaimed Beatrice. "Every day's precious, now. We --"

"My children," hurriedly interrupted the patriarch, "I never yet have shown you my book -- my one and greatest treasure. The book!

"You have told me many things, of sun and moon and stars, which are mocked at as idle tales by my unbelieving people; of continents and seas, mountains, vast cities, great ships, strange engines moved by vapor and by lightning, tall houses; of words thrown along metal threads or even through the air itself; of great nations and wars, of a hundred wondrous matters that verily have passed away even from the remotest memories of us in the Abyss!

"But of our history I have told you little; nor have you seen the book! Yet you must see it, for it alone remains to us of that other, better time. And though my folk mock at it as imposture and myth and fraud, you shall judge if it be true; you shall see what has kept the English speech alive in me, kept memories of the upper world alive. Only the book, the book!"

His voice seemed strangely agitated. As he spoke he raised his hands toward them, sitting on the stone bench in the hut, while outside the rain still thundered louder than the droning roar of the great flame. Stern, his curiosity suddenly aroused, looked at the old man with keen interest.

"The book?" he queried. "What book? What's the name of it? What date? What -- who wrote it, and --"

"Patience, friends!"

"You mean you've really got an English book here in this village? A --"

"A book, verily, from the other days! But first, before I show you, let me tell you the old tradition that was handed down to me by my father and my father's fathers, down through centuries -- I know not how many."

"You mean the story of this Lost Folk in the Abyss?"

"Verily! You have told me yours, of your awakening, of the ruined world and all your struggles and your fall down into this cursed pit. Listen now to mine!"

33. The Patriarch's Tale

"In the beginning," he commanded, slowly and thoughtfully, "our people were as yours; they were the same. Our tradition tells that a great breaking of the world took place very many centuries ago. Out of the earth a huge portion was split, and it became as the moon you tell of, only dark. It circled about the earth --"

"By Jove!" cried Stern, and started to his feet. "That dark patch in the sky! That moving mystery we saw nights at the bungalow on the Hudson!"

"You mean --" the girl exclaimed.

"It's a new planetoid! Another satellite of the earth! It's the split-off part of the world!"

"Another satellite?"

"Of course! Hang it, yes! See now? The great explosion that liberated the poisonous gases and killed practically everybody in the world must have gouged this new planet out of the flank of Mother Earth in the latter part of 1920. The ejected portions, millions of millions of tons, hundreds of thousands of cubic miles of solid rock -- and with them the ruins of Chicago, Milwaukee, St. Louis, Omaha, and hundreds of smaller cities -- are now all revolving in a fixed, regular orbit, some few thousand miles or so from the surface!

"Think! Ours are the only living human eyes that have seen this new world blotting out the stars! This explains everything -- the singular changes in the tides and in the direction of the magnetic pole, decreased gravitation and all the other strange things we noticed, but couldn't understand. By Gad! What a discovery!"

The patriarch listened eagerly while Stern and the girl discussed the strange phenomenon; but when their excitement had subsided and they were ready again to hear him, he began anew:

"Verily, such was the first result of the great catastrophe. And, as you know, millions died. But among the canyons of the Rocky Mountains -- so says the tradition; is it right? Were there such mountains?"

"Yes, yes! Go on!"

"In those canyons a few handfuls of hardy people still survived. Some perished of famine and exposure; some ventured out into the lowlands and died of the gas that still hung heavy there. Some were destroyed in a great fire that the tradition says swept the earth after the explosion. But a few still lived. At one time the number was only eighteen men, twelve women and a few children, so the story goes."

"And then?"

"Then," continued the patriarch, his brow wrinkled in deep thought, "then came the terrible, swift cold. The people, still keeping their English tongue, now dead save for you two, and still with some tools and even a few books, retreated into caves and fissures in the canyons. And so they came to the great descent."

"The what?"

"The huge cleft which the story says once connected the upper world with this Abyss. And --"

"Is it open now," cried Stern, leaning sharply forward.

"Alas, no; but you hurry me too much, good friend. You understand, for a long time they lived the cave-life partly, and partly the upper life. And they increased a great deal in the hundred years that followed the explosion. But they never could go into the plains, for still the gas hung there, rising from a thousand wells -- ten thousand, mayhap, all very deadly. And so they knew not if the rest of the world lived or died."

"And then?" queried the engineer. "Let's have it all in outline. What happened?"

"This, my son: that a still greater cold came upon the world, and the life of the open became impossible. There were now ten or twelve thousand alive; but they were losing their skill, their knowledge, everything. Only a few men still kept the wisdom of reading or writing, even. For life was a terrible fight. And they had to seek food now in the cave-lakes; that was all remaining.

"After that, another fifty or a hundred years, came the second great explosion. The ways were closed to the outer world. Nearly all died. What happened even the tradition does not tell. How many years the handful of people wandered I do not know. Neither do I know how they came here.

"The story says only eight or ten altogether reached this sea. It was much smaller then. The islands of the Lanskaarn, as we call them now, were then joined to the land here. Great changes have taken place. Verily, all is different! Everything was lost -- language and arts, and even the look of the Folk.

"We became as you see us. The tradition itself was forgotten save by a few. Sometimes we increased, then came pestilences and famines, outbreaks of lava and hot mud and gases, and nearly all died. At one time only seven remained --"

"For all the world like the story of Pitcairn Island and the mutineers of the *Bounty*!" interrupted the engineer. "Yes, yes -- go on!"

"There is little more to tell. The tradition says there was once a place of records, where certain of the wisest men of our Folk placed all their lore to keep it; but even this place is lost. Only one family kept any knowledge of the English as a kind of inheritance and the single book went with that family --"

"But the Lanskaarn and the other peoples of the Abyss, where did they come from?" asked Stern eagerly.

The patriarch shook his head.

"How can I tell?" he answered. "The tradition says nothing of them."

"Some other groups, probably," suggested Beatrice, "that came in at different times and through other ways."

"Possibly," Stern assented. "Anything more to tell?"

"Nothing more. We became as savages; we lost all thought of history or learning. We only fought to live! All was forgotten.

"My grandfather taught the English to my father and he to me, and I had no son. Nobody here would learn from me. Nobody cared for the book. Even the tradition they laughed at, and they called my brain softened when I spoke of a place where in the air a light shone half the time brighter even than the great flame! And in every way they mocked me!

215

"So I -- I" -- the old man faltered, his voice tremulous, while tears glittered in his dim and sightless eyes --" I ceased to speak of these things. Then I grew blind and could not read the book. No longer could I refresh my mind with the English. So I said in my heart: 'It is finished and will soon be wholly forgotten forever. This is the end.'

"Verily, I laid the book to rest as I soon must be laid to rest! Had you not come from that better place, my thought would have been true --"

"But it isn't, not by a jugful!" exclaimed the engineer joyously, and stood up in the dim-lit little room. "No, sir! She and I, we're going to change the face of things considerably! How? Never mind just yet. But let's have a look at the old volume, father. Gad! That must be some relic, eh? Imagine a book carried about for a thousand years and read by at least thirty generations of men! The book, father! The book!"

Already the patriarch had arisen and now he gestured at the heavy bench of stone.

"Can you move this, my son?" asked he. "The place of the book lies beneath."

"Under there, eh? All right!" And, needing no other invitation, he set his strength against the massive block of gneiss.

It yielded at the second effort and, sliding ponderously to one side, revealed a cavity in the stone floor some two feet long by about eighteen inches in breadth.

Over this the old man stooped.

"Help me, son," bade he. "Once I could lift it with ease, but now the weight passes my strength."

"What? The weight of a book? But -- where is it? In this packet, here?"

He touched a large and close-wrapped bundle lying in the little crypt, dimly seen by the flicker of the oily wick.

"Yea. Raise it out that I may show you!" answered the patriarch. His hands trembled with eagerness; in his blind eyes a sudden fever seemed to burn. For here was his dearest, his most sacred treasure, all that remained to him of the long-worshipped outer

world -- the world of the vague past and of his distant ancestors
-- the world that Stern and Beatrice had really known and seen,
yet which to him was only "all a wonder and a wild desire."

"Lay the book upon the bench," he ordered. "I will unwrap
it!"

Complex the knots were, but his warped and palsied fingers
deftly undid them as though long familiar with each turn and
twist. Then off came many a layer of the rough brown seaweed
fabric and afterward certain coverings of tough shark-skin neatly
sewn.

"The book!" cried the patriarch. "Now behold it!"

"That?" exclaimed Beatrice. "I never saw a book of that
shape!"

"Each page is separately preserved, wherefore it is so very
thick;," explained the old man. "See here?"

He turned the leaves reverently. Stern, peering closely by the
dim light, saw that they were loosely hung together by loops of
heavy gold wire. Each page was held between two large plates of
mica, and these plates were securely sealed around the edges by
some black substance like varnish or bitumen.

"Only thus," explained the patriarch, "could we hope to save
this precious thing. It was done many hundreds of years ago, and
even then the book was almost lost by age and use."

"I should say so!" ejaculated Stern. Even sealed in its air-tight
covering, he saw that every leaf was yellow, broken, rotten, till the
merest breath would have disintegrated it to powder. A sense of the
infinitudes of time bridged by this volume overwhelmed him; he
drew a deep breath, reached out his hand and touched the wondrous relic of the world that was.

"Long ago," continued the old man, "when the book began to
crumble, one of my ancestors copied it on gold plates, word by
word, letter by letter, every point and line. And our family used
only that book of gold and put away the other. But in my grandfather's time the Lanskaarn raided our village and the gold plates
went for loot to make them trinkets, so they were lost.

"My father meant to begin the task again, but was killed in a

217

raid. I, too, in my fighting youth, had plans for the work; but blindness struck me before I could find peace to labor in. So now all that remains of the mother tongue here is my own knowledge and these tattered scraps. And, if you save us not, soon all, all will be lost forever!"

Much moved, the engineer made no reply, yet thoughts came crowding to his brain. Here visibly before him he beheld the final link that tied these lost Folk to the other time, the last and breaking thread. What history could this book have told? What vast catastrophes, famines, pestilences, wars, horrors had it passed through? In what unwritten cataclysms, in what anguish and despair and long degeneration had the human mind still clung to it and cherished it?

No one could tell; yet Stern felt the essence of its unknown story. An infinite pathos haloed the ancient volume. And reverently he touched its pages once again; he bent and by the guttering light tried to make out a few words here or there upon the crackled, all but perished leaves.

He came upon a crude old woodcut, vague and dim; then a line of text caught his eye.

"By Gad! *Pilgrim's Progress!*" he exclaimed. "Look, Beatrice - - *Pilgrim's Progress*, of all books! No wonder he says 'Verily' and talks archaic stuff and doesn't catch more than half we say. Well, I'll be --"

"Is this then not the English of your time?" asked the patriarch.

"Hardly! It was centuries old at the epoch of the catastrophe. Say, father, the quicker you forget this and take a few lessons in the up-to-date language of the real world that perished, the better! I see now why you don't get on to the idea of steamships and railroads, telephones and wireless and all the rest of it. God! but you've got a lot to learn!"

The old man closed up the precious volume and once more began wrapping it in its many coverings.

"Not for me, all this, I fear," he answered with deep melancholy. "It is too late, too late -- I cannot understand."

"Oh, yes, you can, and will!" the engineer assured him. "Buck up, father! Once I get my biplane to humming again you'll learn a few things, never fear!"

He stepped to the door of the hut and peered out.

"Rain's letting up a bit," he announced. "How about it? Do the signs say it's ready to quit for keeps? If so -- all aboard for the dredging expedition!"

34. The Coming of Kamrou

The storm, in fact, was now almost at an end, and when the engineer awoke next morning he found the rain had wholly ceased. Though the sea was still giving forth white vapors, these had not yet reached their usual density. From the fortifications he could see, by the reflected lights of the village and of the great flame, a considerable distance out across the dim, mysterious sea. He knew the time was come to try for the recovery of the machine, if ever.

"If I don't make a go of it today," said he, "I might as well quit for good. There'll never be a better opportunity. And if it's left down there very much longer, Heaven only knows what kind of shape it'll be in. I make good today or it's all off."

Beatrice eagerly seconded his plans. The old man, too, was impatient as a child to learn more of this wonder of the upper world. And, translating to the Folk the directions that Stern gave him, he soon had a great throng on the beach, where lay not only the Folk's canoes, but also many left by the slaughtered and dispersed Lanskaarn.

Two hours after the crude meal that must be called breakfast for want of a better name, the expedition was ready to start.

Twenty-five of the largest boats, some holding twelve men, set out, to the accompaniment of shouting and singing much like that when the captives had been brought in. Stern, Beatrice and the patriarch all sat in one canoe with eight paddlers. In the bottom lay Stern's heavy grapple with the ten long ropes, now twisted into a single cable, securely knotted to its ring.

To Stern it seemed impossible that any means existed for locating, even approximately, the spot where the machine had fallen. As the shore faded away and the village lights disappeared in the gloom and mist, all landmarks vanished. Everywhere about them the dim, oily sea stretched black and gloomy, with here and there the torches of the little fleet casting strange blue-green lights that wavered like ghostly will-o'-the-wisps over the water.

The boatman's song wailed high, sank low, trembled and ceased; and for a while came silence, save for the dipping of the paddles, the pulling of the waters at the bow of the canoe. The engineer, despite his hard-headed practicality, shuddered a little and drew his mantle closer round him.

Beatrice, too, felt the eerie mystery of the scene. Stern put an arm about her; she slid her hand into his, and thus in silence they sat thinking while the boats drew on and on.

"They really know where they're going, father?" the engineer asked at length. "It all looks alike to me. How can they tell?"

"Verily, I cannot explain that to you," the old man made answer. "We know, that is all."

"But --"

"Had I been always blind you could not expound sight to me. A deaf man cannot understand sound."

"You mean you've developed some new sense, some knowledge of direction and location that we haven't got?"

"Yea, it must be so. In all these many centuries among the dark mists we have to know. And this gloom, this night, are the same to us as you have told me a lake on the surface would be to you in the brightness of that sun which none of us have ever yet beheld."

"Is that so? Well, hanged if I get it! However, no matter about that just so they locate the place. Can they find the exact spot, father?"

"Perhaps not so. But they will come near to it, my son. Only have patience; you shall see!"

Stern and the girl relapsed into silence again, and for perhaps a quarter-hour the boats moved steadily forward through the vapors in a kind of crescent, the tips of which were hidden by the mist.

Then all at once a sharp cry rang from a boat off to the right, a cry taken up and echoed all along the line. The paddles ceased to ply; the canoes now drifted idly forward, their wakes trailing out behind in long "slicks" of greasy blackness flecked with sparkles from the reflected light of all those many torches.

Another word of command; the boatmen slowed their craft.

"Drop the iron here, son, and drag the bottom," said the patriarch.

"Good!" answered Stern, thrilled with excitement and wonder.

He pitched the dredge into the jetty sea. It sank silently as he payed out the cable. At a depth he estimated -- from the amount of cable still left in the boat -- as about thirty fathoms, it struck bottom.

He let out another five fathoms.

"All right, father!" he exclaimed sharply. "Tell our boatmen to give way!"

The old man translated the order: "Ghaa vrouaad, m'yaun!" (Go forward, men.) The paddles dipped again and Stern's canoe moved silently over the inky surface.

Every sense alert, the engineer at the gunwale held the cable. For a few seconds he felt nothing as the slack was taken up; then he perceived a tug and knew the grapple was dragging.

Now intense silence reigned, broken only by the sputter of the smoking torches. The canoes, spaced over the foggy sea, seemed floating in a void of nothingness; each reflected light quivered and danced with weird and tremulous patterns.

Stern played the cable as though it were a fish-line. All his senses centered on interpreting the message it conveyed. Now he felt that it was dragging over sand; now came rocks -- and once it caught, held, then jerked free. His heart leaped wildly. Oh, had it only been the aeroplane!

The tension grew. Out, far out from the drifting line of boats the canoe went forward; it turned at a word from the patriarch and dragged along the front of the line. It criss-crossed on its path; Stern had to admire the skill and thoroughness with which the boatmen covered the area where their mysterious sixth sense of location told them the machine must lie.

All at once a tug, different from all others, yielding, yet firm, set his pulses hammering again.

"Got it!" he shouted, for he knew the truth. "Hold fast, there -- she's hooked!"

"You've got it, Allan? Really got it?" cried the girl, starting up. "Oh --"

"Feel this!" he answered. "Grab hold and pull!"

She obeyed, trembling with eagerness.

"It's caught through one of the ailerons, or some yielding part, I think," he said. "Here, help me hold it tight, now; we mustn't let the hook slip out again!" To the patriarch he added: "Tell 'em to back up, there -- easy -- easy!"

The canoe backed, while Stern took up the slack again. When the pull from below was vertical he ordered the boat stopped.

"Now get nine other boats close in here," commanded he.

The old man gave the order. And presently nine canoes stood in near at hand, while all the rest lay irregularly grouped about them.

Now Stern's plan of the tenfold cable developed itself. Already he was untwisting the thick rope. One by one he passed the separate cords to men in the other boats. And in a few minutes he and nine other men held the ropes, which, all attached to the big iron ring below, spread upward like the ribs of an inverted umbrella.

The engineer's scheme was working to perfection. Well he had realized that no one boat could have sufficed to lift the great weight of the machine. Even the largest canoe would have been capsized and sunk long before a single portion of the Pauillac and its engine had been so much as stirred from the sandy bottom.

But with the buoyant power of ten canoes and twenty or thirty men all applied simultaneously, Stern figured he had a reasonable chance of raising the sunken aeroplane. The fact that it was submerged, together with the diminished gravitation of the Abyss, also worked in his favor. And as he saw the Folk-men grip the cords with muscular hands, awaiting his command, he thrilled with pride and with the sense of real achievement.

"Come, now, boys!" he cried. "Pull! Heave-ho, there! Altogether, lift her! Pull!"

He strained at the rope which he and two others held; the rest

-- each rope now held by three or four men -- bent their back to the labor. As the ropes drew tense, the canoes crowded and jostled together. Those men who were not at the ropes, worked with the paddles to keep the boats apart, so that the ropes should not foul or bind. And in an irregular ring, all round the active canoes, the others drew. Lighted by so many torches, the misty waters glittered as broken waves, thrown out by the agitation of the canoes, radiated in all directions.

"Pull, boys, pull!" shouted the engineer again. "Up she comes! Now, all together!"

Came a jerk, a long and dragging resistance, then a terrific straining on the many cords. The score and a half of men breathed hard; on their naked arms the veins and muscles swelled; the torchlight gleamed blue on their sweating faces and bodies.

And spontaneously, as at all times of great endeavor among the Folk, a wailing song arose; it echoed through the gloom; it grew, taken up by the outlying boats; and in the eternal dark of the Abyss it rose, uncanny, soul-shaking, weird beyond all telling.

Stern felt the shuddering chills chase each other up and down his spine, playing a nervous accompaniment to their chant.

"Gad!" he muttered, shivering, "what a situation for a hard-headed, practical man like me! It's more like a scene from some weird pipe-dream magazine story of the remote past than solid reality!"

Again the Folk strained at the ropes, Stern with them; and now the great weight below was surely rising, inch by inch, up, up, toward the black and gleaming surface of the abysmal sea.

Stern's heart was pounding wildly. If only -- incredible as it seemed -- the Pauillac really were there at the end of the converging ropes; and if it were still in condition to be repaired again! If only the hook and the hard-taxed ropes held!

"Up, boys! Heave ho!" he shouted, pulling till his muscles hardened like steel, and the canoe -- balanced, though it was by five oarsmen and the patriarch all at the other gunwale -- tipped crazily. "Pull! Pull!"

Beatrice sprang to the rope. Unable to restrain herself, she, too, laid hold on the taut, dripping cord; and her white hands, firm, muscular, shapely, gripped with a strength one could never have guessed lay in them.

And now the ropes were sliding up out of the water. faster, ever faster; and higher rose the song of all those laboring Folk and all who watched from the outlying ring of boats.

"Up with it, men! Up!" panted the engineer.

Even as he spoke the waters beneath them began to boil and bubble strangely, as though with the rising of a monstrous fish; and all at once, with a heave, a sloshing splatter, a huge, weed-covered, winglike object, sluicing brine, wallowed sharply out into the torchlight.

A great triumphal howl rose from the waiting Folk -- a howl that drowned Stern's cheer and that of Beatrice, and for a moment all was confusion. the wing rose, fell, slid back; into the water and again dipped upward. The canoes canted; some took water; all were thrown against each other in the central group; and cries, shouts, orders and a wild fencing off with paddles followed.

Stern yelled in vain orders that the old man could not even hear to translate; orders which would not, even though heard, have been obeyed. But after a moment or two comparative order was restored, and the engineer, veins standing out on his temples, eyes ablaze, bellowed:

"Hold fast, you! No more, no more -- don't pull up any more, damn you! Hey, stop that -- you'll rip the hook clean out and lose it again!

"You, father -- here -- tell 'em to let it down a little, now -- about six feet or so. Easy -- does it -- easy!"

Now the Pauillac, sodden with water, hanging thickly with the luxuriant weed clusters which even in a fortnight had grown in that warm sea, was suspended at the end of the ten cords about six or eight feet below the keels of the canoes.

"Tell 'em to let it stay that way now," continued the engineer. "Tell 'em all to hold fast, those that have the ropes. The others paddle for the shore as fast as they can -- and damn the man that loafs now!"

The patriarch conveyed the essence of these instructions to the oarsmen, and now, convoyed by the outlying boats, the ten canoes moved very slowly toward the village.

Retarded by the vast, birdlike bulk that trailed below, they seemed hardly to make any progress at all. Stern ordered the free boats to hitch on and help by towing. Lines were passed, and after a while all twenty-five canoes, driven by the power of two hundred and fifty pairs of sinewy arms, were dragging the Pauillac shoreward.

Stern's excitement -- now that the machine was really almost in his grasp again -- far from diminishing, was every minute growing keener.

The delay until he could examine it and see its condition and its chances of repair, seemed interminable. Continually he urged the patriarch -- himself profoundly moved -- to force the rowers to still greater exertion. At a paddle he labored, throwing every ounce of strength into the toil. Each moment seemed an hour.

"Gad! If it's only possible to make it fly again!" thought he.

Half an hour passed, and now at length the dim and clustered lights of the village began to show vaguely through the mist.

"Come on, boys; now for it!" shouted Stern. "Land her for me and I'll show you wonders you never even dreamed of!"

They drew near the shore. Already Stern was formulating his plans for landing the machine without injuring it, when out from the beach a long and swift canoe put rapidly, driven by twenty men.

At sight of it the rowing in Stern's boats weakened, then stopped. Confused cries arose, altercations and strange shouts; then a hush of expectancy, of fear, seemed to possess the boat crews.

And ever nearer, larger, drew the long canoe, a two-pronged, blazing cressets at its bows.

Across the waters drifted a word.

"Go on, you! Row!" cried Stern. "Land the machine, I tell you! Say, father, what's the matter now? What are my men on strike for all of a sudden? Why don't they finish the job?"

The old man, perplexed, listened intently.

Between the group of canoes and the shore the single boat had stopped. A man was standing upright in it. Now came a clear hail, and now two or three sentences, peremptory, angry, harsh.

At sound of them consternation seized certain of the men. A number dropped the ropes, while others reached for the slings and spears that always lay in the bottoms of the canoes.

"What the devil now'" shouted Stern. "You all gone crazy, or what?"

He turned appealingly to the old man.

"For Heaven's sake, what's up?" he cried. "Tell me, can't you, before the idiots drop my machine and ruin the whole thing? What --"

"Misfortune, O my son!" cried the patriarch in a strange, trembling voice. "The worst that could befall! In our absence he has come back -- he, Kamrou! And under pain of death he bids all men abandon every task and haste to homage. Kamrou the Terrible is here!"

35. Face to Face With Death

For a moment Stern stared, speechless with amazement, at the old man, as though to determine whether or not he had gone mad. But the commotion, the mingled fear and anger of the boat crews convinced him the danger, though unknown, was very real.

And, flaring into sudden rage at this untimely interruption just in the very moment of success, he jerked his pistol from its holster, and stood up in the boat.

"I'll have no butting in here!" he cried in a loud, harsh voice. "Who the devil is Kamrou, I'd like to know? Go on, on, to shore!"

"My son --"

"You order these men to grab those ropes again and go ashore or I warn you there's going to be a whole big heap of trouble!"

Over the waters drifted another hail, and the strange long boat, under the urge of vigorous arms, now began to move toward Stern's fleet. At the same time, mingled cries arose on shore. Stern could see lights moving back and forth; some confusion was under way there, though what, he could not imagine.

"Well," he cried, "are you going to order these men to go forward? Or shall I -- with this?"

And menacingly he raised the grim and ugly gun.

"Oh my son!" exclaimed the patriarch, his lips twitching, his hands outstretched -- while in the boats a Babel of conflicting voices rose --" O my son, if I have sinned in keeping this from you, now let me die! I hid it from your knowledge, verily, to save my people -- to keep you with us till this thing should be accomplished! My reckoning was that Kamrou and his men would stay beyond the Great Vortex, at their labor, until after --"

"Kamrou?" shouted Stern again. "What the deuce do I care about him? Who is he, anyhow? A Lanskaarn, or --"

The girl seized Allan's hand.

"Oh, listen, listen!" she implored. "I --"

"Did you know about this? And never told me?"

"Allan, he said our work could all be done before they --"

"So you did know, eh?"

"He said I must not tell you. Otherwise --"

"Oh, hang that! See here, Beatrice, what's the matter, anyhow? These people have all gone crazy, just in a second, the old man and all! If you know anything about it, for God's sake tell me! I can't stand much more!

"I've got to get this machine to land before they go entirely nutty and drop it, and we lose all our work for nothing. What's up? Who's this Kamrou they're talking about? For Heaven's sake, tell me!"

"He's their chief. Allan -- their chief! He's been gone a long time, he and his men. And --"

"Well, what do we care for him? We're running this village now, aren't we?"

"Listen. The old man says --"

"He's a hard nut, eh? And won't stand for us -- is that it?" He turned to the patriarch. "This Kamrou you're talking about doesn't want us, or our new ideas, or anything? Well, see here. There's no use beating around the bush, now. This thing's going through, this plan of ours! And if Kamrou or anybody else gets in the way of it -- goodby for him!"

"You mean war?"

"War! And I know who'll win, at that! And now, father, you get these men here to work again, or there'll be some sudden deaths round here!"

"Hearken, O my son! Already the feast of welcome to Kamrou is beginning, around the flame. See now, the boat of his messenger is close at hand, bidding all those in this party to hasten in, for homage. Kamrou will not endure divided power. Trust me now and I can save you yet. For the present, yield to him, or seem to, and --"

"Yield nothing!" fairly roared the engineer, angrier than he had ever been in his whole life. "This is my affair now! Nobody else butts in on it at all! To shore with these boats, you hear? or I begin shooting again! And if I do --"

"Allan!" cried the girl.

"Not a word! Only get your gun ready, that's all. We've got to handle this situation sharp, or it's all off! Come, father," he delivered his ultimatum to the patriarch; "come, order them ashore!"

The old man, anguished and tremulous, spoke a few words. Answers arose, here, there. He called something to the standing figure in the despatch-boat, which slackened stopped, turned and headed for the distant beach.

With some confusion the oarsmen of the fleet took up their task again. And now, in a grim silence, more disconcerting even than the previous uproar, the boats made way toward land.

Ten minutes later -- minutes during which the two Americans kept their revolvers ready for instant action -- the aeroplane began to drag on the bottom. Despite the crowd now gathered on the beach, very near at hand and ominously silent, Stern would not let the machine lie even here, in shallow water, where it could easily have been recovered at any time. Like a bulldog with its jaws set on an object, he clung to his original plan of landing the Pauillac at once.

And, standing up in the boat with his pistol leveled, he commanded them, through the mediumship of the patriarch, to shorten the ropes and paddle in still closer. When the beach was only a few rods distant he gave orders that all should land, carrying the ropes with them. He himself was one of the first to wade ashore, with Beatrice.

Ignoring the silent, expectant crowd and the tall figure of Kamrou's messenger -- who now stood, arms crossed, amazed, indignant, almost at the water's edge -- he gave quick commands:

"Now, clear these boats away on both sides! Make a free space, here -- wider -- so, that's right. Now, all you men get hold of the ropes -- all of you, here, take hold, you! Ready, now? Give way, then! Out she comes! Out with her!"

The patriarch, standing in fear and keen anxiety beside him, transmitted the orders. Truly the old man's plight was hard, torn as he was between loyalty to the newcomers and terror of the implacable Kamrou. But Stern had no time to think of aught but the machine and his work.

For now already the great ungainly wings of the machine were wallowing up, up, out of the jetty waters; and now the body, now the engine showed, weed-festooned, smeared with mud and slime, a strange and awesome apparition in that blue and ghastly torch-flare, as the toiling men hauled it slowly, foot by foot, up the long slope of the beach.

Dense silence held the waiting throng; silence and awe, in face of this incomprehensible, tremendous thing.

Even the messenger spoke not a word. He had lost somewhat of his assurance, his pride and overbearing haughtiness. Perhaps he had already heard some tales of these interlopers' terrible weapons.

Stern saw the man's eyes follow the revolver, as he gestured with it; the highlights gleaming along the barrel seemed to fascinate the tall barbarian. But still he drew no step backward. Still in silence, with crossed arms, he waited, watched and took counsel only with himself.

"Thank God, it's out at last!" exclaimed the engineer, and heaved a sigh of genuine, heartfelt relief. "See, Beatrice, there's our old machine again -- and except for that broken rudder, this wing, here, bent, and the rent where the grapple tore the leather covering of the starboard plane I can't see that it's taken any damage. Provided the engine's intact, the rest will be easy. Plenty of chance for metalwork, here, and --"

"Going to take it right up to the village, now?" queried she, anxiously glancing at the crowd of white and silent faces, all eagerly staring -- staring like so many wraiths in a strange dream.

He shrugged his shoulders.

"That depends," he answered. He seemed already to have forgotten Kamrou and the threatening peril in the village, near the great flame. Even the sound of distant chanting and the thudding of dull drums stirred him not. Fascinated, he was walking all round the great mechanical bird, which now lay wounded, weed-covered, sodden and dripping, yet eloquent of infinite possibilities, there on that black, unearthly beach.

All at once he spoke.

"Up to the village with it!" he commanded, waving his pistol-hand toward the causeway and the fortified gates. "I can't risk leaving it here. Come, father, speak to them! It's got to go into the village right now!"

Then Kamrou's messenger, grasping the sense if not the words of the command, strode forward -- a tall, lithe figure of a man, well-knit and hard of face. Under the torchlight the dilated pupils of his pinkish eyes seemed to shine as phosphorescent as a cat's.

Crying out something unintelligible to Stern, he blocked the way. Stern heard the name "Kamrou! Kamrou!"

"Well, what do you want now?" shouted the engineer, a huge and sudden anger seizing him. Already super-excited by the labors of the day and by the nervous strain of having recovered the sunken biplane, all this talk of Kamrou, all this persistent opposition just at the most inauspicious moment worked powerfully upon his irritated nerves.

Cool reason would have dictated diplomacy, parley, and, if possible, truce. But Stern could not believe the Folk, for so long apparently loyal to him and dominated by his influence, could work against their vital interest and his own by deserting him now.

And, all his saner judgment failing him, heeding nothing of the patriarch's entreaties or of the girl's remonstrance as she caught his arm and tried to hold him back, he faced this cooly insolent barbarian.

"You, damn you, what d'you want?" he cried again, his finger itching on the trigger of the automatic. "Think I'm going to quit for you, or Kamrou, or anybody? Quit, now?"

"Think a civilized white man, sweating his heart out to save your people here, is going to knuckle under to any savage that happens to blow in and try to boss this job? If so, you've got another guess coming! Stand back, you, or you'll get cold lead in just one minute!"

Quick words passed from the old man to the messenger and

back again. The patriarch cried again to him, and for a moment Stern saw the barbarian's eyes flicker uneasily toward the revolver. But the calm and cruel face never changed, nor did the savage take one step backward.

"All right, then!" shouted Stern, seeing red in his overpowering rage. "You want it -- you'll get it -- take it, so!"

Up he jerked the automatic, fair at the big barbarian's heart -- a splendid target by the torch- light, not ten feet distant; a sure shot.

But before he could pull trigger the strange two-pronged torch was tossed on high by somebody behind the messenger, and through the dull and foggy gloom a wild, fierce, penetrant cry wailed piercingly.

Came a shooting, numbing pain in Stern's right elbow. The arm dropped, helpless. The boulder which, flung with accurate aim, had destroyed his aim, rolled at his feet. The pistol clattered over the wet, shining stoles.

Stern, cursing madly, leaped and snatched for it with the other hand.

Before he could even reach it a swift foot tripped him power-fully. Headlong he fell. And in a second one of the very ropes that had been used to drag the Pauillac from the depths was lashed about his wrists, his ankles, his struggling, fighting body.

"Beatrice! Shoot! Kill!" he shouted. "Help here! Help! The ma-chine -- they'll wreck it! Everything -- lost! Help!"

His speech died in a choking mumble, stifled by the wet and sodden gag they forced into his mouth.

About him the mob seethed. Through his brain a quick anguish thrilled, the thought of Beatrice unaided and alone. Then came a wonder when the death-stroke would fall -- a frightful, sick de-spair that on the very eve of triumph, of salvation for this Folk and for the world as well as for Beatrice and himself, the unforeseen should have befallen.

He struggled still to catch some glimpse of Beatrice, to cry aloud to her, to shield her; but, alone against five hundred, he was powerless.

Nowhere could he catch even a glimpse of the girl. In that shoving, pushing, shouting horde, nothing could be made out. He knew not even whether civil war had blazed or whether all alike had owned the rule of Kamrou the Terrible.

Like buoys tossing upon the surface of a raging sea, the flaring torches pitched and danced, rose, fell. And from a multitude of throats, from beach and causeway, walls and town, strange shouts rang up into the all-embracing, vague, enshrouding vapor.

Still striving to fight, bound as he was, he felt a great force driving him along, on, on, up the beach and toward the village.

Mute, desperate, stark mad, he knew the Folk were half carrying, half dragging him up the causeway.

As in a dark dream, he vaguely saw the great fortified gate with its huge, torch-lighted monolithic lintel. Even upon this some of the Folk were crowded now to watch the strange, incredible spectacle of the man who had once turned the tide of battle against the Lanskaarn and had saved all their lives, now hauled like a criminal back into the community he had rescued in its hour of sorest need.

His mind leaped to their first entry into the village -- it seemed months ago -- also as prisoners. In a flash he recalled all that had happened since and bitterly he mocked himself for having dared to dream that their influence had really altered these strange, barbarous souls, or uplifted them, or taught them anything at all.

"Now, now just as the rescue of these people was at hand, just as the machine might have carried us and them back into the world, slowly, one by one -- now comes defeat and death!"

An exceeding great bitterness filled his soul once more at this harsh, cynic turn of fate. But most of all he yearned toward Beatrice. That he should die mattered nothing; but the thought of this girl perishing at their hands there in the lost Abyss was dreadful as the pangs of all the fabled hells.

Again he fought to hold back, to try for some sight, even a fleeting glimpse of Beatrice; but the Folk with harsh cries drove him roughly forward.

He could not even see the patriarch. All was confusion, glare, smoke, noise, as he was thrust through the fortified gate, out into the thronged plaza.

Everywhere rose cries, shouts, vociferations, among which he could distinguish only one a thousand times repeated: "Kamrou! Kamrou!"

And through all his rage and bitter bafflement and pain, a sudden great desire welled up in him to see this chief of the Folk, at last -- to lay eyes on this formidable, this terrible one -- to stand face to face with him in whose hand now lay everything, Kamrou!

Across the dim, fog-covered expanse of the plaza he saw the blue-green shimmer of the great flame.

Thither, toward that strange, eternal fire and the ghastly circle of the headless skeletons the Folk were drifting now. Thither his captors were dragging him.

And there, he knew, Kamrou awaited Beatrice and him. There doom was to be dealt out to them. There, and at once!

Thicker the press became. The flame was very near now, its droning roar almost drowning the great and growing babel of cries.

On, on the Folk bore him. All at once he saw again that two-pronged torch raised before him, going ahead; and a way cleared through the press.

Along this way he was carried, no longer struggling, but eager now to know the end, to meet it bravely and with calm philosophy, "as fits a man."

And quite at once he found himself in sight of the many dangling skeletons. Now the quivering jet of the flame grew visible. Now, suddenly, he was thrust forward into a smooth and open space. Silence fell.

Before him he saw Kamrou, Kamrou the Terrible, at last.

36. Gage of Battle

The chief of the People of the Abyss was seated at his ease in a large stone chair, over which heavy layers of; weed-fabric had been thrown. He was flanked on either side by spearsmen and by drummers, who still held their iron sticks poised above their copper drums with shark-skin heads.

Stern saw at a glance that he was a man well over six feet tall, with whipcord muscles and a keen, eager, domineering air. Unlike any of the other Folk, his hair (snow-white) was not twisted into a fantastic knot and fastened with gold pins, but hung loose and was cut square off at about the level of his shoulders, forming a tremendous, bristly mass that reminded one of a lion's mane.

Across his left temple, and involving his left eye with a ghastly mutilation, ran a long, jagged, bright red scar, that stood out vividly against the milk-white skin. In his hands he held no mace, no symbol of power; they rested loosely on his powerful knees; and in their half-crooked fingers, large and long, Stern knew there lay a formidable, an all but irresistible strength.

At sight of the captives -- for Beatrice, too, now suddenly appeared, thrust forward through another lane among the Folk -- Kamrou's keenly cruel face grew hard. His lips curled with a sneer of scorn and hate. His pinkish eyes glittered with anticipation. Full on his face the flare of the great flame fell; Stern could see every line and wrinkle, and he knew that to beg mercy from this huge barbarian (even though he would have begged), were a task wholly vain and futile.

He glanced along the circle of expectant faces that ringed the chief at a distance of some fifteen feet. Surely, thought he, some of the many Folk that he and the girl had saved from butchery, some to whom they had taught the rudiments of the world's lost arts, would now show pity on them -- would stand by them now!

But no; not one face of all that multitude -- now that Kamrou had returned -- evinced other than eager interest to see the end of everything. To Stern flashed the thought that here, despite their seeming half-civilization in the use of metals, fire, dwellings, fabrics and all the rest, dwelt within them a savagery even below that of the ancient, long-extinct American Indians.

And well he knew that if both he and Beatrice were not to die the death this day, only upon themselves they must depend!

Yes, one face showed pity. But only one -- the patriarch's.

Stern suddenly caught sight of him, standing in the front rank of the circled crowd, about twenty feet away to the left, just beyond the girl. Tears gleamed in the old man's sightless eyes; his lips quivered; the engineer saw his hands tremble as he twisted the feeble, impotent fingers together in anguish.

And though he could catch no sound in that rising, falling, ever-roaring tumult of the flame, he knew the patriarch, with some vague and distant remnant of the old-time and vanished religion of the world, was striving to pray.

Stern's eyes met the girl's. Neither could speak, for she, too, was gagged with a rough band of fabric which cruelly cut her beautiful, her tender mouth. At sight of her humiliation and her pain, the man's heart leaped hotly; he strained against his bonds till the veins swelled, and with eyes of terrible rage and hate stared at Kamrou

But the chief's gaze was now fixed insolently upon Beatrice. She, as she stood there, stripped even of her revolver and cartridge-belt, hands bound behind her, hair disheveled, had caught his barbarous fancy. And now in his look Stern saw the kindling of a savage passion so ardent, so consuming, that the man's heart turned sick within him.

"Ten thousand times better she should die!" thought he, racked at the thought of what might be. "Oh, God! If I only had my revolver for a single minute now! One shot for Kamrou -- one for Beatrice -- and after that, nothing would matter; nothing!"

Came a disturbance in the Folk. Heads craned; a murmur of voices rose.

The patriarch, no longer trembling, but with his head held proudly up, both hands outstretched, had stepped into the circle. And now, advancing toward Kamrou, he spoke in quick and eager sentences -- he gestured at the engineer, raised his hand on high, bowed and stepped back.

And all at once a wild, harsh, swelling chorus of cries arose; every face turned toward Stern; the engineer, amazed, knew not what all this meant, but to the ultimate drop in the arteries he pledged his fighting-blood to one last, bitter struggle.

Silence again.

Kamrou had not stirred. Still his great hands rested on his knees; but a thin, venomous smile lengthened his lips. He, too, looked at the engineer, who gave the stare back with redoubled hate. Tense grew the expectation of the Folk.

"What the devil now?" thought Stern, tautening every muscle for the expected attack.

But attack there came none. Instead the patriarch asked a question of those who stood near him; and hands now guided the old man toward the place where Stern was standing, bound.

"O friend; O son!" exclaimed the old man when he had come close. "Now hearken! For, verily, this is the only way!

"It is an ancient custom of the Merucaans that any man captive or free, can ever challenge our chief, whosoever he be, to the death-combat. If the chief wins, he remains chief. If he loses, the victor takes his place. Many hundreds of years, I know not how long, this has been our way. And many terrible combats have been seen here among our people.

"Kamrou has said that you must die, the girl must be his prize. Only one way remains to save her and yourself -- you must struggle with Kamrou. I have delivered to him your challenge already. Let fate decide the issue!"

Everything seemed to whirl before Stern's eyes, and for a moment all grew black. In his ears sounded a great roaring, louder than the roar of the huge flame. Quick questions flashed through his mind. Fight Kamrou? But how? A duel with revolvers? Spears? Maces?

He knew not. Only he knew that in whatever way the ancient combats must be held he was ready!

"You affirm the challenge I have given in your behalf?" Demanded the patriarch. "If you accept it, nod."

Stern nodded with all the vigor of his terrible rage. Kamrou's eyes narrowed; his smile grew fixed and hard, but in it Stern perceived the easy contempt of a bully toward any chance weakling. And through him thrilled a passion of hate such as he had never dreamed in all his life.

Came a quick word from the patriarch. Somebody was slashing the engineer's bonds. All at once the ropes gave way. Free and unfettered, he stepped forward, stretching his arms, opening and closing his cramped, numbed hands, out into the ring toward Kamrou, the chief.

Off came the gag. Stern could speak at last.

His first word was to the girl.

"Beatrice!" he called to her, "there's one chance left! I'm to fight this ruffian here. If I beat him we're free -- we own this tribe, body and soul! If not --"

He broke off short. Even the possibility was not to be considered.

She looked at him and understood his secret thought. Well the man knew that Beatrice would die by her own hand before Kamrou should have his way with her.

The patriarch spoke again.

"My son," said he, "there is but one way for all these combats. It has been so these many centuries. By the smooth edge of the great boiling pit the fights are held. Man against man it is. Verily, you two with only your hands must fight! He who loses --"

"Goes into the pit?"

The old man nodded.

"There is no other way," he answered. "The new, terrible weapons you cannot use. The arrows, slings and spears are all forbidden by ancient custom. It is the naked grasp of the hands, the strong muscles of two men against each other! So we decide our chief!

"I, alas, can help you in nothing. I am powerless, weak, old. Were

I to interfere now and try to change this way, my own body would only go to the pit, and my old bones hang, headless, in the place of captives and criminals. All lies in your hands, my son!

"All; everything! Our whole future, and the future of the world! If you lose, the wonderful machine will be destroyed and all its metal forged into spears and battle axes. Barbarism will conquer; darkness will continue, and war, and death. All will be forever lost!

"The last ray of hope, of light, from the great past of the upper world, will vanish forever! Your own death, my son, and the fate of the girl, will be as nothing beside the terrible catastrophe, if you are beaten.

"For, verily, it will be the death of the world!

"And now, my son, now go to battle -- to battle for this woman, for yourself, for us, for the future of our race, for everything!

"Kamrou is ready. The pit is boiling.

"Go now! Fight -- and -- and --"

His voice was lost in a great tumult of cries, yells, shouts. Spears brandished. Came a sound of shields struck with clubs and axes. The copper drums again began to throb and clang.

Kamrou had risen from his seat.

Stern knew the supreme moment of his life was at hand.

37. The Final Struggle

Kamrou flung off his long and heavy cloak. He stood there in the flamelight, broad-chested, beautifully muscled, lean of hip, the perfect picture of a fighting man. Naked he was, save for his loincloth. And still he smiled.

Stern likewise stripped away his own cloak. Clad only like the chief, he faced him.

"Well, now," said he, "here goes! And may the best man win!"

Kamrou waved the circle back at one side. It opened, revealing the great pit to southward of the flame. Stern saw the vapors rising, bluish in that strange light, from the perpetual boiling of the black waters in its depths. Oddly enough, even at that moment a stray bit of scientific thought nicked into his consciousness -- the memory that under compressed air water boils only at very high temperatures. Down here, in this great pressure, the water must easily be over three hundred degrees to seethe like that.

He, too, smiled.

"So much the better," thought he. "The hotter, the sooner it's all over for the man who goes!"

Up rose numbers of the two-pronged torches. Stern got confused glimpses of the Folk -- he saw the terrible, barbaric eagerness with which they now anticipated this inevitable tragedy of at least one human death in its most awful form.

Beatrice he no longer saw. Where was she? He knew not. But in a long, last cry of farewell he raised his voice. Then, with Kamrou, he strode toward the steaming, boiling pit in the smooth rock floor.

Two tall men broke through the tensely eager throng. In their hands they bore each a golden jar, curiously shaped and chiseled, and bearing a whimsical resemblance to a coffee-urn.

"What the devil now?" wondered Stern, eager to be at work.

He saw at once the meaning of the jars. One of the bearers approached Kamrou. The other came to him. They raised the vessels, and over the antagonists' bare bodies poured a thin, warm stream of some rank-smelling oil. All over the skin they rubbed it, till the bodies glistened strangely in the flamelight. Then, with muttered words he could not catch, they withdrew.

All seemed confused and vague to Stern as in a painful dream. Images and pictures seemed to present themselves to his brain. The light, the fog and heat, the rising steam, the roaring of the flame, and over all the throb-throb-throb of those infernal copper drums worked powerfully on his senses.

Already he seemed to feel the grip of Kamrou, the pangs of the hard struggle, the sudden plunge into the vat of scalding death.

With a strong effort he flung off these fancies and faced his sneering foe, who now -- his red-wealed face puckered into a malicious grin -- stood waiting.

Stern all at once saw the patriarch once more.

"Go, son!" cried the old man. "Now is the moment! When the drums cease, lay hold of him!"

Even as he spoke, the great drums slowed their beat, then stopped.

Stern, with a final thought of Beatrice, advanced.

All the advantage lay with Kamrou. Familiar with the place was he, and with the rules of this incredible contest. Everywhere about him stood crowding hundreds of his Folk, owing him their allegiance, hostile to the newcomer, the man from another world. Out of all that multitude only two hearts' beat in sympathy and hope for him; only two human beings gave him their thoughts and their support -- a helpless girl; a feeble, blind old man.

Kamrou stood taller, too, than Stern, and certainly bulked heavier. He was in perfect condition, while Stern had not yet fully recovered from the fight in the Abyss, from the great change in living conditions there in the depths, and -- more important still -- from the harsh blow of the rock that had numbed his elbow on the beach.

His arms and hands, too, still felt the cramping of the cords that had bound him. He needed a few hours yet to work them into suppleness and perfect strength. But respite there was none.

He must fight now at once under all handicaps, or die -- and in his death yield Beatrice to the barbaric passions of the chief.

Oddly enough there recurred to his mind, as he drew near the waiting, sneering Kamrou, that brave old war-cry of the Greeks of Xenophon as they hurled themselves against the vastly greater army of the Persians --" *Zeus Sotor kal Nike!* -- Zeus Savior and victory!"

The shout burst from his lips. Forward he ran, on to the battle where either he or the barbarian must perish in the boiling pit -- forward, to what? To victory -- to death?

Kamrou stood fast till Stern's right hand had almost gripped his throat -- for Stern, the challenger, had to deliver the first attack.

But suddenly he slipped aside; and as Stern swerved for him, made a quick leap.

With an agility, a strength and skill tigerlike and marvelous, he caught Stern round the waist, whirled him and would have dashed him toward the pit. But already the engineer's right arm was under Kamrou's left; the right hand had him by the throat, and Kamrou's head went sharply back till the vertebrae strained hard.

Eel-like, elusive, oiled, the chief broke the hold, even as he flung a leg about one of Stern's.

A moment they swayed, tugging, straining, panting. In the old days Stern would not for one moment have been a match for this barbaric athlete, but the long months of life close to nature had hardened him and toughened every fiber. And now a stab of joy thrilled through him as he realized that in his muscles lay at least a force to balk the savage for a little while.

To Stern came back his wrestling lore of the very long ago, the days of Harvard, in the dim, vanished past. He freed his left arm from the gorilla-like grip of Kamrou, and, quick as lightning, got a jiu-jitsu stranglehold.

The savage choked, gurgled, writhed; his face grew purple with stagnant blood. Then he leaped, dragging the engineer with him; they fell, rolled, twisted -- and Stern's hold was broken.

A great shout rose as Kamrou struggled up and once more seized the American. He raised him like a child, and took a step, two, three, toward the infernal cauldron in the rock floor.

Stern, desperate, wrenched his oiled arms clear. A second later they had closed again about the chief's throat -- the one point of attack that Stern had chosen for his best.

The barbarian faltered. Grunting, panting, he shook the engineer as a dog shakes a rat, but the hold was secure. Kamrou's great arms wrapped themselves in a formidable "body-scissors" grip; Stern felt the breath squeezed from his body.

Then suddenly the chief's oily heel slipped on the smooth-worn rock, not ten feet from the lip of the bubbling vat -- and for the second time both fell

This time Stern was atop. Over they rolled, once, twice, straining with madness. Stern's thumbs were sunk deep in the throat of the barbarian at either side. As he gouged harder, deeper, he felt the terrific pounding of the chief's jugular. Hot on his own neck panted the choking breath of Kamrou. Oh, could he only hold that grip a minute longer -- even a half-minute!

But already his own breath was gone. A buzzing filled his ears; sparkling lights danced, quivering before his eyes. The blood seemed bursting his brain; far off and vague he heard the droning of the flame, the shouts and cries of the great horde of watchers.

A whiff of steam -- hot, damp, terrifying -- passed across his face, in which the veins were starting from the oily skin. His eyes, half closed, bulged from the sockets. He knew the pit was very close now; dully he heard its steady bubbling.

"If I go -- he goes, too!" the engineer swore to himself. "He'll never have -- Beatrice -- anyway!"

Over and over they rolled, their grips tight -- locked as steel. Now Kamrou was on top, now Stern. But the chief's muscles were still strong as ever; Stern's already had begun to weaken.

Strive as he might, he could not get another hold, nor could he throw another ounce of power into that he already had. Up, up, slowly up slipped the chief's arms; Stern knew the savage meant to throttle him; and once those long, prehensile fingers reached his throat, goodby!

Then it seemed to him a voice, very far and small, was speaking to him, coolly, impersonally, in a matter-of-fact way as though suggesting an experiment.

Dazed as he was, he recognized that voice -- it was the voice of Dr. Harbutt, who once had taught him many a wily trick upon the mat; Harbutt, dead and gone these thousand years or more.

"Why not try the satsu-da, Stern?" the voice was saying. "Excellent, at times."

Though Stern's face was black and swollen, eyes shut and mouth all twisted awry in this titanic struggle with the ape-hold of the huge chief, yet the soul within him calmly smiled.

The satsu-da -- yes, he remembered it now, strongest and best of all the jiu-jitsu feats.

And, suddenly loosening his hands from the chief's throat, he clenched his right fist, hard as steel.

A second later the "killing-blow" had fallen on the barbarian's neck, just where the swelling protuberance behind the ear marked the vital spot.

Terrible was the force of that blow, struck for his own life, for the honor of Beatrice, the salvation of the world.

Kamrou gave a strange grunt. His head fell backward. Both eyes closed; the mouth lolled open and a glairy froth began to trickle down.

The frightful grip of the long, hairy arms relaxed. Exhausted, Stern fell prone right on the slippery edge of the boiling pit.

He felt a sudden scalding dash of water, steam and boiling spray; he heard a sudden splash, then a wild, barbarous, long-drawn howling of the massed Folly.

Lying there, spent, gasping, all but dead in the thick steam-drift of the vat, he opened his eyes.

Kamrou was nowhere to be seen.

Seemingly very distant, he heard the copper drums begin to beat once more with feverish haste.

A great, compelling lassitude enveloped him. He knew no more.

38. The Sun of Spring

"What altitude now? Can you make-out, Allan?"

"No. The aneroid's only good up to five miles. We must have made two hundred, vertically, since this morning. The way the propeller takes hold and the planes climb in this condensed air is just a miracle!"

"Two passengers at that!" Beatrice answered, leaning back in her seat again. She turned to the patriarch, who, sitting in an extra place in the thoroughly overhauled and newly equipped Pauillac, was holding with nervous hands to the wire stays in front of him.

"Patience, father," she cheered him. "Two hours more -- not over three, at the outside-and you shall breathe the upper air again! For the first time the sunlight shall fall upon your face!"

"The sun! The sun! Oh, is it possible?" murmured the aged man. "Verily, I had never thought to live until this day! The sun!"

Came silence between these three for a time, while the strong heart of the machine beat steadily; and the engineer, with deft and skilful hand, guided it in wide-swept spirals upward, ever up, up, up, back toward the realms of day, of life, once more; up through the fogs and clouds, away from heat and dark and mystery, toward the clear, pure, refreshing air of heaven again.

At last Stern spoke.

"Well, father," said he, "I never would have thought it; but you were right, after all! They're like so much clay in the potter's hand now, for me. I see I can do with them whatever I will.

"I was afraid some of them might object, after all, to any such proposition. It's one thing for them to accept me as boss down there, and quite another for them to consent to wholesale transplanting, such as we've got under way. But I can't see any possible reason why -- with plenty of time and patience -- the thing can't be accomplished all right. The main difficulty was their consent; and now we've got that, the rest is mere detail and routine work."

"Time and patience," repeated the girl. "Those are our watchwords now, boy. And we've got lots of both, haven't we?"

"Two passengers each trip," the engineer continued, more practical than she, "and three trips a week, at the most, makes six of the Folk landed on the surface weekly. In other words, it'll take --"

"No matter about that now!" interrupted Beatrice. "We've got all the time there is! Even if it takes five years, what of that? What are months or even years in the life-history of the world?"

Stern kept silence again. In his mind he was revolving a hundred vital questions of shelter, feeding, acclimatization for these men, now to be transported from a place of dark and damp and heat to the strange outer regions of the surface-world.

Plainly he saw it would be a task of unparalleled skill, delicacy, and difficult accomplishment; but his spirits rose only the higher as he faced its actual details. After all that he and Beatrice had been through since their wakening in the tower, he feared no failure to solve any questions that now might rise. By care, by keeping the Folk at first in caves, then gradually accustoming them to stronger and brighter light, more air, more cold, he knew he could bridge the gap of centuries in a few years.

Ever adaptable, the human body would respond to changed environments. Patience and time -- these would solve all!

And as for this Folk's barbarism, it mattered not. Much better such stock to rebuild from than some mild, supine race of far higher culture. To fight the rough battles of life and re-establishment still ahead, the bold and warlike Merucaans were all that he could wish.

"Imagine me as a school-teacher," suddenly exclaimed the girl, laughing: "giving the children A B C and making them read: 'I see the cat' -- when there aren't any cats nowadays -- no tame ones, anyhow! Imagine --"

"Sh-h-h!" cautioned Stern. "Don't waste your energies imagining things just yet. There's more than enough real work, food-getting, house-building in caves, and all that, before we ever get to schools. That's years ahead yet, education is!"

Silence again, save for the strong and ceaseless chatter of the engine, that, noisy as a score of mowing machines, flung its indomitable challenge to gravitation out into the fathomless void on every hand.

"Allan! Allan! Oh, a star! Look, look! A star!"

The girl was first to see that blest and wondrous thing. Hours had passed, long, weary hours; steadily the air-pressure had sunk, the vapors thinned; but light had not yet filtered through the mists. And Allan's mind had been sore troubled thereat. He had not thought of the simple reason that they were reaching the surface at night.

But now he knew, and as she cried to him "A star!" he, too, looked and saw it, and as though he had been a little child he felt the sudden tears start to his weary eyes.

"A star!" he answered. "Oh, thank God -- a star!"

It faded almost at once, as vapors shrouded it; but soon it came again, and others, many more; and now the first breath of the cool and blessed outer air was wafted to them.

Used as they had been, all these long months -- for now the year had turned again and early spring was coming upon the world -- used to the closed and stifling atmosphere of the Abyss, its chemicalized fogs and mists, the first effect of the pure surface-air was almost intoxicating as they mounted higher, higher, toward the lip of the titanic gulf.

The patriarch, trembling with eagerness and with exhaustion -- for he was very old and now his vital forces were all but spent -- breathed it only with difficulty. Rapid was his respiration; on either pallid cheek a strange and vivid patch of color showed.

Suddenly he spoke.

"Stars? You see them -- really see them?" faltered he. "Oh, for my sight again! Oh, that I might see them once, only once, those wonderful things of ancient story! Then, verily, I should be glad to die!"

Midnight.

Hard-driven now for many hours, heated, yet still running true, the Pauillac had at length made a safe landing on the western verge of the Abyss. Again the voyagers felt solid earth beneath their feet. By the clear starlight Stern had brought the machine to earth on a little plateau, wooded in part, partly bare sand. Numb and stiff, he had alighted from the driver's seat, and had helped both passengers alight,

The girl, radiant with joy, had kissed him full upon the lips; the patriarch had fallen on his knees, and, gathering a handful of the sand -- the precious surface of the earth, long fabled among his Folk, long worshipped in his deepest reveries -- had clasped it to his thin and heaving breast.

If he had known how to pray he would have worshipped there. But even though his lips were silent, his attitude, his soul were all one vast and heartfelt prayer -- prayer to the mother-earth, the unseen stars, the night, the wind upon his brow, the sweet and subtle airs of heaven that enfolded him like a caress.

Stern wrapped the old man in a spare mantle, for the night was chill, then made a crackling fire on the sands. Worn out, they rested, all. Little they said. The beauty and majesty of night now -- seen again after long absence -- a hundred times more solemn than they had ever known it, kept the two Americans from speech. And the old man, buried in his own thoughts, sat by the fire, burning with a fever of impatient longings for the dawn.

Five o'clock.

Now all across the eastern sky, shrouded as it was with the slow, silent mist-wreaths rising ghostly from the Abyss, delicate pink and pearl-gray tints were spreading, shading above to light blues and to purples of exquisite depth and clarity.

No cloud flecked the sky, the wondrous sky of early spring. Dawn, pure as on the primal day, was climbing from the eastern depths. And, thrilled by that eternal miracle, the man and woman, hand in hand, awaited the full coming of the light.

The patriarch spoke.

"Is the sun nigh arisen now?" he queried in a strange, awed voice, trembling with eagerness and deep emotion. "Is it coming, at last -- the sun?"

"It'll be here now before long, father," answered Stern.

"From which direction does it come? Am I facing it?" he asked, with pitiful anxiety.

"You're facing it. The first rays will fall on you. Only be patient. I promise you it shall not fail!"

A pause. Then the aged man spoke again.

"Remember, oh, my children," said he, with terrible earnestness, "all that I have told you, all that you must know. Remember how to deal with my people. They are as children in your hands. Be very patient, very firm and wise; all will be well.

"Remember my warnings of the Great Vortex, so very far below our sea, the Lanskaarn, and all those other perils of the Abyss whereof I have spoken. Remember, too, all the traditions of the Cave of Records. Some day, when all else is accomplished, you may find that cave. I have told you everything I know of its location. Seek it some day. and find the history of the dead, buried past, from the time of the great catastrophe to the final migration when my ancestors sought the lower sea."

Another silence. All three were too deeply moved for any speech. And ever mounting higher, brighter and more clear, dawn flung its glories wide across the sky.

"Help me that I may stand, to greet the day!" at last the patriarch said. "I cannot rise, alone."

Stern and the girl, each taking an arm, got him to his feet. He stood there facing the east, priestlike in venerable and solemn worship of the coming sun.

"Give me each a hand, my children," he commanded. In Stern's hand, strong, corded, toil-worn, he laid the girl's.

"Thus do I give you each to each," said he. "Thus do I make you one!"

Stern drew Beatrice into his arms. Blind though the old man was, he sensed the act, and smiled. A great and holy peace had shrouded him.

"Only that I may feel the sun upon my face!" breathed he.

All at once a thinning cloud-haze let the light glow through.

Beatrice looked at Stern. He shook his head.

"Not yet," he answered.

Swiftly uprose the sun. The morning wind dispelled the shrouding vapors.

"Oh, what is this warmth?" exclaimed the patriarch, trembling violently. "What is this warmth, this glow upon my face? This life, this --"

Out toward the east he stretched both hands. Instinctively the priestlike worship of the sun, old when the world was still in infancy. surged back to him again after the long, lost centuries of darkness and oblivion.

"The sun! The sun!" he cried, his voice triumphant as a trumpet-call. Tears coursed from his blind eyes; but on his lips a smile of joy unutterable was set.

"The sun! At last! The --"

Stern caught his feeble body as he fell.

Down on the sands they laid him. To the stilled heart Stern laid his ear.

Tears were in his eyes, too, and in the girl's, as Stern shook his head, silently.

Up over the time-worn, the venerable, the kindly face they drew the mantle, but not before each had reverently kissed the wrinkled forehead.

"Better thus," whispered the engineer. "Far better, every way. He had his wish; he felt the sunshine on his face; his outgoing spirit must be mingled with that worshipped light and air and sky -- with dawn -- with springtime --"

"With life itself!" said Beatrice.

And through her tears she smiled, while higher rose the warm, life-giving sun of spring.

LEONAUR

ALSO FROM LEONAUR
AVAILABLE IN SOFTCOVER OR HARDCOVER WITH DUST JACKET

SFI CLASSIC SCIENCE FICTION SERIES
BEFORE ADAM & Other Stories
by Jack London

Volume 1 of The Collected Science Fiction & Fantasy of Jack London.

SOFTCOVER   : **ISBN 1-84677-008-4**
HARDCOVER : **ISBN 1-84677-015-7**

SF2 CLASSIC SCIENCE FICTION SERIES
THE IRON HEEL & Other Stories
by Jack London

Volume 2 of The Collected Science Fiction & Fantasy of Jack London.

SOFTCOVER   : **ISBN 1-84677-004-1**
HARDCOVER : **ISBN 1-84677-011-4**

SF3 CLASSIC SCIENCE FICTION SERIES
THE STAR ROVER & Other Stories
by Jack London

Volume 3 of The Collected Science Fiction & Fantasy of Jack London.

SOFTCOVER   : **ISBN 1-84677-006-8**
HARDCOVER : **ISBN 1-84677-013-0**

WFI THE WARFARE FICTION SERIES
NAPOLEONIC WAR STORIES
by Sir Arthur Quiller-Couch

Tales of soldiers, spies, battles & Sieges from the Peninsular & Waterloo campaigns

SOFTCOVER   : **ISBN 1-84677-003-3**
HARDCOVER : **ISBN 1-84677-014-9**

LEONAUR

ALSO FROM LEONAUR
AVAILABLE IN SOFTCOVER OR HARDCOVER WITH DUST JACKET

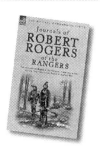

.